Books in the Terminal City Saga

Book One: Terminal City
Book Two: Winter's End
Book Three: Reaper's Edge

BOOK TWO IN THE TERMINAL CITY SAGA

WINTER'S END

Trevor Melanson

EDGE SCIENCE FICTION AND FANTASY PUBLISHING
An Imprint of HADES PUBLICATIONS, INC.
CALGARY

Winter's End
Book Two in the Terminal City Saga

Copyright © 2017 by Trevor Melanson

EDGE SCIENCE FICTION AND FANTASY PUBLISHING
An Imprint of HADES PUBLICATIONS, INC.
P.O. Box 1714, Calgary, Alberta, T2P 2L7, Canada

The EDGE Team:
Producer: Brian Hades
Acquisitions Editor: Michelle Heumann
Edited by: Brian Hades
Cover Design: Brian Hades
Cover Art: Lyn Perkins
Book Design: Mark Steele

ISBN: 978-1-77053-144-4

EDGE Science Fiction and Fantasy Publishing and Hades Publications, Inc. acknowledges the ongoing support of the Alberta Foundation for the Arts and the Canada Council for the Arts for our publishing programme.

Library and Archives Canada Cataloguing in Publication
CIP Data on file with the National Library of Canada
ISBN: 978-1-77053-144-4
(e-Book ISBN: 978-1-77053-143-7)

FIRST EDITION
(20170521)
Printed in USA
www.edgewebsite.com

Publisher's Note:

Thank you for purchasing this book. It began as an idea, was shaped by the creativity of its talented author, and was subsequently molded into the book you have before you by a team of editors and designers.

Like all EDGE books, this book is the result of the creative talents of a dedicated team of individuals who all believe that books (whether in print or pixels) have the magical ability to take you on an adventure to new and wondrous places powered by the author's imagination.

As EDGE's publisher, I hope that you enjoy this book. It is a part of our ongoing quest to discover talented authors and to make their creative writing available to you.

We also hope that you will share your discovery and enjoyment of this novel on social media through Facebook, Twitter, Goodreads, Pinterest, etc., and by posting your opinions and/or reviews on Amazon and other review sites and blogs. By doing so, others will be able to share your discovery and passion for this book.

Brian Hades, publisher

Dedication

For Ariane, who was literally by my side for most of this book, and always so in spirit

It is change, continuing change, inevitable change, that is the dominant factor in society today. No sensible decision can be made any longer without taking into account not only the world as it is, but the world as it will be.

—Isaac Asimov

Chapter 1

While incredibly rare, spirit-stealing spells may be the most heinous, most unforgivable known to necromancy. For victims, the outcome is worse than death.

—*Samuel Benedict, Advanced Necromancy*

— ‹› —

Kyle MacDonald knew that tonight was inevitable. Everything was inevitable.

Dragging his razor over his Adam's apple up to his chin, Kyle cut against the grain of his stubble, once, twice, then again, shaving until his skin was perfectly smooth. Bleeding in two spots but smooth. He washed the blood away, splashing his face with handfuls of tap water, then pulled a white towel off its rack. The metal bar twirled and squeaked. He patted his cheeks, eyeing the curved corners of his round face, as soft and slippery as a wet melon — as inoffensively bland too. Thirty years to the day, Kyle was, but people often told him he looked twenty. Looked innocent, cordial, unremarkable. Looked like a Kyle.

Kyle, however, was none of these things, though that was hardly his fault. The universe was clockwork, he had learned. Every moment, every birth, every death, every human being the consequence of what came before them. Cause and effect. Kyle was who he was, what he was, and nothing could change that. His future was already written, his victims already chosen.

Next came his hair. With his final black comb, Kyle meticulously parted each thin brown strand to one side. Finally, he brushed his teeth, and he was ready.

Kyle used to resent his illness. Psychopath: it sounded more like an accusation. People didn't understand. And then one day he had a life-changing epiphany: it didn't matter. Nothing did. Free will was a facade, he realized. Humans were mere products of nature, and his nature compelled him to consume, to grow. You can't blame a tornado for destroying a few trailers.

Or a psychopathic necromancer for stealing spirits.

The first one had been the hardest. First times usually were, but it wasn't just the chant that proved difficult. More, it was the price: not only a person's life but their afterlife too. A stolen spirit couldn't enter the Spirit Realm, couldn't fade peacefully into nothing. It remained a prisoner within its captor, within Kyle MacDonald. It went against everything his parents, talented necromancers in their own right, had taught him. But each time he grew more powerful, albeit increasingly less so. The returns were diminishing. Though not his desire. Nor the voices in his head, dozens of them now, screaming and begging for release — for a real death.

What's more, everyday spirits no longer satiated Kyle's appetite. These days, he had to kill his fellow necromancers. It was the difference between gruel and steak. Necromancers had a special connection to the Spirit Realm, and each spirit was unique. "Like a fine wine," he often said. Thing was, he could only tap into that special connection if he consumed it, and Kyle needed to grow. That was simply a fact. Simply his nature.

He flicked off the bathroom light and stepped into the living room, a simple space that was clean and overwhelmingly beige. It looked like every other hundred-dollar hotel room. Kyle had stayed in a lot of them over the years. There were only so many necromancers out there, after all, and a bit of traveling was required. Kyle liked to think of himself as a sort of hunter-gatherer, roaming to survive.

He grabbed his blazer off the bed before sliding it over top his freshly ironed dress shirt — appearances were important — then fetched his collar stays from the nightstand. Kyle pushed them in one at a time, checking himself out in the small oak mirror above the dresser. "Your name is Leonard Sutton," he said aloud and then walked out the front door, locking it behind him.

Kyle made his way to the elevator, politely nodding to an old woman who passed him in the hallway, a smile stretched across his plain face, as ready as ever to face the inevitable.

— «» —

"You must be Leonard." The man was in his late forties but youthfully groomed. His suit looked new — silver, sharp at the edges, and a pretty good fit save for the waist. A modest gut poured over his belt and under a skinny black tie that matched his thick-rimmed glasses. Untailored, his suit, but meticulously chosen. Diego Castillo wasn't quite as wealthy as he appeared from a distance, but then Kyle wasn't here for his money.

Diego leaned forward to shake hands. His was rough and tan, but his grip was soft and warm. He smiled before reclining into his seat. Kyle joined him, grinning as he sunk into the leather upholstery. It was a small, intimate table, a candle and two cocktails all that lay between them.

"I hope you don't mind," said Diego. Kyle could feel his breath. "I got you an old fashioned. It's my favorite, so if you don't want it..." He trailed off teasingly.

"You shouldn't have." Kyle took a small sip. "I'm not much of a drinker, but I think I can make an exception tonight. Cheers."

"Cheers," said Diego. "To exceptions."

"To exceptions."

"It's not often I meet a fellow, shall we say, hobbyist in Salt Lake City." Diego eyed the room around them, but the dim hotel bar was mostly deserted.

"It's my first time," replied Kyle. "I wish I could stay a little longer."

Diego looked incredulous. "You wish you could stay longer," he said, eyebrows raised, "in Salt Lake fucking City?"

"Hah, hah, hah." When Kyle laughed, he spoke each "hah."

"Don't get me wrong," added Diego. "I grew up here and all that. But let me tell you, boy, as soon as my kids — whom I love to bits." He took a deep, melodramatic breath. "As soon as those wonderful bastards go off to college, I am out of here. And I mean for good. Being a gay man in Salt Lake City is like being a butterfly in a hornet's nest."

"Lucky for me, I found the butterfly." Kyle feigned a sip of his old fashioned.

Diego rolled back in his chair, guffawing, his whole body rocking as his cheeks grew redder and redder. His laugh was everything Kyle's was not. "Oh God, Leonard." Diego wiped both eyes with the back of his hand, one after the other. "You are too goddamn cute."

"Hah, hah, hah."

Diego let out a satisfied sigh. "So, you're in sales, are you? How do you like that?"

"It suits me. I like people. Heck, I even like small talk." Kyle hated small talk.

"Well, you're very good at it." Diego drank down the last of his old fashioned as if it were a shot and then signaled the server for another.

"Your profile said you're a lawyer." Kyle was referring to the dating website the two had met on three weeks earlier. For a baby-faced millennial like Kyle, meeting men was hardly a challenge. Meeting necromancers, on the other hand — now that was trickier.

Kyle's dating profile said nothing of necromancy. It was spotless, cheerful, almost abnormally innocent. He was a fun-loving salesman from Seattle who traveled a lot ("for work AND pleasure"). Leonard Sutton was a cliché. Unless, of course, you knew what to look for. Unless you were a fellow necromancer.

A single line gave him away: "People say I have a lot of spirit — realms of it!" To most readers, it was merely an awkward phrase (Leonard was no master wordsmith). But to necromancers, the words *spirit* and *realm* side-by-side stuck out like a blot of blood on white canvas. And sometimes, on those rare occasions, one of them would reach out.

If there was one hole in Kyle's plot, it was the possibility of drawing unwanted attention, of attracting inquisitors — the religious fanatics who hunted and killed his kind for a living. They were always searching for subtle clues that might lead them to their next target. But Kyle didn't fear inquisitors. There seemed to be fewer of them these days, and he'd already killed a couple. He was the real predator, after all, the tornado — and he'd swallow up anyone who crossed him.

Diego, on the other hand, was a gentle soul. Kyle could sense that much. He harbored no ill will toward the man, but then he rarely did. It wasn't about who deserved what, because in Kyle's universe, no one deserved anything. If people were snowflakes, as they say, then humanity was an avalanche, each individual barreling down the mountainside, a prisoner to physics. And here, in this hotel bar, Diego had hit ground.

Soon, he would melt into Kyle.

"Sad to say it." Diego rolled his eyes. "I am indeed a lawyer." He leaned forward on one elbow. "Did you know that seventy-five percent of lawyers regret becoming lawyers?" He poked the table with his index finger. "Seventy-five percent."

"Wow, really?" Kyle pretended to look surprised, to care.

"Actually, I have no idea." Diego chuckled. "I think I read that somewhere. Could be true."

"Hah." Kyle tried not to overdo it this time. He sometimes wondered what it felt like, having a good laugh. He heard once that some women went their whole lives without ever experiencing an orgasm, mistaking ripples of pleasure for the real thing. Kyle wondered if he was like those women, smirking and chuckling but never truly laughing — never knowing how hilarious life could be.

"You know what I don't regret, though," said Diego. Then, under his breath: "Becoming a necromancer."

A grin spread across Kyle's face, and for the first time that night, it was an authentic one. "That," he said, "makes two of us."

Once more, they clinked glasses.

— «» —

"Make yourself at home."

They were back in Kyle's hotel room. Diego kicked off his shoes and went straight for the bed, unfurling onto his back, arms outstretched. "Mmm. Comfy."

Kyle locked the door then headed to the bathroom. "To freshen up."

"I haven't been this drunk in some time," said Diego.

Kyle could see him reflected in the bathroom mirror, rolling and giggling, crinkling his crisp sheets. "There's nothing wrong with having a little fun," he replied. "You've earned it."

"Have I, now?"

"Sure," said Kyle, splashing water on his face — he liked to stay clean. "We all deserve to have what we want. To do what we want."

"Is that so?" Diego could see Kyle's reflection too; he was staring back at him, lust in his eyes. "I don't always know what I want, Leonard — lovely, lovely Leonard — but right now, in this moment, I am dead certain of it."

Kyle flicked off the bathroom light and stepped out from behind the doorframe. "That makes two of us," he said.

Diego sat upright with renewed energy, downplaying his drunken demeanor. He watched every step Kyle took toward the bed like a cat trailing a fly.

Kyle sat down beside him, close enough that their hips touched. Diego lifted his hand from the bed, tracing Kyle's spine, up and down, then in swirls. He leaned in, inhaling Kyle's neck and cheek before kissing him.

Truth be told, Kyle had never figured out his sexuality. Though he generally preferred women, gender mattered less than the act itself. They were all just bodies, after all, some more pleasurable than others. In a sense, his psychopathy freed him: he felt no remorse, no pressure to be straight or gay. He simply wanted what he wanted when he wanted it — and he would take it without hesitation.

But Kyle did not desire Diego, at least not sexually — he was too old, too drunk. All the same, he was a necromancer. Not a particularly gifted one, granted, but that would only make him easier to consume, to contain. And Kyle was hungry.

"You smell like soap." Diego chuckled, his hand crawling down Kyle's stomach, making its way to his belt.

Kyle said nothing, nor did his eyes. His hand, however, moved up to Diego's throat. Kyle had learned the hard way that if you're going to attack another necromancer, you best stop them from chanting — stop their ability to reflect your spells, to strike back. So Kyle squeezed.

For a second, Diego seemed to think he was just playing rough. It wasn't until the air in his throat was cut off like a closed valve that he noticed Kyle chanting. That his eyes were no longer unassuming and kind but a venomous crimson.

Diego took a swing at him, but his fist struck Kyle's cheek like a pillow, his strength diminished to a child's. The younger necromancer remained unblemished and unfazed, staring through him with his red eyes, through a man who was vanishing by the second. The spell had already taken hold. The air between them was a veritable strainer, Diego's spirit being pulled through as Kyle consumed its mangled remains.

Once Diego could no longer move his body, he knew it was over. His gaze said as much, but now Kyle could hear his thoughts. The thoughts of a dying man, because though Diego wouldn't truly die — held prisoner in the Living Realm, in Kyle — the very thing that made life worth living in his view, his autonomy, would be left behind like his corpse. If Diego had possessed free will, it was evaporating in the space between them.

Kyle, of course, did not believe in such things.

The two men fell to the carpet. Diego's body landed on its side, Kyle on his ass. He gasped for air, sweat streaming down his pale, round face. Consuming another man's spirit was like swallowing an apple whole — getting it down was the hardest, if not seemingly impossible, part.

But Kyle had done this many times before and knew that pain was just part of the process. He crawled off the floor onto his bed, clinging to the sheets, his fingers curled into claws.

Sometimes Kyle passed out afterward, but not today. He was getting better at this, growing stronger. His body was adapting, evolving, transforming into an impossible creature.

Impossible — if only Kyle MacDonald were not inevitable.

Chapter 2

It was unusually balmy for 1 a.m. Unusually balmy for Terminal City, anyway, even with the ocean breeze slipping through Mason Cross's slender frame, tousling his dark hair. The summers here weren't supposed to be this hot, but this year was different.

"Climate change, man," said Craig, kicking a piece of driftwood five feet into the ocean.

"Yeah, I guess so," replied Mason, looking out at the water. He was digging his toes into the beach's moist sand, seeing how deep he could go. Anything, after all, was more entertaining than his present conversation.

Craig and Mason were quintessential acquaintances. They'd had enough time to become friends, and Craig was certainly friendly enough — in fact, he was too friendly. It made Mason uncomfortable because he couldn't reciprocate Craig's enthusiasm. The problem was that Craig was boring. Everyone insisted he was a fun guy, and perhaps he was, but Mason found him unbearably dull. Even just getting through a cigarette, it turned out, was an arduous endeavor when Craig was involved.

"Asha said you quit." Craig nodded toward Mason's cigarette, his own flopping from between his pouty lips.

"I did," said Mason. "More or less. This one doesn't count." He held it up and took another puff. "I came up with a rule, you see: I no longer buy cigarettes. I just smoke them when other people offer."

"So you're a mooch." He smiled. Craig was always smiling. Always joking around, sometimes using his stocky body as a prop, as if he'd been born into this world to be some leading man's second, the comic relief.

Mason shrugged, forcing a chuckle. "Yeah, I guess I'm a mooch."

"My friend, AJ, guy used to mooch my cigarettes like every fucking day. Then he started to get addicted, and so his girlfriend made him stop." Craig made a whipping noise.

Mason rolled his eyes, his face turned toward the ocean so that Craig couldn't see. "Should we get back to the group?"

"F'sho." Craig threw his cigarette butt into the ocean.

Mason carried his back to their bonfire, flicking it into the flames as he sat down next to Asha. She was laughing at a joke he'd apparently missed.

"Did you hear about Jessica?" Asha turned toward him, brushing a long lock of her boisterous black hair behind one ear.

Mason shook his head and met her gaze with an expectant half-grin.

"Jasmine was just saying that she had a bit of a panic attack last night," explained Asha.

"Why's that funny?" Mason was laughing anyway.

"From smoking her first joint," Jasmine chimed in from across the fire. "She kept saying she was having a heart attack. This 20-year-old, one-hundred-pound girl with low-blood pressure — a fucking heart attack. She was so dead certain of it that she made us take her to the hospital, I shit you not. You should have seen the look on the doctor's face."

Mason was prodding the fire's embers with a blackened stick, an empty package of veggie dogs flapped open on the log beside him. "Better safe than sorry," he said, more or less jokingly. Jasmine had a penchant for exaggeration.

There were just the four of them tonight: Mason, Asha, Craig, and Jasmine. Even after the better part of two years, Mason still felt that Craig and Jasmine — along with most of the people they hung out with — were Asha's friends, not his. But he wasn't complaining. If not for his girlfriend, the infinitely more likeable half of the couple (coined "Masha" by Jasmine), Mason probably wouldn't have had much of a social life. Back when he'd started classes at Carwin University, nearly two years ago now, he'd at least had Lester — even if Lester had only been there because Mason's father had asked him to be. But Lester had promptly joined Dad in the Spirit Realm, compliments of the inquisition.

In short, Asha was the reason Mason was not alone.

Except when he was, of course. Mason needed a little alone time most days, and not just because he was a necromancer but rather because he was Mason.

Jasmine was still chuckling at her own story. She was pretty when she laughed. Not as pretty as Asha but radiant in a shiny, done-up kind of way. Laughter cracked her otherwise permanent facade. Jasmine sighed then said, "Jessica is such a Taurus, man."

Mason visibly cringed.

Asha noticed. "Mason hates astrology." She poked his shoulder. "Isn't that right?" Asha did this a lot: prodded Mason out of his shell, speaking on his behalf when she knew he was holding back an opinion. Once the spark was lit, she knew, he had no choice but to speak up. What Mason couldn't quite figure out was her end — whether she was trying to encourage him to be more social or just having fun. Both were in her nature: Asha tried to help everyone with everything, but she could also be mischievous. It was her release, he figured — these small transgressions.

In any event, they were both smiling before long, looking like she'd told a joke only Mason had heard.

"Yeah," he said finally and then took a swig from his bottle of Corona. "Look." He addressed Jasmine. "Astrology is just totally made up, is all. Totally... bullshit."

"Or maybe you're just not open-minded enough," Jasmine shot back, tilting her head to one side the way she did whenever she let loose a real zinger.

Mason looked painfully unimpressed. "Do you know how far a light year is?" he asked her.

Jasmine shrugged.

"It's the distance light can travel in a year." Mason tried not to sound like a know-it-all, like an asshole. "Light is the fastest thing in the universe," he said, mimicking motion with his free hand. "It takes just eight minutes for light to get here from the sun. The sun is hundreds of times farther away than the moon, hundreds of times farther than humans have ever traveled, and light does it in eight minutes. Now imagine how far something going that fast could travel in a year — that's a light year. The stars in the sky are light years away — some of them millions of light years. The universe itself is billions of light years." He emphasized the word *billions*, like an asshole. "And you're telling me, Jasmine, that these impossibly distant, impossibly massive stars are in some way — in any way — related to whether, I don't know, Craig gets a goddamn promotion at Starbucks next month?"

Craig didn't jump in, but his expression clearly said, *Don't drag me into this.*

Secretly, Mason wondered if his spiel was a little rich considering he was a self-described necromancer. The difference was, of course, that he'd seen necromancy firsthand, and as unlikely as it would have once seemed to him — as it had when Lester introduced the topic over dinner during the fall of his first year at Carwin — he was so neck-deep in necromancy at this point that he'd have an easier time denying gravity. Plus, necromancy had a logic to it. It was crazy as hell, sure, but it made sense. The connections astrology made did not.

Jasmine was squinting at him. "All right, Mr. Philosopher." She was referring to Mason. "Since you're so smart, enlighten me: what's guiding all of us?" She swung her arm around like an oar out of water. "You, me, Craig, Asha. You obviously think horoscopes are stupid, so what would you recommend instead?"

Mason shrugged.

"No answer this time?" Jasmine was being an asshole too.

"I think people should just admit that they don't know what's coming," said Mason. "Maybe the universe does, but we're running blind down here. Life is, I don't know, a labyrinth."

"Always so dark, Mason." It was Asha, clearly having a good time.

Mason rested one arm behind her back. "Labyrinths aren't so bad," he said. "Anyway, my point is that we can't see too far ahead of ourselves. We reach these intersections in

life and pick a way we think is best, but we don't really know
— we never really know. We can't see around the corner. We
can only guess."

"So, what's at the end?" asked Asha.

"What do you mean?" replied Mason.

"Of the labyrinth," she said. "If life is a labyrinth,
shouldn't it have an exit? You're going to say death, aren't
you? Because you're so dark."

Mason was still poking the fire with the same charred
stick. "I don't know that there is an exit," he said smiling,
staring through the flames. "I think people think there's one,
an exit, that if they live a certain way, walk down a certain
path, they'll eventually reach happily ever after or heaven
— whatever it is they're chasing. Someplace uncomplicated,
someplace complete. But me, I don't think that place exists. I
think we live and die in the maze. Might as well embrace it."

Though that was easier said than done, he knew.

"My mom said something like that to me once." It was
Craig, looking uncharacteristically serious; he even took off
his hat, a Toronto Blue Jays baseball cap, folding it between
his knees. "She wasn't so, you know, philosophical about it
or whatever — but same idea."

Everyone in the group turned their heads.

"My dad was kind of a shithead," said Craig. "More than
kind of, actually. I mean, I don't think he ever hit her, my
mom, but he would intimidate her, you know? He was a
bully. And he'd hit me, 'cause he believed in that, in hitting
kids. I saw right through that fucker, though. But my mom,
he'd, like, manipulate her. I think she knew she was being
manipulated too, which was the fucked-up thing, but she
stuck with him anyway."

Craig didn't look any of them in the eyes as he spoke;
he looked past them, into himself. Wherever he was, it was
someplace Mason hadn't realized Craig had in him.

"Then one day he cheated on her," Craig continued. "I
wasn't even mad about that, not really. I mean, their marriage
was a sham anyway. But that's what did it for my mom. I
guess until that moment their marriage had been this, I don't
know, idea in her mind. It didn't matter how messed up the

reality was because the idea was pure — until, of course, he banged someone else. After she found out, they got a divorce, and I haven't spoken to my old man since.

"She was super depressed about it at first, but then she did this total one-eighty. Suddenly, she was, like, happier than I'd ever seen her. Anyway, I was fifteen, I think, and my mom and I, we sat down and had this talk. I wanted to understand why she'd stuck with him so long. Ever since I was a kid, I hated my dad. My mom was older and wiser and all that shit, except when it came to him, and I didn't get why.

"She let me have a beer that night." Craig held up his bottle like a prop. "My first one. And what she said was that it wasn't really about him. It was about the finish line, this perfect family she thought she could have, the family she'd always dreamed of. She just couldn't give that up, couldn't stop chasing happily ever after, like Mason said, until finally that dick cheated on her, which turned out to be a good thing in the end. Anyway, she told me that night that life is simply what's right in front of you. Everything else is fantasy.

"That's why I live in the moment." Craig smiled. "That's why I'm so damn chill all the time. Anyway, she's dating this new guy now, bit of a dweeb, but she seems happy so whatever." Craig shrugged then made use of the beer in his hand, chugging the last of it. The circle went silent save for his audible gulps and the fire crackling between them.

Mason and Asha exchanged a glance, both of them looking a little surprised and a little impressed. Mason had been wrong about Craig, dismissing him as more caricature than man. The truth was, Craig's worldview wasn't so different from his own. His approach to life, which seemed ridiculous to Mason just five minutes ago, suddenly made sense. Maybe Mason had it wrong. Maybe, like Craig said, he ought to be more chill.

If only that were still an option. Mason had died and come back to life, a favor from the Spirit Realm (which he'd repaid in full, repaid by killing Rowland), and that left a chill of its own.

"Good story, Craig." It was Asha. None of them knew what else to say.

Mason was about to chime in — with something nice for once — until the air around him rose five degrees. It was as if hot water had been poured over Mason, minus the obvious splash. He could feel his skin prickling. He looked at each of them in turn, Asha, Craig, and Jasmine, but no one else seemed to notice. Of course not. Only Mason felt necromancy.

"Anyone want another beer?" Jasmine reached for the box of Corona, which was closer to the fire than it should have been. She dragged it backward through the sand then grabbed two bottles, one for herself and one for Craig, who was waving both arms overhead like a stranded survivor in need of saving — or just another Corona.

Meanwhile, Mason was lost in his head, lost chasing an overwhelming necromantic pull. And a pull it was: he could feel it beckoning him down the shore. Someone was waiting for him there, he knew.

"I'm gonna take a piss." Mason stood up. "Be right back." He chugged the last of his beer before standing up, in case he might be a while. He didn't know who was waiting for him, after all, and as a rule didn't like leaving drinks behind.

Mason, who was not overly drunk but still probably too drunk for this, trudged down the sandy shore, pulled by a feeling — and his own damn curiosity. It was necromancy, all right, but it didn't feel... nefarious. It felt like an invitation from a friend.

The ocean crashes grew louder and the fire behind him fainter. Mason's friends were but dark silhouettes now. He could hear them laughing — Craig especially — but their words had turned into distant mumbles. From here, they were just humans around a fire, the millennia-old image of humanity.

Mason marched on, realizing he actually did kind of need to take a piss. But his bladder would have to wait. His whole body was tingling now, from his fingers to his face, tingling as if something was about to pop. Hopefully, it wasn't him. Until finally he realized it was a cue for him to act. Mason had to make the next move.

Luckily, he knew just the right spell. It was one of the first that Lester had taught him. In Mason's basement was a plain cement wall that was, well, anything but plain. The right necromantic spell revealed that there was, in fact, a glowing red door in its midst, a door into a library brimming with necromantic grimoires.

"The gates of hell," Mason had said to Lester. Now he carried the key.

Mason cast the spell without even chanting, nonchalantly like a seasoned pro. He rarely chanted these days. Unlike other necromancers, he no longer needed to — another favor from the Spirit Realm. With Rowland gone, among the world's couple-thousand necromancers, only Mason truly understood Deathspeak, the language of the dead. Perhaps because, deep down, he wasn't fully alive — and never would be.

Suddenly, a flash of red.

Shit. Mason hoped his friends hadn't noticed. He whirled around, tripping over his own feet and falling into the sand. But they were still sitting around their fire, laughing. *Good.* Mason picked himself up, brushing off his jeans, then turned back toward the ocean to see what he'd revealed.

And there she was, her navy blue dress billowing in the wind, a woman Mason recognized immediately.

"It's you," he said.

Chapter 3

Dear Hiroshi,

Thanks eternally for your kind message. Samuel was always so fond of you, and I know how much his friendship meant to you, as well. I wish I could say more right now, but I am... all out of words.

I'll see you soon,

Joan

—jworthington@nmail.com

— ⟨⟩ —

Joan Worthington was trimmer than the last time Mason had seen her, two years earlier. Trimmer and her hair grayer. The last time was, in fact, the only time the two had ever met, and yet for both of them, it ranked among the hardest nights they'd ever lived through — a night they'd only barely lived through. On nights that change everything, you don't forget the players, you don't forget the faces, and Mason certainly hadn't forgotten hers.

"Hello, Mason," said Joan. "It's nice to see you again."

"Yeah, you too," replied Mason. "If I recall right, you did say we'd meet again."

"That sounds like something I would say." She inhaled deeply, savoring the ocean air. "How have these last couple years treated you?"

"Good." They truly had, largely thanks to Asha. He turned back around to check on her and the others. Asha, Craig, and Jasmine were still huddled around their fire, swigging back beers.

"Oh, don't worry," said Joan, catching his gaze. "They can't see us. If their eyes wandered our way, all they would see is the ocean. We're both hidden under the umbrella of my spell."

Indeed, Mason could feel it, like a warm breath of fog had settled over their small patch of beach. He was more sensitive to spirit energy than he used to be. He nodded knowingly and then asked, "What brings you to Terminal City?"

"You, Mason." She sat down on a nearby log, crossing her legs and leaning back as far as physics would allow. "Well, not just you."

"Figures," said Mason. "There's always another guy."

Joan chuckled. "Tell me, Mason: have you ever met a man named Eli Abelman?"

"Eli Abelman?" Mason let the name sink in. "Sounds familiar."

"He's a medieval history professor at Carwin University," she went on. "About fifty, curly gray hair."

"That sounds like half the professors here." Mason pondered some more. "Actually, I think I have met him once or twice. I think he was friends with my dad. Yeah. I remember now. He was at my father's funeral, standing off to the side, not saying much to anyone. Not that that would have struck me as unusual, mind you — my dad had a lot of strange friends. Anyway, what about him?"

"What about him, indeed." Joan stared out at the ocean, hair dancing over her eyes, her weightless blue dress hugging her limbs like plastic wrap. "You may not know this, Mason, but not every necromancer agrees with what we do, with what the guardians do. Not everyone believes necromancy should be kept secret."

"I take it you don't think the world is ready for that?" asked Mason.

"The world will never be ready for us," she said resolutely. "Inquisitors are but a painful lesson in the power of human ignorance, of human fear. There are so few of us, so few necromancers. We cannot protect ourselves from the whole world, Mason. We can only hide."

"I don't know. Maybe." The inquisitors were certainly a painful lesson, like she said, but he still wasn't sure how he felt. "So, what's this have to do with Eli? Is he one of these necromancers who want to come out of the, umm, necromancy closet?" Mason would need to come up with a better line for future reference.

"I suspect as much," she said.

"Based on what?"

"I wish I could say more," replied Joan. "For now, however, I must apologize. I cannot disclose the source of my suspicion."

Mason took a seat down on the log beside her, cracking his stiff legs. He was also still a bit drunk. "And where do I come into all this?"

"I want you to meet him," she said. "I want you to find out what his plans are."

Mason shrugged. "Why the hell would he tell me?"

"He won't, at first," she replied. "You'll have to get to know him, befriend him even. You're a necromancer. We're a small club, and he did know your father. Eli will want to be your friend, I have no doubt about that, and perhaps eventually he will want to open up too. Introduce yourself, tell him that Lester told you about him, that he was a necromancer."

"He didn't," Mason shot back. He was also surprised she knew that Lester had been his mentor, a detail that Mason had never shared with Joan, who clearly had done her research before coming here. "It just seems wrong, lying about the dead," he continued, "using them as a means."

"That's what we do, Mason. We're necromancers, remember." She sighed those last words, like it was a heavy burden, being a necromancer. A sense of dark duty, however, wasn't Joan's only bargaining chip. "If you do this for us, I can't promise anything, but... it would go a long way with the other guardians."

"What do you mean?" Mason turned toward her, eyebrows furrowed.

"With Samuel gone, there remains a vacant seat on our council, a particularly important one," said Joan. "I cannot fill both his shoes and mine. We are still considering who should take over his responsibilities. Among the names on the list, and my personal choice for Samuel's successor, is, well, it's you, Mason."

He was a little flattered but no less confused. The guardians were the gatekeepers of necromancy. No one took charge of necromancers, which would've proven harder than herding cats, but when it came time to take responsibility for the bigger picture, it was left to them. Samuel, who had taken responsibility for North America, had been older, with decades of necromancy under his belt. At least, that was all true until he took a bullet from the inquisition, leaving this world alongside Rowland. The night that changed everything. Still, Mason? "I'm like… twenty-two." He had to think about it for a moment. "Almost twenty-three."

"And already one of the most powerful necromancers on the planet," said Joan.

Mason blushed.

"With Rowland gone, you are the only necromancer left alive who has been to the Spirit Realm and back," she added. "You told me that yourself, remember. Because of this, because of your unique connection to the Spirit Realm, sooner or later, you will be the most powerful among us, perhaps even as powerful as Rowland was. But power is all I hope you ever share in common with that man. I'm thinking long-term, Mason. We want you on our side. And I believe that you have good judgment. Two years ago, when we first met, you understood what needed to be done to keep us safe, and you did it."

That he had, although truth be told, he was less sure than she was that he'd done the right thing, killing Rowland. Rowland had saved his life, had protected him under his barrier as inquisitors surrounded them both, and Mason had repaid that favor by murdering him. He'd thought that after enough time had gone by, the cold, dark shadow of what he'd done would fade until he could see clearly again, see in the daylight of reason, see that he had indeed done the right thing, the thing that needed to be done, like Joan said. But that shadow still lingered, even after two years, or perhaps it was the truth that stayed. Perhaps the shadow had long since retreated and the ground underneath was just black and rotten.

"This world has more than its fair share of old, entitled fools leading us astray," Joan continued. "The others may be wary of your youth, but I, for one, am not. Plus, it pays quite well. We have generous donors."

Mason smiled. "It would be nice to pay off my student loan."

"That is what I'm offering you, Mason — a chance to pay off your student loan."

He laughed, running one hand through his hair, which was overdue for a good cut. "I don't know."

"I realize religion is falling out of favor among your generation, but this world is still by and large a deeply religious one," said Joan. "If our existence ever became public, the inquisitors would gain more allies than you might think. With most of those bastards dead now — one thing I must credit Rowland for — we're safer than we've been for some time. Yes, the inquisition will rebuild and strike back, but an even war is better than a chase. If the world knew the truth about necromancy, about people like us, we would be seen as... spiritual terrorists."

She shifted her body closer to his, resting her left hand on his pant leg, staring him in the eyes until he stared back. "Find out what he believes," she said, "and find out what he plans to do about it. Eli is not a bad man, Mason, but if he believes what I think he believes, then he is wrong — and sometimes that is worse."

Mason didn't do things impulsively, didn't say yes before thinking yes. Instead, he broke free from her insistent gaze and looked past her, past the ocean waves crashing not far from their feet. The end of Terminal City, its downtown peninsula, stretched past the evergreen trees behind them and into view, shining golden, a gem of civilization. Mason often wondered how humanity could build such bright towers and still be so awful in so many ways. Rowland would have credited the experts, the few who propelled humanity forward, boat builders in a sea of deadweight. Was that what Joan was asking Mason to be? A guardian. One of the few who would matter, who would make it all a little better for everyone else.

"What would you do to him?" asked Mason. "To Eli, I mean. If he's planning something... dangerous."

"Hopefully just talk," said Joan. "But ultimately, we'll do what needs to be done to keep our kind safe. I know you can see the bigger picture. I was there. I remember."

Mason sighed. He didn't like the sound of that, but he supposed he could have his say on the matter if it came to it. Better him than someone else. Hell, maybe this was an opportunity for Mason to save a life — rather than end another one. "Okay," he said. "I'll talk to him. I'll find out if he's planning anything."

Joan smiled, more with appreciation than joy. "You're doing the right thing," she said. "And if I have anything to say about it, you will be rewarded for it."

Mason nodded, hoping she was right on both counts. "Where are you off to now?" he asked.

"Back home to London," she answered, and then she handed him a white slip of paper, pressing it into his palm. "My phone number. Keep me updated about Eli. And if you have any questions about anything, anything at all, just ask. I hope we can be friends."

"I suppose I could use another necromancer friend," he replied. "I've been flying solo for a while now."

"I know the feeling," she said.

Mason stood up and stretched. "You asked how I'd been doing, but I never asked you. How have you been since, you know, that night?"

Joan got up too, looking ready to leave. "The thing about life, Mason, is that it never gets any easier. You just grow more used to it." She patted his shoulder. "I'll let you get back to your friends now. Call me after you've had a chance to speak with Eli."

Mason nodded once more — "See you, Joan" — and then turned away, walking forward until he felt her spell cool off, like stepping out from a small room into the crisp outdoors, if the walls had been invisible. When he whirled back around to see if she was still there, he saw only the ocean, like she said he would. No woman, no Joan, just waves rolling up and down the sand.

It was an odd sensation: feeling alone yet knowing someone was standing not twenty feet away, staring back. Mason felt blind. But at least he knew how to see. His friends down the beach, his girlfriend — their blindness was permanent. They were blind to necromancy, to the true nature of death, to a sixth sense he now possessed. But Mason knew that, somewhere beyond the smattering of stars shining faintly overhead, between the fourteen-billionth light year and Earth, some alien creature existed that wouldn't believe just how blind he was too.

Halfway back, Mason veered left into the woods. Unsure if Joan was still watching him, he positioned himself behind the trunk of a tree before unzipping the fly of his jeans. "Ah, yeah." Pissing seemed somehow simpler when you were a little drunk. Mason sidetracked once more, this time to the ocean, and bent down onto his knees. He held his hands beneath the water like two spatulas, letting the waves roll over his knuckles until he felt acceptably clean. It was more ritual than hygiene, he knew. Finally, Mason meandered toward the fire.

"Welcome back," said Craig. "Did you get lost or just break the Guinness world record for longest piss?"

Mason seated himself in the sand beside Asha and cracked open another Corona. "Just took some time to enjoy the scenery," he replied.

"Mason likes to stare out at the ocean and think about the meaning of life," added Asha, who wasn't entirely wrong.

"So, anyway, like I was saying." Craig turned his attention back toward Jasmine, both of them red-faced and smiling. "Kevin is essentially a giant douchebag."

Mason leaned into Asha, kissing her temple, and then rocked backward, a strand of her hair still stuck to his lips. She fell into his chest, curling inward like a cat, purring a soft moan.

He felt warmer again, and not just from the fire crackling between them. Mason remembered something that cop had said to him that night two years ago, the night he saw so many people die. "Knowing I have her," he'd said about his girlfriend (who also happened to be Mason's favorite professor), "it just makes all the dark stuff a little less dark." Mason understood that now. He understood it as well as he understood anything.

With yet another heavy task at hand, which he'd stupidly accepted — was it responsibility that chased him like some ceaseless ex-lover, or was it Mason who was the addict? — he knew he'd appreciate Asha's warmth even more in the coming weeks. Mason sometimes wondered what he'd do without her. Probably take up smoking again.

Chapter 4

One year later, still no answers
by Vivian Woo

It was a year ago today that the clouds over Terminal City turned crimson, a year since the blood rain poured from our sky. So startling the phenomenon was, so unreal, it seemed safe to assume that an answer would come quickly. Surely, there had to be a good reason, a big reason.

But a year on, we're no closer to finding it.

It was not the first time that red had poured from above, but we now know our blood rain was different. We know it was not just sand being carried in the clouds and then released in the rain, as has happened before. Ours left no trace, no evidence, no answers. The rain simply turned back to blue and washed itself away, leaving us to wonder if it was a collective delusion.

But of course, we know it was not. We all saw it, and we can still see it in the countless videos that were recorded. Crimson rain, rain as red as blood, poured from our sky, and we haven't the faintest clue why. It's a strange feeling in the information age: having no answer.

We are certainly not the first people in history to be unable to explain our weather. Many ancient civilizations believed that rain, lightning, earthquakes: all were operated by the gods. Gods who could be appeased with the right, often fatal, sacrifice. Indeed, more dangerous than not knowing is mistakenly thinking you do. The truth, after all, was always out there, lost in some far-flung future, des-

tined to be discovered by those who were intelligent and patient.

The truth of our red rain may too be over the great mountains of time, just out of view. And so long as we keep our eyes open, we will get there. It is impatience, our need to think we know now, that makes us blind.

—*The Terminal City Chronicle*

— «» —

Clayton Stark cleared his throat. "Can I get the, uh, gnocchi? I don't think I'm saying that right."

The server smiled and nodded, collecting their menus before she went.

"*Nyo-key*," said Alicia from beside him, looking humored.

"What did I say?" he asked.

"Sounded like *naw-chee*."

"Not even close, then. At least I didn't pronounce the g." Clayton glanced across the table toward his girlfriend's parents. "Sorry, I'm not much of a food guy. More of a consumer than a connoisseur."

Fred, Alicia's father, shrugged. "I suppose there are worse ways to be ignorant." He was half-joking. He often half-joked with Clayton, torn between the fact that they were quite different, the two of them, and their unlikely friendship. Fred was the sort of guy who wore cufflinks to dinner, silver ones tonight, slipping out the arm of his navy blazer as he reached for his glass of Pinot gris; the sort of guy who spent seventy dollars on a haircut, even if he didn't have a lot of hair; the sort of guy who'd gone to university for a decade and surrounded himself with people who'd done likewise — like his daughter and wife, sitting next to him, smirking; the sort of guy who, despite his nurtured appreciation of the finer things in life, was fiercely smart and recognized and respected intelligence above all else. And so he liked Clayton, even more than he liked gnocchi.

"It's quite good here," said Fred, "the gnocchi."

"I think I actually prefer Clayton's version," said Brenda, Alicia's mother. "*Naw-chee*. It's more intuitive, no? Language is always changing, darling, shedding its archaic forms for more intuitive ones. *Naw-chee*: that's how I'm going to say it from now on." Brenda was a linguistics professor with long silver hair and a good sense of humor. Clayton liked her.

He liked them both, in fact, which was good given that he'd been dating their daughter for three years now. Certainly, they were a stark contrast to his own folks. His mom worked at a Walmart in the suburbs, and his dad was in Florida, or was it California these days? The two didn't talk. Clayton, meanwhile, had been the first person in his family to graduate high school, let alone get his degree, and to Mom his bachelor's made him academic royalty. To the folks sitting across the table, however, it made him just barely qualified to date their daughter. Everyone lived in their own bubbles, he supposed.

The restaurant they were sitting in, an old Italian eatery with classic white table cloths and smartly dressed servers, was certainly one type of bubble. Thirty-dollar plates were the cheap option. The clientele was a mix of old money and new money, but they all had that one thing in common, that thing that defined who you were, and who you could be, more than anything else: money. Not necessarily crazy money, but growing up the way he did, Clayton had a very different definition of wealth than the people around him.

Except Alicia. She got it. Looking beautiful as ever, her blonde hair grown out longer than usual — pouring over one shoulder like a mane of gold — she was still the best thing in Clayton's life. Her dress tonight was red, the same shade as her maroon-framed glasses, which were the one constant in her otherwise fluid wardrobe. Alicia could rock a million different looks a million different ways; Clayton, meanwhile, was all jeans and neutral-colored collared shirts.

"Brenda and I were watching this documentary the other day, *Red Night*." It was Fred. "Some subpar television production. The channel eludes me. Did you happen to catch it?"

Alicia shook her head, rotating toward Clayton, who shrugged.

"You didn't miss anything," said Fred. "It was mediocre, but—"

"Which was it?" Brenda faced her husband. "Subpar or mediocre? Below average or simply average?"

Fred smiled. "It was bad."

"Go on." Brenda nodded.

"Anyhow." Fred appeared more amused than annoyed. "It had me pondering on the red rain from two years ago — that's what it was about, the documentary. But what can you say about a phenomenon for which there is no good explanation? There's a doomsday cult, did you know that? Wearing white robes, talking about the Maker. These folks might as well be straight out of the seventies." He laughed at his own reference. "God-fearing brutes notwithstanding, still nothing has come to light. We're as dumbfounded today as we were the night it happened. It's a nagging curiosity for me, this rain."

"He talks about it a lot," affirmed Brenda, "which is why we watched that subpar documentary."

"How can you not talk about it?" Fred spoke with both hands outstretched. "It amazes me," he continued, "how so many people have simply moved on. How time has turned it normal, just a thing that happened — blood-red rain pouring over the city. Just another Friday, folks."

"People want to be comfortable," said Alicia, "more than they want an answer. If you cannot explain something away, the easiest alternative is to ignore it."

Like Fred, Clayton hadn't ignored it. Couldn't, even if he wanted to, but he supposed he wouldn't be a very good detective were he in the habit of ignoring things. It was more than just the rain; it was that night — the night he killed a man. And so more than most people, even an insatiably curious man like Fred, Clayton needed an answer.

"It's not just the rain," said Clayton, twirling the red wine in his glass. "The explosion on the bridge: we still don't know who did it, or why that helicopter went down. And I still don't know anything about that guy I shot, as hard as I try. His identity was, well, bullshit. As far as we know, he's still just some John Doe with a suit and a gun. And there was this…" —he shook his head— "this puddle of human blood we found a couple days before it all went down. Again, no answers. How does all that happen? The rain turns red, a goddamn bridge explodes, and then some guy who looks like a government agent pulls a gun on me for no clear reason. One night." Clayton held up his index finger. "This all happened in one night, in this city, and two years later... well, it's like you said, Fred: we still don't understand shit." Clayton took a swig.

"So, you believe all these things are connected?" asked Fred, who, unlike his daughter, had never heard Clayton's unabridged opinion on the matter.

"I'm not in the business of ignoring coincidences," said Clayton. "That's a few too many to ignore. It's too damn unbelievable to ignore. Whatever happened that night with the rain, I think we did it. Humans, not nature."

Fred scratched his clean-shaven chin then nodded from shoulder to shoulder, a *perhaps* look on his face. "I'm not one for conspiracy theories," he said, "but I see your point. I suppose an event as unlikely as this one could have an equally unlikely explanation. As I said before, it is a nagging curiosity of mine."

"I think we have that in common." Clayton looked over to Alicia, who understood just how true that was. She smiled. Hers was effortlessly regal, accentuating her high cheekbones. She was an angular woman, her statuesque qualities a gift from her mother's side.

"The linguine?"

Brenda raised her hand.

The server, a dark-haired twenty-something, had returned with dinner. As she began setting down their plates, Clayton realized just how hungry he was, eagerly eyeing his—

"And one *naw-chee*."

Alicia laughed first.

— ⟨⟩ —

Clayton shut the door behind them, dropping his keys into a dish beside the door. He ran one hand through his brown hair — sopping wet from the rain — feeling foolish for thinking he could forgo an umbrella for once. Hair used to be simpler, dryer, but he'd recently grown his longer on top. Alicia said it suited him better.

"I'm glad you two get along so well," she said.

"Eh?" Clayton shrugged off his black leather coat.

"You and my father," she clarified. "I wasn't sure you gentlemen would hit it off, at least not as well as you do. Although he'd never admit it, I suspect my dad wishes he too were a police detective, perhaps in a different life."

"That's hard to picture." Clayton smirked, hanging up his jacket. "What would you have done if he didn't like me, your dad?"

"That would have been his problem." Alicia kissed him on his wet cheek.

They were back home now. Home, specifically, was a condo at the edge of Terminal City's downtown peninsula, in a glass tower that looked like all the other glass towers piercing the shore. Clayton and Alicia had made the move six months ago, a move that had taken them out of their respective comfort zones. Neither of them had ever lived with a significant other despite being in their mid-thirties, and so the prospect had been met with virginal anticipation, a concoction of worry and excitement. In retrospect, Clayton wondered what he'd ever been afraid of.

"Stupid rain." Alicia extended a lock of her yellow hair, eyeing the wet strands between her fingers, and then marched into the bathroom.

Clayton, meanwhile, meandered into the living area, past their leather sofas and the 50-inch TV (his purchase), and then gazed out the wall of windows at the end of the room, hands on his hips. The view below their twenty-seventh-floor home was all that justified what they paid for the place. Beyond the reflective skyscrapers, ocean peaks shimmered with lights from above. Terminal was a city of mirrors, where everything masked itself with something else, something beautiful — just never what was right in front of you. Still, the ocean was Clayton's favorite sight, at least after the woman in the bathroom, her hair dryer going.

Across the inlet, Clayton could see the forest that encapsulated Carwin University, where Alicia taught philosophy, reminding him of his conversation with Fred. That's where he'd been the night the red rain came down:

lost on Carwin's campus and then, somehow, in a shootout with a stranger. He still suspected that young guy, Mason, knew more than he'd let on. He had come in for questioning and said little, but Clayton thought he'd caught a glimpse of recognition in his eyes at the sight of the body — the body of the man Clayton had killed. Alicia, who taught Mason, spoke highly of him, though that didn't mean he wasn't hiding something.

But all that happened two years ago. As he often did, Clayton told himself he should let it go even as he booted up his laptop, planning to do anything but. A smoker telling himself, sure, tomorrow, last one, promise. The files were hidden within a labyrinth of inconspicuously named folders, searchable only to him, or so he hoped. Alicia sometimes used his computer, and he'd rather keep his lingering suspicions to himself. She'd rather he left "the poor kid who just lost his father" alone.

Clayton popped in a single ear bud and clicked play, listening to his recorded conversation with Mason through one ear and Alicia's hair dryer through the other. He couldn't say how many times he'd listened to this ten-minute audio clip over the last two years. Enough times that he could probably recite most of it by memory. Enough times that he couldn't believe he'd missed something.

"Where did you find Mr. Huhhh — what was his name again?" asked Mason through Clayton's headphone, for the hundredth time. "The guy you showed me in the morgue."

"Outside your house." Clayton hated the sound of his own voice on tape; how do you say "umm" that much and not realize? "Then he broke in. Kicked the freaking door open."

Mason: "Jeez. That's weird."

Clayton: "Yeah."

Clayton rewound the clip back to Mason: "Where did you find Mr. Huhhh." Once more, this time sped down: "Mr. Hu — uhhh."

There.

It was subtle, a quick shift in tone, but the more Clayton thought about it — the more he replayed that "huh" — the less it sounded like a "huh," and the more it sounded like a Mr. Hu-something.

"Mr. Hudson," Clayton mused aloud. "Mr. Hunter. Mr.... Humphrey?"

A band of yellow light expanded from the bathroom door.

Clayton yanked out his ear bud and closed the evidence on his laptop. He slapped the monitor shut and stood back up, returning his gaze to the ocean outside his window. But his mind stayed where it was, processing this new revelation — unless, of course, he was kidding himself, growing obsessive, seeing clues where there were none.

Alicia approached him from behind, wrapping her bare arms around his chest. She kissed his shoulder.

Beyond the water, Carwin's campus was all but obscured by its shield of trees. Somewhere in that forest was Mason Cross, stirring in his strange house. Clayton was picturing him now, picturing what he might be doing, what he might be thinking. And most of all, what he would say to him the next time they met. Because now Clayton was sure of something: there would be a next time.

"This view never gets old, does it?" Alicia whispered into his ear.

A faint foghorn echoed across the ocean.

"No," said Clayton. "It really doesn't."

Chapter 5

Carwin's campus was a strange sight in the summer months: half a ghost town, with most students gone till fall. This suited Mason, ever an introvert, just fine.

He was on his way to Sherwood Hall, meandering down University Avenue, listening to the birds chirp. Last night's rain had already evaporated, and the sun was making cameos from behind failing clouds.

Mason was enjoying this summer more than past ones. Maybe because it truly was better, or maybe because he no longer felt disappointed by summer's empty promises. The season of expectation. But Mason already had what he wanted. He wished he were on his way to see Asha now, but a different person demanded his attention.

Eli Abelman. He was a professor of medieval studies here. Mason had researched him on the faculty page of Carwin's website, but beyond that, he hadn't found much on Eli. He was the opposite of Mason's father, a former professor here and one of Carwin's more public intellectuals. Google had endless pages to offer on John Cross. Or almost endless; his son had reached the end a couple times.

In any event, Eli's profile provided all that Mason had needed: his email address. Mason had written that he was interested in taking one of Eli's classes — which was true, if after the fact — and that he remembered he was a friend of his father. He was hoping that he had a minute to chat. Eli provided his office hours and, he added, was sorry for Mason's loss. Even after two-and-a-half years, Mason was still receiving condolences, as if any mention of Dad's death made it new again.

It did still hurt sometimes, usually when he thought about it too long and realized that time didn't make losing your dad any less terrible. Some people had shitty fathers, but Mason didn't count himself among them. Flawed as Dad was — as they both were — Mason was one of the lucky ones. He only wished he'd realized that sooner.

Sherwood Hall was a brutalistic beast of a building: a giant gray slab of cement pockmarked with small square windows. Mason had most of his classes here. It was nicer on the inside, though not by much. He yanked open the same glass door he always did and stepped through. Eli's office was up a floor and down the hall. After two years, Mason knew this labyrinth of hallways well enough not to get lost.

He knocked twice on Eli's office door.

Eli flung it open, squinting and seeming half-befuddled. "Mason," he said.

"That's me."

"Umm." Eli looked out of his element. "Come in. Sit."

Mason sat. Eli did likewise, across from him behind a gray desk, its surface hidden under a mess of books and papers. The room felt cramped, not from a lack of space but rather from a lack of tidying up. Behind Eli, a faded poster of a crumbling castle, silhouetted by an orange sunset, read, "History is our window into the future."

"So, Mason." Eli shuffled sheets around on his desk — as if there were still time to make things presentable — never making eye contact for more than a stolen second. "It's, umm, it's good to see you again. You said you were interested in taking one of my classes this fall?"

"That's right." Mason had two years left in his philosophy degree, and while not the real reason he was here, he did need to take a few electives. Medieval studies sounded fun, a feeling that was likely the result of Mason growing up reading dictionary-sized fantasy novels. "Maybe something introductory."

"Mhmm, mhmm." Eli nodded, staring down at whatever was, or wasn't, between his feet. Though it had been a while, he looked as Mason remembered him. Same expressions. Same style. Today it was a crumpled dress shirt beneath his green sweater vest, ill-fitting khakis, and a pair of faded loafers. His salt-and-pepper hair was the same too: bushy all over. Old men never changed their hair.

"I'll be teaching a two-hundred-level course on myths and legends from the Middle Ages," said Eli. "Very popular with students, that one. And I'm launching a new three-hundred-level on the Medieval Inquisition."

How appropriate, thought Mason, who knew a thing or two about inquisitors. And of course he would definitely take that one, the three-hundred-level. Mason, whose grades were north of average but south of great, had learned that class difficulty wasn't *his* biggest difficulty. He needed passion. He needed to care about what he was learning.

"Do you have any, umm—" Eli twirled a pen, dropped it. "Do you have any questions? I can certainly go into more detail."

Terrible as he was at lying, Mason was struggling to transition to the truth, to the real reason he was here. Or rather, a version of it. He wouldn't tell Eli that Joan suspected him of being treacherous to her cause, to keeping necromancy a secret — that she thought he was a dangerous radical. No, he wouldn't mention Joan at all. Lester: that was the approved lie, Mason reminded himself.

"So, I'm not really here to take your class," said Mason, so awkwardly. "I mean, I am going to take that inquisition one because it actually sounds really cool, but that's not why I'm here."

Eli shifted farther back into his chair, eyes squinting defensively. He picked his pen back up off the desk.

"Lester Wright. You know him?" asked Mason.

"Not exceedingly well," said Eli, "but yes."

"He told me about you back when he was, you know, alive. He told me you were one of us. I didn't think to reach out until now."

"One of… *whom?*"

Mason sighed, pondered, then shrugged. Sometimes it was easier to prove your point than state it — another lesson he'd learned from Lester — so he did just that. The air under Mason's palm began glowing red. He held the crimson orb beneath his chest like a secret, like a drug dealer who'd brought the shit.

Eli's eyes widened. "I see."

Mason let the orb die, and the room went stale again, losing its faint red aura.

Eli cleared his throat. "Interesting," he said, wagging an index finger. "I, umm, I didn't hear you chant. Why didn't I hear you chant?"

"Just a trick I learned," said Mason. A trick bestowed on him by death itself, but he left that part out. He wasn't sure why he held this particular truth back, why he couldn't nonchalantly mention that the Spirit Realm had revived him two years earlier. It was the reason for his improved power, the reason he could cast spells without chanting when other necromancers could not, and yet — on a purely emotional level — his resurrection felt like an Achilles heel, his kryptonite. As if the truth would disarm him somehow. There was a dash of vanity in there too: he'd be a good necromancer even without this gift, his curse, whatever it was, and Mason wanted some credit for being smart.

"So, when did you first learn necromancy, Mason?" asked Eli.

"About two years ago," replied Mason, who noticed Eli's eyes calculating. "Lester taught me, not my father."

Eli nodded and then shook his head downward. "He was a brilliant man, your father. We worked on a few spells together, did you know that? We did, we did. It was mostly him, I suppose. I had my head in the books. Your dad, he was the artist, the one who turned my theories into realities. He was a man who took action, you see, made things come alive. I envied that. He sure was something, whereas I..." Eli shrugged then said casually, "I'm not always entirely sure what kind of man I am."

Mason wasn't entirely sure either.

"I'm so sorry, Mason." Eli's eyes had turned a soft shade of red, but not from necromancy.

"Thanks.... It's been three years, though." Mason was rounding up liberally. "Almost three years."

"I suppose at your age, three years feels like a lot," replied Eli. "I forget these things."

Someone knocked on the window behind Mason.

Eli gazed past him, half-grinned, then waved whoever it was into the room. The door squeaked as she stepped into the office. She was short but slender, her heart-shaped face lightly freckled, with straight black hair broken by a streak of blue. She had a tattoo on her forearm, written in Latin, but Mason was far from fluent in that particular dead language.

She smiled at Mason. "Hello."

"Hey."

"Liana." She extended her hand.

"Mason." He shook it, encompassing her small fingers in his.

"Mason, meet Liana Park," said Eli. "Liana, this is Mason Cross. His father was John Cross, whom you met once, I believe. Yes, yes."

"Oh," she said. "Yeah."

Mason caught that look in her eyes, that look he'd seen a dozen times before, and waited for her to cough out the obligatory condolences, as if she'd just swallowed something that couldn't go down without first coming back up.

But she didn't. "What are you studying here, Mason?"

"Philosophy."

"Nice." Liana nodded enthusiastically.

"You?"

She pointed toward Eli, her fingers forming a pistol. "Medieval studies."

"Liana is one of my grad students," said Eli. "I'm her supervisor. And not only..." —he hesitated— "not only in medieval studies."

Liana was in no rush to fill in the blank, her mood going from cheery to surprised with the flick of a switch. Mason, whose emotional reactions festered like failed experiments, looked intensely at the wall and waited for Eli to explain.

"Mason," the professor continued, looking at her, "is, umm, one of us. A necromancer."

And Liana was back to cheery just like that. "Oh, cool!"

Mason forced a smile and nodded.

"Hey, check this out." Liana held out a finger and began chanting, her eyes glowing red. A pinpoint of crimson sparkled into existence, atop the tip of her nail, and then she drew. The red light followed her finger until she had handwritten her name in the air between them.

"That is way cooler than Etch A Sketch," said Mason, who didn't know how she'd done it, either. He was impressed, excited even, distracted from his mission — or whatever it was.

"I know, right," said Liana, waving off her signature like a second thought. Red coils curled and faded back to nothing, as all necromancy does.

"Mason." It was Eli. "I must head out. A prior engagement. I did not realize that we would be talking about — well, you know. I would like to converse further, however. I am busy this weekend until Sunday evening. Can you meet me at Holy Trinity Cathedral downtown? At nine sharp, preferably."

Mason shook his head but not to say no, a what-the-fuck look about him. "You want me to meet you at a church? On Sunday night?"

Eli was already standing up, packing paper into his leather shoulder bag. "Yes, yes. Does that work for you?"

"Yeah... sure," said Mason. "Why not. I'll meet you at Holy Trinity on Sunday."

"Let me just jot down the details for you." Eli was opening and slamming drawers, looking for a pen or perhaps just his head.

"It's okay." Mason pointed to his own. "I'll remember. I can find it on Google."

Eli stood up straight — he was taller than Mason had realized when he didn't slouch — and led them out of his office, locking the door.

"Good to meet you, Mason," he said.

They shook hands. Liana watched on, smirking for some reason.

"See you Sunday," said Mason.

"Oh." Eli suddenly sounded flustered, more so than usual anyhow. "Liana. I'm so sorry. What did you need?"

She smiled. "It can wait."

"Okay." Eli waved with both hands. "I'm off, then." And so he was, long legs marching down the hallway and around the corner, out of sight.

Mason and Liana walked out together, escaping the maze that was Sherwood Hall to the sunlit campus. Liana put on sunglasses. Mason squinted. He'd already lost two pairs this summer. Sunglasses and umbrellas: the two things Mason couldn't hold onto for more than a few months.

In the sunlight, he noticed Liana was dressed in all black, a contrast to the white hot cement they walked on. A tight black T-shirt and black jeans, black boots too, but she wore them well, had a way about her.

"So." She spoke first. "Mason. How long you been a necromancer, bud?"

"Couple years," he said. "You?"

"Five or so," she replied, "but some years were more productive than others."

"Has Eli always been your mentor?"

"Not always, no," she said. "I had another teacher once, a long time ago, then I was on my own for a spell."

"I've been on my own for quite some time," echoed Mason. "It's not so bad, though. I'm lucky, I guess. I have a whole library of necromancy to learn from thanks to my dad. I've always learned stuff faster on my own, anyway."

Indeed, Mason's drive was all the encouragement he needed, or so he felt. He'd read half that library by now and could, for the most part, figure out most spells on his own. There was something inherently solitary about necromancy, he believed. Perhaps it was the fact that it was a fundamentally mental exercise, not a ritualistic one. There were no potions or sacrifices necessary. It wasn't like the magic in the fantasy novels he'd read (and continued to read). There were chants, sure, but even those Mason could forgo now that he understood Deathspeak. Simply put, spells didn't, couldn't, work until you understood them. Understanding was all that was truly required, and like death, he knew, understanding was something everyone arrived at alone.

"It ain't all just about learning, Mason," said Liana. "When you're really into something, passionate, excited..."

She embodied the word, skipping a little. "When you do something you love, it's nice to know a few people who love it too, people you can talk about it with. Otherwise that part of you will always be, well, not just alone but, you know, lonely."

"I suppose you're right," replied Mason. "I guess we can be friends, you and I."

"You bet your ass we can be friends," she said. "It'll sure as heck be nice to hang out with a necromancer who's not Eli — God bless him — for once. I'll show you how I did that cool light tracing spell sometime if you want."

"That'd be great," he said. "Hopefully I can share a few spells too."

Liana stopped in her tracks. They were at an intersection along University Avenue. She nodded her head one way; he was going the other. "I gotta jet, but I'm glad we met. Shit, that rhymed."

"Yeah." He laughed. "Me too."

She waved and wandered off, leaving Mason alone again, with his thoughts.

Walking home, Mason thought about how nice the day was, how Liana seemed cool, how Eli seemed weird, about this mission he was on and whether or not he wanted to follow through with it, and he thought about Sunday — the church.

Why in God's name did Eli want to meet in a church?

Chapter 6

For we are but of yesterday, and know nothing, be-
cause our days upon earth are a shadow.

—Job 8:9

— «» —

It was just after nine and a hint of orange tinted the city
skyline, a dying flame in a room of mirrors. The sun was
setting alongside Holy Trinity Cathedral's central tower,
vanishing behind one side and then re-emerging from the
other as Mason made his way across the street. It was a gray
stone cathedral with sharp copper roofs, green from age.
There were few century-old buildings in Terminal City, but
Holy Trinity hugged its corner of downtown stubbornly —
the only heritage building at an intersection of glass office
towers.

As Mason stepped through the church's open double
doors — even the doors were artful, with embossed oak,
standing fifteen feet tall — he could already hear them.
Voices, murmuring then singing as he tiptoed farther down
the hallway. The church workers who saw him smiled and
nodded, but Mason felt like a spy, like a demon in lamb's
clothing — or just an atheist in a church.

The sanctuary was dimly lit with the golden hue of
candles, adding intimacy to a room built to show off scale, its
vaulted ceilings and tall windows dark and distant tonight.
Smoke swirled from a thurible making its way around the
room, the extended arm of a slow-moving figure obscured
in old shadows. Metal and chain, back and forth from a
practiced hand, swinging as perfectly as a pendulum.

But more than the sights, the sounds overwhelmed.
Gregorian chanting. Mason had never heard dying music in

person, music from a time too long ago to truly comprehend. He couldn't see them at first, the monks who chanted, and then he looked up. On the balcony behind him, two rows of old men stood slouching, singing far older songs. Latin again. Maybe he should learn the dead language — his father had found it worth his while.

Mason turned his attention back to the wooden pews. Where was Eli? The crowd was small, with as many people sitting and listening as there were singing, some with their heads bowed, their eyes closed, some looking around the room, taking it all in — or perhaps they were just bored. Gregorian chanting probably wasn't for everyone.

But Mason liked it. The voices, the way they echoed through the room, the candles, the small cloud of smoke circling the sanctuary. It wasn't one thing in particular that he liked — it was the whole, the experience. There was something about it, something... not necessarily holy but majestic, in a way he was still grappling to understand.

And there he was.

In the darkest corner sat Eli, his bushy head hanging below his shoulders. Mason wandered over and seated himself slowly, the bench beneath him creaking.

"Hey," he whispered. "Sorry I'm late."

Eli raised his head, looking loose and relaxed, looking, in other words, unlike his usual self. He waved his hand — *Don't worry about it*, his expression said — and then dropped his head once more, eyes closed.

Mason wondered if he should do the same. Instead, he took in the room some more. And then, finally, it hit him: that feeling he couldn't quite explain, that feeling he'd never experienced before. Not spiritual — no, Mason wasn't going to convert, not today, not ever — but rather it was... a sense of history. Time had only ever been a concept to him, but here in this room, this music, it moved more than his mind. It placed him in the grand scheme of time. Mason could feel history — and his place in it.

— «» —

"I wouldn't have pegged you as a religious man." Mason inhaled a mouthful of steam from his white porcelain tea cup, the Earl Grey inside still too hot for comfortable consumption. He slurped a painful sip and returned the tea to its saucer.

Eli let out a single chuckle. "Religious?" he said. "No, no. And even if I were" —he pointed toward his curly gray hair, which was tousled to one side— "wrong religion. Reminds me of a joke: what do you call a Jew in a church?"

"I'm not going to touch that one." Mason leaned back in his chair.

"An atheist." Eli snickered, succumbing to his own joke.

Mason smirked. "The town I grew up in, Sanford, most people there were Protestant," he replied, "and believing in God and being part of the religion, well, Protestants treat them as inseparable."

Eli nodded knowingly.

They were sitting at a small table across from one another, in the back corner of a quaint café a block down the road from Holy Trinity. Outside the window beside them, car after car zoomed by. A choir of honks, a loud motorcycle trumpeting a symphony of insecurity. Inside, a coffee grinder whizzed incessantly. The inescapable sounds of life downtown.

"Obvious question, then," said Mason, "why meet at a church?"

Eli pointed at Mason with his whole hand, which shook slightly from too much caffeine. "First," he replied, "I have a question for you. Did you enjoy the performance?"

"Gregorian chanting?" Mason thought about it. "Yeah," he said. "It was… meditative. It made me think about history, about people who lived a thousand years ago, and about how maybe they'd had a similar experience, sitting in a similar room, listening to similar sounds. Yeah, I enjoyed it."

Eli smiled. "Well, I think you just answered your own question." He seemed calmer than the last time they'd met. Maybe it was the music. "Sorry I couldn't see you sooner," he said. "It was my weekend with my boy, Charles. Thirteen now. Nothing like me, Charles, no matter how hard I try to get him to pick up a goddamn book. I've somehow become my son's antithesis." Eli shook his head and, briefly, looked more like the bewildered professor Mason remembered from last week. "In any event," he continued, "this weekend was good, which is to say it wasn't explicitly bad."

Eli took a gulp of his coffee, which Mason had noticed was heavy on the cream and sugar.

Mason preferred his black and said as much. "Isn't it a little late for coffee, anyhow?" he added, trying again to drink his scalding tea. Nope. "I'm not normally a tea drinker, but less caffeine, you know."

"My mistress, Coffee, she makes a fool of me," said Eli. "Perhaps you should have opted for herbal tea, no?"

"What did I get?" asked Mason.

"Black tea."

"What's the difference?"

"Black tea has caffeine in it." Eli swigged his sweetened coffee. "Herbal tea does not."

"Ah," replied Mason. "Like I said, I'm not much of a tea drinker."

"So, tell me... how are your, umm, non-academic studies going?" Eli paused and straightened his neck to survey the half-empty café, as if an inquisitor might be within ear shot. He leaned forward on his elbows. "Are you practicing with any fellow necromancers?" he whispered.

Mason shook his head. "Just me and my spells," he said at normal volume, less concerned with secrecy than Eli evidently. If anyone overheard them, Mason figured they'd be mistaken for a couple of nerdy Dungeons & Dragons players — not a couple of nerdy necromancers. Plus, he knew the inquisition was all but done for, at least for the time being. He'd watched Rowland kill the majority of those bastards. He wondered if other necromancers knew this, but these days Mason was a solitary spellcaster, lost to his herd until just recently, until Joan showed up.

"It's honestly not been all bad, though," Mason continued. "Being on my own, I mean. I've always learned things fastest that way. I think I learn better from problem solving than I do from listening to other people. I'm rather... logical."

Eli nodded. "If you don't mind me saying, you sound like your father."

Mason hadn't heard that one in a while. "I wasn't trying to take after him," he said. "It just sort of happened." He sipped his tea, and for once it didn't burn.

"That's how it goes," said Eli. "Sneaks up on you. I was thirty before I could admit how much I was like my father. My boy, Charles, on the other hand..." He sighed. "I think it goes one of two ways, two extremes, like a magnet: your children either attract your qualities or repel them with a vengeance." Eli pulled his hands apart in the manner of a volcano. "I'd rather the former, but, well, we don't choose our children. It's best not to dwell on such things, I suppose."

"I dwell on everything," said Mason. "Constantly."

"As do I." Eli smiled. "Just don't forget to dwell out loud on occasion, with good company. I'm sure you've learned many things on your own — if you're anything like your father — but there are lessons you can only learn from other people, lessons you cannot find in books."

"Liana actually said something similar the other day," replied Mason.

Eli nodded knowingly. "She's a smart young lady, that one," he said. "Indeed, Mason, if you are interested, I, umm, we would welcome your company on an upcoming expedition. What do you know about Winter's End?"

Mason shook his head. "Not much. Lester once said it was the closest thing necromancy had to an academy, and I've read mentions of it. I've always wanted to go, but I have no idea where it is."

"Of course, of course. That is by design," said Eli. "Winter's End is a secret within a secret, unknown even to many necromancers. Admittance is invite-only, but I am an invited guest, as was your father, as you will be too if you choose to join us."

"When are you going?" Mason contained his excitement — he was better at holding in emotions than he was at expressing them.

"Next weekend," said Eli. "Short notice, I realize, but alas, we only just met."

"Fair enough. Second question: why the trip? What's at Winter's End?"

"Right, right." Eli stalled, stirring his coffee, his small silver spoon clinking against the cup. "I have a project that I'm working on." He hesitated once more, eyes squinting away from Mason. "A, uhh, rather sizable project. You see, Mason, unlike your father, I have failed to bring my ideas to fruition. Not this time, however. I've promised myself not this time. And to complete my project, I must go to Winter's End."

"That's... vague," replied Mason. "I take it you don't want to tell me about this project."

Eli faked a smile. "Another time, perhaps. Yes, another time."

Perhaps this was it: the first clue that Eli was guilty of Joan's accusations — that he had a plan to put necromancy's secrets in peril. Mason didn't answer immediately. A table of middle-aged women made their way out the front door, and it was a small enough space that the café felt suddenly, significantly emptier.

"Can I get back to you," asked Mason, "about Winter's End?"

"Of course, of course," said Eli. "Do let me know in a few days, however. Preparations and all that."

Mason nodded, his teacup bobbing on his bottom lip.

Eli's smile seemed real this time. "I am glad you joined me tonight, Mason. I recall I invited your father a few times, to Gregorian chanting I mean. I've been listening to these monks chant for a decade now, but he never did come out. Not a fan of religion, your father." Eli shook his head for emphasis. "I tried to explain to him that it wasn't about religion, not for me. Perhaps for those other men and women in the pews, the feeling they get is spiritual, or at least that's what they would call it. Word choices: sometimes they're all that separate us. The sensation, though, I think it's the same for them and for us, for believers and atheists alike. Even for necromancers. We just call it something else."

Eli dropped his chin to his palm like a philosopher of old, staring out the window into the bright city night. "Even excruciatingly rational people like you and me, like your father — we're emotional beings, no? Our means may be logical, sure, but our ends, our desires, what gets under our skin, what excites us, what motivates us — our foundations are biological. We're towers built on grass and dirt, even the skyscrapers among us. Otherwise, Mason, why not act like a psychopath? Is it any less logical to want the world to wither?

"Only," said Eli, "if you care that it does not."

Chapter 7

Everybody has met these people, been deceived and manipulated by them, and forced to live with or repair the damage they have wrought. These often charming — but always deadly — individuals have a clinical name: psychopaths. Their hallmark is a stunning lack of conscience; their game is self-gratification at the other person's expense. Many spend time in prison, but many do not. All take far more than they give.

—Robert D. Hare, Without Conscience: The Disturbing World of the Psychopaths Among Us

— «» —

Denver, 21 years earlier

Kyle had two best friends. There was the boy across the street, Brian — a bit weird, that one, but Kyle took what he could get — and then there was Jason. Jason was the opposite of weird, its foil, achingly normal by choice.

What he lacked in height — he was a short kid for his age — Jason compensated for in hair. His was an unkempt, unshowered mess of brown, bouncing against his shoulders whenever he ran, and he was already running, eternally excited. Kyle hated Jason's hair.

He also hated Jason's stupid skateboard. Jason carried it with him wherever they went, but he wasn't good enough to do tricks. Still, he tried sometimes, asking his friends to watch, asking Kyle to watch, as every failed kickflip sent his skateboard flying out from underneath his feet like a car careening off the highway, flipping and skidding. Kyle sometimes imagined them that way — imagined the skateboard was a car with a mom and dad, with kids and a dog. He imagined their deaths, bloodied bodies flying through the windshield. Sometimes, Kyle imagined Jason was in the car.

Jason did have an impressive pog collection, however, and this Kyle envied.

But Kyle hated Jason.

Kyle hated all of his friends.

— «» —

Kyle also hated carrots. Mom had made him a peanut butter and jelly sandwich for lunch — he never tired of peanut butter and jelly sandwiches — but the price, there was always a price, was a side of baby carrots. They're good for your eyes, she'd say, but Kyle's eyes were just fine. When school was in session, he'd simply toss his carrots into the cafeteria trashcan, where they belonged, and lie to her. Easy peasy. But it was summer, and he was sitting at home at the breakfast table all by himself.

Or almost all by himself. Mom was in the living room, talking through the wall.

"How was your sleepover last night?" she asked.

"Fine," said Kyle, still chewing.

He wasn't in the mood for chatter. Mom was boring. She bored him over breakfast and lunch, and then she bored him in the evenings. Lately, she was boring him more than usual. She was a teacher, his mom, which meant she had the summers off too. Other nine-year-olds had babysitters or went to summer camp. Kyle was jealous of the kids who went to camp, not because he wanted to go too — he knew he'd hate camp, what with all those people, and rules, and dumb games — but rather because he'd never been asked. Had never even been given the option. Someone should have asked Kyle what *he* wanted, but adults never did that.

There was a whole world Mom and Dad refused to see.

"You've been spending a lot more time with Jason and Travis," she said, approval apparent in her tone. "Dr. Fleischmann will be glad to hear you've made such good friends."

Kyle didn't reply, rolling a single carrot along the table under the palm of his hand. He didn't give a damn what Dr. Fleischmann thought. Kyle wasn't some stupid shrink's science project and owed her nothing, not a grain of truth.

And he definitely didn't give a damn what Mom thought either, or Dad for that matter. Jason and Travis were good for one thing, however: they got Kyle away from all the awful adults in his life.

The doorbell rang.

He could hear Mom's footsteps through the wall (Kyle had no reason to answer the door himself) and then the front door swing open. He could hear his squeaky voice from outside: "Hey, Ms. MacDonald, can Kyle come out and play?"

"Kyle!" she called in a shrill tone, despite the fact that he was fifteen feet away and could hear her just fine. "Jason's here."

Kyle sighed, stuffing the last of his baby carrots into his back pocket.

— ⟨⟩ —

Jason had one foot on his skateboard and was launching himself ahead of Kyle, who made no effort to catch up. They were on the sidewalk two blocks from home, heading to the forest: a stretch of green beside the elementary school, just a few trees deep. It was a forest through nine-year-old eyes.

Kyle reached into his back pocket and pulled out a handful of carrots. "Want a carrot?"

"Nah," said Jason from ten feet ahead, standing with his skateboard mounted upright like a cane. "Carrots are gay."

Kyle flung them into the nearest bush.

"Yo, watch this." Jason was on his skateboard again, crouching. Kyle knew what came next.

To his credit, Jason actually got the skateboard spinning this time, turning in the air between his sneakers and the cement like a torpedo engine. Skateboarder's purgatory. For a brief second, Kyle thought he was actually going to pull it off this time. For a brief second, he resented him for it.

"Aw, hell!"

The skateboard had spun half a turn too far, landing upside down. Jason tripped over the wheels. He fell onto his elbows and said nothing, but Kyle could see him cringing.

Kyle snickered.

"I hit a stupid rock." In general, Jason hit a lot of rocks. He rolled over and examined a scuff on his elbow. He was bleeding, but not badly. He brushed away the pebbles sticking to his forearm and jumped to his feet.

Kyle contained his smiled. "Need to go home?" he asked.

"Nah." Jason snatched his skateboard off the ground, angry at it. "I'm fine."

Kyle shrugged. They continued on.

The school was eerily quiet in the summer months. Classrooms with clean desks, a playground with still swings: it looked like a scene after the rapture. An adult told Kyle once that all children go to heaven. Kyle couldn't say why, but deep down he felt that heaven held no place for him. Kyle was nine, but he wasn't a child. He wasn't an adult either. He simply wasn't his body.

Jason sprinted as they neared the forest. Skateboards, after all, didn't work so well on grass. Kyle crossed the rest of the field at a leisurely pace, fanning Jason's irrational impatience.

"C'mon," said Jason, pacing between two tall evergreens, kicking out clumps of bark mulch.

They wandered past a few more trees and to their usual spot. Their hangout was a small clearing where the dirt had been smoothed and packed tightly, transforming it into a natural surface. The trees here were covered in carved markings— "J+L 4ever," a picture of a dick, "Matt's gay" — but otherwise it was nothing special. Save for the fact that Jason and he (and sometimes Brian, when they were feeling socially generous) hung out here more summer days than not.

Jason collapsed to his knees, his skateboard falling with him, and reached into his pocket. He pulled out a neon green plastic tube and clicked open the lid. Carefully, or at least as carefully as Jason did anything, he poured out his collection of pogs onto the clearing.

Kyle joined him, sitting cross-legged before unveiling his own collection, a more modest one than Jason's.

Jason's parents had more money than Kyle's.

"Check this out." Jason dug into his other pocket. It was a new slammer, this one polished metal with a ring of black skulls circling the surface. He held it before him like a prize.

Kyle had to admit that it was pretty fucking badass. "Nice," he said flatly, jealousy bubbling up beneath his plain expression. Kyle had only ever had one slammer, made of plastic and colored a hazardous orange — and increasingly, chipped at the edges. He remembered how he saw it six months ago: bright and fiery. New. Now it looked dull and cheap and old, especially next to Jason's Porsche of a slammer.

"Play for keeps?" asked Jason.

Kyle hesitated. He knew it was a bad idea. That slammer was dangerous. But right now, he wanted more than anything to get the better of Jason, even if it meant risking getting exactly the opposite.

"Fine," said Kyle, and they began stacking their pogs upside down.

The game was simple, talentless really, but even so, Kyle's nature compelled him to compete. To win. Slammers were thrown at the pile of cardboard pogs and whichever pogs flipped right side up on your turn, you kept. Those were the rules. It was a stupid game.

Kyle went first. He fucked up. His slammer barely brushed the pile, flipping only the top pog over. He took his meager reward and swallowed hard.

"My turn," said Jason, biting his bottom lip as he raised his slammer, ready to strike.

Boom.

An explosion of pogs.

He'd just won half the goddamn pile in a single turn. He scooped them up, all his new pogs — Kyle's pogs — beaming with the shit-eating grin of an unprofessional poker player.

They played the next few turns in silence.

Kyle hated his friends.

"It's not fair," he said after the game was over and he was down a dozen pogs. "Metal slammers aren't fair."

Jason made fists and scrubbed his cheeks, mimicking crying. (No one actually cries like that, thought Kyle.) "Better luck next time, man," he said. "Not my fault your slammer sucks. Get a better slammer."

Well, if he was going to insist.

It was the first time Kyle ever hurt anyone. At least, the first time he'd *really* hurt someone. He almost didn't realize he was doing it. The animal in him took over, took Jason's steal slammer, clenched it— "Hey, give that back!" —and then did just that, hurling it into Jason's cheek.

Jason keeled over then curled into a ball, hiding his face. It was the quietest Kyle had ever seen him. Then came soft sobs, muffled by his sleeve.

Kyle stared down at him, wondering what to do next, wondering how to get out of this. He hadn't a clue. The only thing he knew for sure was what he wanted in that moment, and it was lying in front of him. Not Jason but his silver, skull-laced slammer. Kyle picked it up and pocketed it. Jason, who still had his head buried in his arm, didn't notice.

Then Kyle collected his pogs — plus a few of Jason's — and piled them neatly into his blue plastic tube. Slowly, he backed away.

That's when Jason looked up, looked straight at him. He sniffled. "I'm going to tell," he said.

Kyle said nothing. He turned away, a stoic expression on his face, and walked off. He walked all around the neighborhood until evening set in, avoiding going home for as long as he could — avoiding punishment.

He'd screwed up big time. He could see his grounding coming from a mile away, a big one this time, chugging toward him like a freight train, and he'd gone and tied himself to the tracks. He could see Mom's expression, and Dad's, and stupid Dr. Fleischmann's.

Idiot. You're better than this. You're better than them.

And still, despite everything, despite the adult-ocalypse that loomed over the horizon, a smile sprung up on Kyle, a smile he couldn't suppress. It was, in fact, a real smile.

He'd wanted that for so long, he realized: to put Jason in his place. And God, it had felt every bit as good as he'd imagined it would.

But next time, Kyle decided, next time he'd be more careful.

Next time, no one would find out.

Chapter 8

The basement was a dim crimson and everything in it tinted red. The only aura came from the black chandelier in the middle of the room, but it held no light bulbs. Rather, six red orbs hovered over the chandelier's wiry arms, lighting the windowless space with a palette of blood. Mason's library of necromantic texts, a gift passed down from his father, operated on spells alone.

At its center was a large wooden table, old and oak — a place to experiment, write, or simply soak up a good read unbothered by the world outside — and that's where Mason was sitting now, bent over a book. It wasn't the first time he'd read this particular one.

It was the only "published" piece of prose he'd found by his father written about necromancy. Sure, in his public life Dad had been a famous academic with an impressive bibliography, but when it came to necromancy, John Cross had been a doer, a spellcaster, not a writer, or so Mason had been told.

But here was an essay written by Dad for other necromancers — necromancers like his son — of which perhaps a hundred copies (a generous estimation) had been published and distributed in secret. There was one part in particular that Mason had read over and over:

> It is not heaven, and it is certainly not hell. From what we know, the Spirit Realm is an afterlife unlike any in myth, offering neither reward nor punishment. It is simply the place we all go when we die.
>
> No god oversees the Spirit Realm, which instead oversees itself. The Spirit Realm is formed from spir-

its, from what they perceive and imagine, and all eventually fade into its collective consciousness. Thus, the place itself and its overseer are, for the most part, one and the same.

Think of it like rain. Each human life is a raindrop, and death arrives when we hit the ground. Eventually, we evaporate. We still exist then, but our individuality is pulled apart as we become a piece of something far bigger, far greater: a cloud. The Spirit Realm is a conscious cloud. The difference being that it never rains again. The cloud only keeps collecting.

Indeed, the Spirit Realm is massive and powerful, but it is not omniscient or omnipotent. Nor is it infinite. The collective consciousness grew without guidance, absorbing spirits as they faded into human libraries: collections of information without self-awareness. Over time, an overarching self-awareness must have grown out of all this information, perhaps not unlike the robotic singularity speculated by futurists: that point when machines become conscious, when information creates life. The Spirit Realm evolved out of darkness, from faded memories, and created order where once there was none.

Thus, the Spirit Realm is more like humanity than any god. It has not always been, it may not always be, and it can make mistakes, though it learns from them. It continues to evolve — it is a spiritual civilization — and in this sense, too, the Spirit Realm and humanity are existential brethren: always growing and, hopefully, getting better.

There were a handful of other essays in this book, all about the Spirit Realm — its title, *Essays on the Spirit Realm*, was less inspiring than its contents — but Mason thought Dad's was the most interesting. He was biased of course, but the truth was his father had been a genius, exhaling insight like others did air.

This library was a testament to that. If you didn't count sleeping, Mason spent more time in this basement, reading and spellcasting — and occasionally doing his homework down here for some inexplicable reason — than he did in any other room of his house.

His stupidly big house.

After Lester died, Mason was left living all by himself, although he supposed Asha stayed over a lot. She kept a toothbrush, deodorant, and makeup in his upstairs bathroom, a hair dryer too. Oh, and most recently, her own bottle of shampoo because she didn't like the cheap man shampoo Mason used. "Just some essentials," as she put it, but Mason didn't mind. It made the place feel a little more lived in. He'd briefly considered getting a cat — a black one alluding to the fact that he was sort of like a witch, necromancy and all that, a joke no one else would be permitted to understand — but at the end of the day, Mason didn't want to have to take care of a fucking cat.

And so it was just him and his books, hanging out in a windowless bunker when he had a whole damn house, one with bedrooms he forgot even existed. But curiosity was his companion, his mentor, his roommate, and it hung out downstairs. Curiosity had kept him moving forward these past two years, reading necromantic text after necromantic text, though he knew there were only so many books to read. Mason would run out eventually.

He couldn't say how many spells he knew now. Hundreds. Mason could create complex illusions, for example, like the image of a concrete wall that hid the door to this room (which he'd recreated a dozen times in the past year). Some spells he knew only in theory, as they required another human being, but he was quite sure that, if it ever came to it, there was nothing he couldn't cast. His unique connection to the Spirit Realm, the bridge he'd crossed to death, meant Mason could truly understand Deathspeak (though far from fluently). At twenty-two, the best analogy he'd come up with was that it was like playing a video game with cheat codes enabled.

And so Mason's real challenge was a creative one, in coming up with new ways to use spirit energy, ways that couldn't be found in the books filling the densely packed shelves surrounding him.

This was harder than it might sound. In effect, it meant writing in a language you didn't understand. That was necromancy. Necromancers knew what certain phrases accomplished but not which parts did what — meant what. The result was a lot of trial and error: patching words together from different spells, typically ones that shared something in common with whatever it was you were trying to do, seeing what worked and, far more often, what did not.

Mason at least had the advantage of a gut feeling, a flicker of understanding from time to time. His special connection. But even then, spellcasting was like grammar: you still had to know all the rules.

His current project wasn't as simple as he'd been hoping. Mason was trying to recreate that traceable light Liana had shown him in Eli's office. It looked easy enough, but then so did a good magic trick. Looking easy and being easy were far from the same thing. He put his book down and gave it another go, and then another.

"Stupid fucking..." Mason sighed and started again.

He couldn't get the light to follow his fingertip, try and try as he might. It reminded him of that computer science class he'd taken last semester. With coding, sometimes you just needed to add a bracket somewhere and, voila, suddenly the whole damn program worked. Mason couldn't tell if he just needed to fix some small detail — add the Deathspeak equivalent of a bracket over there — or if he was going about the whole spell wrong. It was aggravating, and the funny thing was he knew Liana would be happy to teach him the spell — she'd said as much — but Mason took pride in doing things on his own.

"Damn it."

Two knocks came from upstairs.

Someone, apparently, was at the front door.

Mason set down his notepad, looking a little surprised. Odd. He wasn't expecting anyone. He supposed either Asha was dropping by unannounced or someone was selling religion. In case of the former, he got to his feet.

Leaving his library was a bit like tying a complicated pair of shoes: there was work to be done before he could get to the door. Mason stepped out of the room and turned to face its exposed entrance, which was glowing red. From a distance, you might mistake it for a photographer's dark room, if only film weren't a dead medium. But Mason practiced in a different dead art, and it wasn't one he was willing to share with the uninitiated (essentially, everyone in his life, even the woman he loved). And so Mason recited a simple spell in his mind and watched the door turn to concrete.

With his secret safe, he climbed the basement's creaky wooden stairs to the main floor.

Another two knocks.

This time, Mason answered — and didn't say anything. He knew this man, but the name stayed stuck on the tip of his tongue.

The man, who looked to be in his thirties, answered for him. "Clayton," he said. "Clayton Stark. We met two years ago."

"Right," said Mason, as much to himself. The cop who'd driven him home that fateful night. The one who'd killed Mr. Huxley. He'd shown Mason the body at the morgue and asked if he knew the man. Of course, Mason had said that he did not.

"Mind if I come in for a minute?" asked Clayton.

Mason didn't want to seem defensive — even if the unexpected visit made him slightly so — and said, "Sure." He nodded and welcomed him in with a swing of his hand.

"Thanks."

Mason led him to the kitchen table, where they both took a seat, opposite of one another.

"So, how can I help you?" asked Mason.

"Just a routine follow-up," replied Clayton. "Sometimes we like to check in again, even with old cases, see if maybe we missed something the first time. This one's still open, you know — this case — even after two years. That John Doe I killed..." Clayton eyed the white tile floor not five feet from him, inside the doorframe— "Right over there" —and then turned to Mason. "We still don't know who the hell that guy was."

"I see." What Mason couldn't see, however, was whether or not this really was a routine follow-up. What did Mason know about police work? Nothing, and perhaps Clayton knew that. "Do you want something to drink?" he asked, unsure what else to say.

"Just water's fine," said Clayton. "Thanks."

Mason fetched two clear glasses from the cupboard.

The thing with Mason, though, was that he was clumsy sometimes, too in his head to pay attention to his hands, too busy wondering what this visit was really about. To his credit, Mason filled the first glass just fine, but when he turned to offer Clayton his drink, it found the other glass first, still resting on the counter. They crashed and tinkled like a broken instrument.

"Aw, shit," spat Mason. Then an "Ow, fuck" as he realized he was bleeding.

"You okay?" Clayton got up from his seat and inched his way over.

"Damn it." Mason sighed. "Yeah, I'm fine. Just a little blood." Certainly nothing he wasn't used to.

Mason rinsed his hand in the sink then tore off a piece of paper towel. He crumpled it into a ball, padding his palm. Blood still seeped out, slowly now, painting the paper towel red.

"I have some bandages in my car," said Clayton, trying to be helpful.

Mason shook his head. "Don't worry about it." He dropped his blooded piece of paper towel onto the counter, ripped off another, and then took a seat.

"Forget the water." Clayton joined him, sitting back down.

"Oh, sorry."

"You're bleeding, man. Don't apologize." Clayton gave a friendly grin, and Mason was reminded of their first encounter, of Clayton's casual demeanor, of how he'd liked the guy.

"Fair enough," said Mason.

"This will only take a minute," replied Clayton, still in his brown leather jacket. "If you don't mind."

Mason saw him staring at his wound. "I'm fine. Fire away."

Clayton nodded. "First question, then. Remind me where you were the night of the altercation. That is, my altercation with the stranger who entered your house."

"I was at my girlfriend's for most of it," replied Mason. "We had a fight, though, and I went for a walk after that."

"What time did you leave for your walk?"

Mason shrugged. "I don't remember. I wasn't really paying attention to the time. We'd just fought, and I was a bit buzzed to be perfectly honest. Anyway, you already asked me these questions two years ago."

"Like I said, this is just routine." Clayton smiled. "Sometimes witnesses don't realize what's important to a case and leave out a key detail. It's probably more common than you think. You know how cops often ask the same question two, three, four times, even? We're not just acting like annoying pricks for nothing. Hard to believe, I get it, but people tend to be..." He considered his words. "Storytellers," he said. "And good stories leave out the boring stuff. But the boring stuff is often where we find our best clues."

Mason still didn't trust him. He liked him, but he didn't trust him. "Makes sense, I guess," he said. "Go on."

Clayton looked him squarely in the eyes. "Do you know a Mr. Humphrey?"

He hadn't asked that one the first time.

"Excuse me?" replied Mason.

"Mr. Humphrey," repeated Clayton. "Name ring a bell?"

It sure as hell did, but it was a dull, broken bell that rang the wrong note. Its vibrations echoed through him all the same. *Did he mean Mr. Huxley?*

Mason shook his head. "No," he said, "I don't know him." But perhaps Clayton wasn't looking for an answer, he considered. Perhaps he was looking for a reaction, and Mason wasn't sure if he'd just given him one. "Where'd you hear that name?" he asked.

"It came up in our investigation," said Clayton. "Never hurts to ask."

"I suppose not." Mason sat upright, like an animal pet against the grain of its fur. "Anything else?" he asked.

Clayton looked around the room and then eventually back toward Mason. "Nah," he said lightly. "I think we're good. We're done our routine follow-up."

They both stood and shook hands.

"So, you think you'll ever figure out who that guy was?" asked Mason, trying to sound conversational. Trying to sound innocent.

Clayton wandered over to the kitchen window and stared out, one hand leaning into the sink. "Honestly..." He breathed a long sigh. "I doubt it."

After that, they walked back to the front door as Clayton said goodbye.

"Best of luck to you," Mason told him.

Clayton nodded, smiling again, and walked to his car.

Mason closed the door, locking it for some reason — from whatever that was. He had killed four men that night two years ago, four times as many as Clayton had, and though they may have had it coming, Mason knew he had little legal recourse. He was a necromancer, and he operated outside the realm of legality. Now that night was coming back like a bad dream he'd thought he'd put to rest.

But some nights never truly ended.

And here he was, about to get himself mixed up in things again. Mixed up in the dangerous world of necromancy that existed outside the safety of his hidden basement, a world of secrets, a world far beneath the surface of society — the last, bloodiest layer before death itself.

Wandering back into the kitchen, Mason thumbed his phone with his uninjured hand. He looked at the text message he'd sent two hours ago, to Joan.

Joan, the message read, *I'm going to Winter's End with Eli.*

Mason set his phone down onto the kitchen counter, figuring he should clean up and take care of his hand. But the bloodied piece of paper towel he'd left on the counter was no longer there. He whirled around, scanning the kitchen. It was gone. Then Mason looked out the kitchen window toward Clayton's car.

But it was gone too.

Chapter 9

Dearest Joan,

My heart is broken beyond repair. Samuel was not just a friend. He was a best friend and one of the finest human beings I have ever known. As are you, Joan. I eagerly anticipate our next meeting. Even in these darkest of times — especially in these darkest of times — good company is life's greatest salvation.

Warm regards,

Hiroshi

—hiroshi.saito@nmail.com

— ‹› —

Joan was sitting in a bar not far from Heathrow. She'd been back in London just a few days now, and despite her proximity to the airport had no intention of leaving again anytime soon. But she would stay at this bar for a while. Her rosé remained relatively untouched and her company understandably absent.

He showed up as soon as he could, with apologies.

"You're here," she said smiling.

They hugged. Hers was awkward, and his was firm — which made hers even more awkward. But Joan had learned long ago to compensate for her illiteracy in body language by speaking clearly.

"I've missed you," she said.

"And I, you." Hiroshi grinned perfectly, authentically, handsomely. He sat down on the barstool next to hers, escorting her back into her seat, her thin fingers held in his thick, leathery palm. Hiroshi was equal parts gentleman and feminist, a contradiction it seemed only he could pull off.

"Planes and punctuality..." Hiroshi sighed dramatically.

"Go together like oil and water, I know," said Joan.

"Like necromancers and inquisitors," he added under his breath.

"That doesn't sound like a particularly fun party," she replied. "So, how long do you have?"

"My flight leaves early. Six in the morning to be exact. A wise man would leave an hour from now. But for you, Joan, I'll gladly make it two."

"Two scotches, then?"

"Or three." Hiroshi waved over the bartender and ordered his drink, neat.

"Where are you going this time?" asked Joan.

He casually unfastened the top button of his ash-colored dress shirt. Hiroshi wasn't one for bold colors. Locations, on the other hand...

"Greenland," he said, and she knew what that meant.

"Winter's End."

He nodded. "After a quick stop in Reykjavik."

"What brings you to Winter's End?" she asked.

"It's been a while," he said. "And a personal project."

"Your scotch, sir."

Hiroshi nodded, took a sip, and sighed. He eased into his seat. Even between flights, he kept himself more put-together than Joan knew how. While Hiroshi was ceaselessly humble, he had — like most humble men — a quiet arrogance. A flame inside an immaculate furnace: that was Hiroshi Saito. You could miss its faint flickers if you didn't look carefully, if you didn't know him well. Joan saw them in his eyes, in his stiff movements, in the seconds he composed himself. Even disheveled, Hiroshi looked perfectly so.

Joan was the opposite, or so she felt. No amount of hairspray could salvage the hornet's nest on her head, but she did at least like this black dress she had on. Samuel had liked it too. He'd always said she was mirror-blind.

"Funny you bring up Winter's End," said Joan.

"Is it?"

"Indeed," she replied. "You remember Mason Cross, yes?"

"The boy who killed Rowland," said Hiroshi. "How could I forget? I have not had the pleasure of meeting him, mind you."

"You may get your chance." Joan straightened and took a quick sip of her rosé. "He told me he was on his way there — to Winter's End."

"I did not realize you two stayed in touch."

"We haven't. Well," she said, "we didn't. He's doing me a favor."

This time, Hiroshi waited for her to continue.

Joan wasn't sure how much she wanted to say, but the truth was all or nothing — that's something she'd always believed. He hadn't loved Samuel as she had, but they'd been good friends. She and Hiroshi were good friends too. Yes, Joan supposed good friends deserved the truth, in all its painful glory.

"I have something to tell you about Samuel," she said.

— «» —

Joan had uncovered the truth about her lover a year ago, a year after his death.

In retrospect, she wondered if she'd already known deep down, if only she'd really looked. Perhaps Samuel had been right about one thing: perhaps she was mirror-blind.

It had been a gray November day when Joan met up with Samuel's daughter, Ashley. Joan didn't know Ashley well, although she was well-acquainted with a version of her. Joan knew Ashley through her father, through the stories Samuel would tell, through the emails he would obsess over, through his end of their arguments. She was a force in Joan's life more than she was a person: an anchor that kept Samuel harbored in America, meaning their time was spent stateside more often than not (Joan had no children) and that any future they might have had together existed there too. Until, of course, it didn't.

Joan, meanwhile, was an asterisk in Ashley's life, "Dad's girlfriend or something like that." Ashley was in college, her first year, and no longer living with her mother, Samuel's ex-wife. She'd emailed Joan in September, but Joan hadn't booked her flight immediately.

They stepped onto the porch of Samuel's red Victorian, a house that had been a second home to Joan. Now she was being ushered in like a hotel guest. Ashley jingled through a ring of keys. Joan had a copy, but she didn't have permission. Not anymore. This was no longer her home away from home.

"How do you like Maine?" asked Ashley, but her tone implied she didn't care.

"It's lovely." Joan didn't care for this conversation either.

"Cool."

The door creaked open. "Here you go," said Ashley. "I'm going to meet up with some friends for lunch. I'll be back in like, I don't know, two hours? That should be enough time to get all your stuff or whatever, yeah?"

Joan didn't bother telling her that she could lock up too. "Yes, that's plenty of time," she said. "Thank you, Ashley."

"Cool. I'll catch you in a bit."

She wandered off, and Joan closed the door behind her.

Joan didn't move at first, her shoes still on, as if the truth waited behind every door of this old house. As if, until she proved otherwise, Samuel might be just upstairs, hiding in a closet this whole time. Stupid thoughts. She had such stupid thoughts sometimes.

It only took Joan a few minutes to gather all her belongings: a hair straightener, a handful of books — nothing that justified the cost of coming to America. Goodbyes, on the other hand, goodbyes were priceless.

The house had a den upstairs with more books than she'd ever owned. A thousand, perhaps, lining two walls, not to mention the pile of manuscripts covering one corner of his desk. Samuel had been a prolific author. A well-read one, too, as well as anyone writing on necromancy could be. Necromancy had been taught inconsistently for centuries before he came along. Different mentors taught different lessons, different spells. There were no best practices. Samuel changed all that; his books provided a logical way in and made necromancy more accessible.

Perhaps that should have been her first clue.

The sky outside the bay window behind his desk was overcast, but its view was no less beautiful. Water had that effect on Joan. The ocean under the clouds was a deeper, blacker blue. It was not the bright ocean of a blue sky, not the ocean of new frontiers. The ocean under the clouds, she felt, was the ocean of an aged planet, primordial, and vast, and quiet. Joan stared out and let it consume her.

And then, finally, she rifled through Samuel's desk.

It wasn't curiosity, though she couldn't deny wondering what she might find, but no, she had a job to do. Like Samuel had been, she was a guardian, which meant her first duty was to protect the secret of necromancy. In short, she couldn't leave evidence lying around, not even locked up. Locks seldom stayed locked, and Samuel had more than just those manuscripts. She would recover what she could today and return for his hidden library (accessible through one of these bookshelves, though she always forgot which one) at a later date. That was another reason she was holding onto her key.

Joan went through one drawer at a time, skimming his piles of notes page by page, flipping through his books to make sure nothing fell out, examining both sides of every picture — a few were of them. Finally, she reached the bottom drawer, and it wouldn't open.

She tugged again. Locked.

Joan knelt and looked a little closer. There was no keyhole, no lock as far as she could tell. Or rather, no lock typical of drawers. There was a lock, but it came in the form of a necromantic spell. She could sense it now, faint and old. It wouldn't last forever.

Joan tried a few different chants, and the third time was the charm. She slid the last drawer open. It was full of faded notes and old pen-written letters. She gathered them all, every last one, then spread them over his desk like a deck of cards before a magic trick.

Some were letters between them, letters he had treasured. But locks hid more than treasure; locks hid secrets too.

Eli,

> *I do not think the time is now, although I sympathize with your cause. You know this. I want change too, but change must come about carefully. Change must come about at the right time.*

Joan stopped reading, preparing herself for what might come next. There was no date, but the letter looked a few years old. Change, of course, could mean a million different things, but her body acted as if it already had its answer. Her heart grew claustrophobic in her chest. She read on.

But change will come, Eli. Necromancy is a gift that cannot, and should not, stay secret forever. We will let the world know. The world deserves to know, but history is full of messy transformations. We need to do this as cleanly as possible. We will talk more at Winter's End.

Warm regards,

Samuel

— «» —

"That is quite a story, Joan," said Hiroshi.

"What you mean," she replied, "is that is quite an accusation."

"It is," he said. "But you know I trust you."

"Thank you. I understand it's..."

"Difficult."

"Yes."

"Even more so for you, I imagine."

Joan traced the stem of her wine glass between two fingers. "I've been lied to before, of course. But there's a difference," she said, "between being lied to and being betrayed. I feel as though I've been blind. How could a man I loved have hidden so much from me? I am a smart woman. How could I have believed I really knew him all these years and not known this, not known that he was plotting to undo every goddamn thing I work so tirelessly to defend? As he said he loved me, as he fucked me, he just... I don't know."

"Among all injuries," said Hiroshi, "betrayal leaves the longest scar. For betrayal is the line between two opposites, between a warm embrace and a cold dagger to the heart.

"And yet," he continued, "nothing can be judged without context. Samuel wronged you, certainly, but he did so believing he was doing what was right, believing he could make the world a better place. That is the Samuel I knew, the Samuel you knew, the Samuel who loved you. His betrayal, however misguided, was a selfless act, not a selfish one."

Joan hated crying. She grabbed a tissue from her purse and dabbed both eyes, wiping tears and smudging mascara. What a mess. "Perhaps," she said. She sighed and smiled a sad smile. "I hate crying."

Hiroshi gave her arm a gentle squeeze. "Most things are good in moderation," he said. "Even crying."

Joan blew her nose one last time before pocketing her tissue. Then she looked up at him, looked done with crying. "There were other letters," she said, "between Samuel and Eli. I got the sense they were moving forward with their plans, however slowly. I know I should have told you sooner, Hiroshi, but I wasn't sure what to believe for a while — or what to do."

"I appreciate you telling me now," said Hiroshi. "It is a complex situation."

"I don't know what their plans were, though," replied Joan, "or what Eli's still are. The letters were vague, intentionally so I expect, in case someone like me ever found them." She swigged the last of her rosé and added, "I have someone investigating the matter."

"Mason Cross," replied Hiroshi.

"Yes. Mason Cross."

"An interesting choice."

"I thought so," said Joan. "I'm not completely mad, though. Mason Cross can't be ignored. He's a good young man, and we need him on our side. We need him to be one of us. He says he's been to the Spirit Realm, and I believe him. Killing Rowland isn't proof, but it comes bloody close. And I've seen the way he casts spells: without chanting. So yes, I believe him."

"It sounds like you have more planned for young Mason Cross than just this task," said Hiroshi, who was always one step ahead of the conversation, or trying to be.

"About that." Joan stalled. "Samuel still hasn't been replaced. North America needs a new guardian. We can't do it all, the four of us."

"Contenders must be considered carefully," he replied, "perhaps even more so now, considering what you just told me about Samuel. We can at least cross Eli Abelman off the list. As for Mason, well, he is young."

"And powerful," she said. "Intelligent. He's a lot like his father, Hiroshi. He's a lot like John." She knew Hiroshi held John Cross in high regard.

The room around them was filling out now. Women at the table behind them were laughing and clinking glasses. Hiroshi whisked away his contemplative aura and grinned, in his usual calm, controlled manner, at the prettiest one. Joan bit her tongue. He ordered them both another round.

"I suppose," said Hiroshi, still smiling, "I will meet Mason soon enough." He looked back toward Joan. "And I shall see for myself."

Chapter 10

Asha. It's me, Mason. I am writing you this letter as you sit five feet away, watching me write it. We're drunk. I love you. I love wine too. Not this wine, but wine in general. This wine is not very good, but you know what? I don't even care. Because I fucking love you, and that makes everything amazing. On second thought, I just had another sip and, well, yeah, maybe not everything. Sorry. I didn't know they made wine this bad. I won't get the cheapest bottle next time. (I'll spring for the second cheapest.)

—Mason

— ‹›› —

"**Where the hell** are you?"

Mason was standing in the middle of his bedroom, his sighs of exasperation turning into sighs of defeat. He couldn't find his goddamn suitcase. He knew he had one. He'd stuffed it full of clothes when he moved into this old place two years ago, but Mason hadn't seen it since. This house was good at hiding things.

A knock came from downstairs.

Unlike his last guest, however, Mason was expecting this one. He headed to the front door to let her in.

"Hey, babe."

"Hey." Asha walked inside and gave him a peck on the cheek. She began unraveling the long laces of her — he'd been told very expensive — black boots. "How's packing going?"

"Not very well," said Mason. "I can't find my suitcase."

Asha paused to think, staring straight ahead as she set down her purse on the nearest chair. "I know where it is."

"You do?"

She nodded. "Follow me."

Mason followed. She led him to his garage and flicked on the light. Over the years, Mason's garage had transformed into a storage room. In fact, about the only thing it didn't store was a car.

"I didn't see it in here," he said.

Asha ignored him, sliding boxes off of other boxes, half of them empty. "You could make a fort with these," she said.

Mason shrugged. "You never know when you might need a box. Or a fort."

"Or a suitcase." She lifted it up triumphantly, a blue one with its tiny black wheels spinning.

He responded with a single clap. "How did you know it was there?"

"Remember that time we went camping?"

"The time we did shrooms?"

"Yeah."

"I remember."

"I went digging through your garage for a tent," said Asha. "You said you had one."

"I said I might have one," replied Mason. "Honestly, someone should program a search engine for all the random shit in this house. I can't keep track of it."

Asha shrugged. "It was more fun without a tent anyway."

"For you maybe," he said. "I didn't sleep at all that night. I actually thought I was going to die. Hell, I thought I was already dead. Someone should have told me four grams was a lot of shrooms."

Asha giggled, stepping around boxes, his newly found suitcase in tow. "You had fun. You were laughing."

"Yeah, when I wasn't doubting my very existence," replied Mason, laughing again. "I thought that forest was a goddamn graveyard of souls. I thought I was in hell — not one of the worst levels of hell, I'll grant you, but still hell — and you know I'm an atheist."

The funny thing was, unlike any version of heaven or hell he'd ever read about, Mason's shroom trip actually wasn't so unlike the Spirit Realm: dark, confusing, and trippy as fuck.

"We won't do shrooms again." She clutched his forearms and kissed him from talking. "Promise."

He kissed her back. "Want a beer?"

Asha looked up at him. "What kind of question is that?"

— «» —

The bottle cap landed on its side and rolled onto the carpet. Asha picked it up and threw it at him.

He threw a pillow at her.

"You're going to make me spill my beer!" She was shielding her face with one elbow.

"You did start it." Mason sipped his beer, slowly. They'd drunk through two-thirds of his six-pack, and he wanted this one to last a little while longer.

She stuck out her tongue.

He raised his eyebrows.

Then the living room went quiet.

"So," she said, "tell me about this trip you're taking tomorrow, with your old high school buddies." The doubt was obvious in her voice, and maybe she wanted it to be.

"With Geoff and Sean?" he replied. They were good, generic names. "Honestly, we hadn't stayed in touch at all. I wasn't even really that close with them back in high school. Well, I wasn't close with anyone in high school, and I guess neither were they. Anyway, Sean came up with this idea out of the blue, said we could use his parents' cabin."

This was the excuse he had come up with to cover for his journey to Winter's End. Like all his excuses, it wasn't very good. It wasn't very good because had a couple of high school acquaintances asked him on a random cabin trip, he would have answered, unequivocally, no thanks. He knew this about himself, and Asha, well, she knew Mason better than he knew himself.

She said nothing before she said something. "Mason." Uh-oh. "I know everyone is entitled to their secrets, but some secrets are too big to keep from your girlfriend of two years."

Mason tried to say that he wasn't lying, but the words wouldn't come out. It would be like hitting her. He just couldn't bear it, and he knew that she couldn't either. "I'm sorry," he said. "It's nothing bad. It's just..." He didn't go on.

He was stuck, a malfunctioning machine. His smart half felt it could solve this, but his good half broke him before he could finish.

"I know you're not cheating on me or anything," said Asha, "but you need to trust me, Mason. I can't handle walls. I can't."

"You know how much I love you," he told her.

She tensed up. "I know you love me. I know you want to protect me. I know you think you're harboring some dark secret, and maybe you are. But you don't get to make that decision for me. You're my partner, not my parent. You know what that means? Partner? It means we fucking tell each other the things that really matter. There's a part of you that's a stranger to me, and I love you, but that stranger is going to ruin us, Mason. And I don't want it to ruin us."

Asha was flushed, first because she was upset and then because she was embarrassed by how upset she'd suddenly gotten. Mason read her carefully as he fought to keep his own face frustratingly stoic.

And that's when he realized that everything around them, all the paintings and lamps and the stupid blue couch they were sitting on, falling apart at the seams, everything in this dim living room once belonged to his father. Products of John Cross. Mason was a product of John Cross. And John specialized in secrets, in compartmentalizing who he was, never giving anyone every piece.

And then Mason was a teenager again, embarrassed by how much he took after Dad.

"I don't want it to ruin us either," he said.

— «» —

She was digging her nails into his back, moving her hips into his. Mason loved sex — obviously — but he couldn't quite feel the way Asha felt when they made love. She was connected to her body in a way he would never be. Every part of her bent and quivered with every movement, every thrust. She was performance art. He was just a guy having sex.

Each performance had its theme. Sometimes it was love, other times lust, or comfort — Mason's favorite, for reasons unknown to him. Sex was a conversation, and Asha was a poet. Tonight, though, her poem was angry. Sharp, intense, at times a little painful. She came first, and he followed shortly after.

He kissed her until she rolled over to her side of his bed. It was the side he took when he slept alone.

"Sometimes, Mason," said Asha, "sometimes you make me feel, I don't know, ashamed for being angry. You don't mean to do it. You just do."

"I know. I'm sorry."

"I'm not wrong to be angry, you know," she said. "I'm not super angry or anything, but I am upset. My parents, they don't talk about stuff. They hide their anger. They fume in private, and the whole time I was a kid, I watched it fester, that unspoken anger, and it was poison. I don't want to end up like them. That's my nightmare. So yeah, I just want you to know that when I'm angry, it's because I care about you, because I care about our relationship."

"I guess I've got my anger on a tight leash," he said.

"Do you think that's healthy?"

"I don't know," he replied. "I get pretty angry at computers sometimes."

She turned over smiling. "That doesn't count."

Mason shrugged. "I don't want to be angry at you."

"There's a difference between not being angry and not showing it."

He nodded. "I know. Still," he said, "I'm not angry at you. I'm not sure I've ever been angry at you. I get angry at myself sometimes, and at things, but usually not people. People are who they are, and getting angry at them won't change anything. It just gives them more power."

"Exactly," said Asha. "It's like you're always holding onto the power, holding onto your anger, holding onto this… secret of yours."

Mason knew this was a turning point. She'd put up with him dodging questions and telling lies for long enough. Again, he couldn't be mad at her. No, she'd been more patient than he deserved, and she was right: he had to give up some of his power. He had to share it. He had to share necromancy. If she left him, she left him, and sure as death, the coldness she kept at bay — the coldness within him — would go full blizzard. But if he didn't put himself on the line, and soon, winter was all but certain. And so the real question was just what the hell was he going to say? What the hell was he going to show her?

Mason needed a few nights to sleep on it.

Asha had her eyes closed now, her anger giving way to sleep, but he knew she was still awake, still listening. They were both naked and exposed. No clothes, no sheets. Blankets were piled on the floor. Mason wasn't dripping sweat, but his skin was soft and sticky all over, every inch of him slightly uncomfortable. Asha's damp hair drew black lines down her cheek. It was a hot summer night, and Mason didn't have an air conditioner. He hadn't thought he'd need one in Terminal City, but this summer was something else.

The room had gotten suddenly, stingingly quiet. Or maybe it just felt quiet. The cheap, white fan by the foot of his bed was buzzing mechanically, trying and failing to cool them. And then, finally, Mason said something.

"Okay. I'm going to let you in. I'm going to tell you the truth."

Hey eyes were back open.

"It's weird," he said. "Not bad, just weird. Like, don't try to guess what it is. You won't."

Asha looked a little offended. "You don't think I know you well enough?"

"You know me better than anyone on the planet," he told her. "But still. You won't guess this one. I need a few days to find the right words, to tell you the truth about me. Well, about one part of me."

She nodded quickly— "That's fine" —and he could see how badly she wanted to know. If there was one emotion Mason understood well, it was curiosity.

"Oh," he said, "I almost forgot. I got you something. It's kind of fitting, actually."

"A gift?"

"You could say that." Mason slipped out of bed and shuffled through the top drawer of his desk. "All right, where are you?" He flicked on his lamp.

"So bright." Asha shielded her eyes.

"Sorry." He was still shuffling. "One second. I put it... right... over... hmm. Shit. Unless..." He knelt down, snatched his jeans off the floor, dug through both pockets, and then smiled.

Mason walked back to her with something in his closed hand. He bounced onto the bed and unfurled his fingers. A brass key. Asha took it in hers.

"It's for the front door," he said. "Now you can come over whenever you want, even if I'm not here. It's a big house. I figured I should share it."

Her eyes smiled even if she didn't.

"I know it's not enough," continued Mason. "I know I have, well, let's just call it a different door to open. And I will," he told her. "As soon as I get back from my trip, I'm going to tell you everything. Just a few more days, I promise."

She paused— "Okay" —and then hugged him, clinging onto her new key. "I love you," she said.

"I love you too."

The room was still hot and uncomfortable, but after all that, Mason managed to get a better night's sleep than he'd been anticipating, which was good. He expected he had a long day ahead of him.

Chapter 11

It was another nice day, which is to say it was another hot day. Mason had always hated that assumption: that a nice day automatically meant a hot and sunny one, as if you couldn't be in the mood for a good downpour. In any event, Mason more or less agreed with it this time. It was indeed a nice, hot, sunny day.

Liana was waiting outside Sherwood Hall with a black bag slung over her shoulder. Eli, however, was nowhere in sight.

"Hey." Mason stopped beside her, rolling his suitcase into a parked position. "How are you?"

Liana smiled. "It's a beautiful day," she said, "and we're going on an adventure. How do you think I am?"

"I don't know." He shrugged. "A seven?"

"What?"

"A seven out of ten on the how-you're-doing scale."

"More like a solid nine, buddy."

"Why not ten?"

"Because… hmm." Liana turned her face toward the sky, tapping her small chin. "Because you've always gotta leave a little room for things to get better, you know," she said. "Imagine, suddenly, you realized that the experience you're having *right now* is the best experience you'll ever have. Your, like, true-ten moment, and then it's over, and that's it. Nothing will ever be better. Oh my god, man, how depressing would that be?"

"I guess it's a good thing that we won't know when it happens," replied Mason. "Seen Eli yet?"

Liana nodded toward the glass doors into Sherwood Hall. "He's just grabbing a few things. Guy's always grabbing a few things. Watch, he'll still forget something. He always forgets something, trust me. That poor man."

"You got everything you need?" asked Mason.

"Sure do," said Liana. "I even bought a new coat for the occasion."

"A coat?"

"You didn't bring a coat?"

"It's August," he said. "I didn't know I needed one. Hell, I don't even know where we're going."

She sighed, shaking her head. "Eli should have told you to bring a coat. See, he always forgets something."

They heard footsteps from inside Sherwood Hall and turned to see Eli barging through the doors back-first, a bag dangling from each shoulder. He whirled around, cradling an open box. Mason couldn't make out what was inside — evidence of Eli's mystery plan, perhaps? Mason doubted it would be that easy.

Eli walked past them, barely making eye contact. "Come on," he said. "The plane leaves in an hour."

"I thought we had two hours," replied Liana.

"I thought so too," mumbled Eli. "Alas, this is the last flight to Greenland for a week."

"Wait, what?" said Mason, matching speed with Eli and Liana. "Greenland?"

Without slowing, Liana looked Mason up and down. "I told you that you'd want a coat."

— «» —

The land below them was impossibly massive, on the one side an ocean speckled with bright icebergs, on the other black and white mountains. Even in summer, Greenland never left winter fully behind. Mason couldn't remember the last time he'd seen a tree. But it was bright, and beautiful, and from their small plane, he could see for hundreds of miles. Farther than you'd think, Eli had explained, because the air in Greenland was dry, not like Terminal City, where mountains were hidden behind sheets of blue. Here, they looked right next door, but everything was bigger than it looked in Greenland, farther away than you'd thought it would be. You could look, but you couldn't touch. It almost seemed unfair.

But this place wasn't meant for people. Of course, that didn't stop them.

"Just shy of 60,000 residents," said Eli, "in the whole country."

"Jeez," replied Mason. "That's about the size of the town I grew up in, which I always thought was so small. But this island is huge."

"Indeed. In fact, it is the biggest island in the world." Eli, who was sitting in the seat ahead of Mason, gazed out the window. "Just wait until we get to Ilulissat, the, umm, third largest city in Greenland. Yes, yes, that's right. Population: five-thousand. It's less than a third the size of Nuuk." Eli hadn't talked much this trip, preferring to dwell in his head, but when he did, it was always about Greenland: history lessons, stats. Eli was a one-man Wikipedia.

Mason, meanwhile, really wished he'd brought a book. This was the third plane he'd been on in the last day — and it had been about a day (with very little internet) —and though Liana made interesting conversation, Mason was simply all talked out. He had brought a notepad and written some crap, but he was all written out too. He was just... out, and he didn't sleep well on planes.

Liana stirred from her slumber. "How much longer till Ilu...whatever?" She held her eyes closed.

Eli checked his watch. "An hour," he said, "I think. It would seem I'm not very good with hours."

Liana smiled. "Don't be so hard on yourself, Eli dear." She opened her eyes and looked over at Mason. "Enjoying the view?"

Mason nodded. "It's quite something. Everything's so... blank. Beautiful, but blank. Like a canvas waiting for a painter, for someone to build a building or even just plant a tree. It's like Earth from billions of years ago, you know? Earth before there was life." He stayed staring out the window. "It reminds me of something I read recently."

Liana looked over. "What's that?"

"An essay," replied Mason, hesitating. "An essay my father wrote."

Liana waited for him to continue. Mason couldn't tell if Eli was paying attention.

"It was about the Spirit Realm," said Mason, "about how it started from nothing. There was just blackness, and then this consciousness evolved and took over. Anyway, this reminded me of that." He nodded toward the world outside the window. "Everything down there is so undeveloped, sort of like the Spirit Realm before it had a mind, I guess."

"Neat theory. I once read one that said it was a really powerful necromancer from way back when that took over. And then that necromancer became the Spirit Realm and hid their old identity and continued to evolve and stuff, sort of like a superhero or whatever." Liana leaned back ponderously. "What about Deathspeak? How do you think that came about?"

"I was wondering that too," said Mason, who then shrugged. "I suspect it came about the same way similar things come about in the Living Realm. Things like language, electricity, programming: they start simple and then, over time, different people add different parts, new rules, until one day they're big and complex — and powerful. We necromancers are a part of that evolution, I suppose."

"Everything always comes back to evolution, doesn't it?" replied Liana.

"Yeah," said Mason. "I've noticed that."

Liana smiled and looked up at the ceiling, for reasons only she knew.

"It is a good essay." The voice was Eli's.

The plane was buzzing loudly. Aside from the pilot, they were its only passengers.

"Your father's, I mean," he added. "Yes, yes, smart man, your dad. You're more like him than my son is like me, that's for sure." It was the last thing Eli said for another hour.

— 《》 —

Mason didn't sleep particularly well. The blackout curtain over his hotel window couldn't quite hide the perpetual daylight that never ceased this time of year in Greenland. Just knowing it was bright outside fucked with him. He showered early and began packing his one bag in his dim hotel room, leaving the curtain closed.

Outside on the porch, it was deathly quiet. A few trucks rolled by, minutes apart, each one leaving a stubborn silence in its wake. It was also quite cool, and a good thing they'd bought an extra jacket for Mason last night — a simple black one, Eli's treat.

"Hey there." Liana, it seemed, was up early too. She wiped one eye, leaning out the front door of their bright blue hotel. "Didn't sleep well either?" She had wrapped herself in a thick, gray blanket.

"Not really, no," replied Mason. "Is Eli up?"

Liana nodded. "In the shower. I suppose I should shower too. Oh, and Eli told me to tell you that if you need to call or text anyone, do so now. No reception where we're going, or so says the professor." She nodded again, this time to herself, and then went back inside. The door squeaked shut.

Figuring he had thirty minutes to kill, Mason wandered his way over to the ocean and sat down on the edge of a wooden dock, dangling his feet over the water. Ilulissat was hardly a winter wonderland in summer, but he could still see icebergs floating by, some small, some magnificent. He'd never seen an iceberg before yesterday.

Mason heard footsteps and turned his head. The stranger looked like a fisher, Inuit, fifty maybe. He was smiling and looking out across the dock.

"Good morning," said Mason.

The man smiled. "Yes. Good morning. Warm."

"Really?" replied Mason. "I'm pretty cold."

The man shook his head. "No. Warm. You not from here. This is warm morning."

"Your English is good," said Mason.

"No." The man laughed.

"Better than my Greenlandic."

"Yes."

So, this is warm, thought Mason. Craig's recent words of wisdom came to mind: *Climate change, man.* Still, Mason zipped up his new jacket all the way, covering his neck. Warm meant different things to different people.

Once more, he looked back toward the stranger, who smiled again. Mason smiled back. Behind the happy fisher, Ilulissat's small buildings formed a palette of bright colors. From this angle, it seemed like such a serene place. Mason wondered what the truth of Ilulissat was. Places, after all, were never what they seemed.

Then he remembered what Liana had just said: text now, before it was too late. There was no reception at Winter's End, apparently, wherever it was on this bizarrely empty island.

Hey...

Mason wondered what to type, thinking he should say something reassuring. But no. Asha was waiting for the truth, and until then perhaps it was best to keep things brief.

I'll be out of cell range for a few days. I'll...

He paused again.

I'll tell you everything when I get back. Love you.

Mason pressed send, pocketed his phone, pushed himself up, and then finally made his way back to the hotel. Eli and Liana were probably just about ready to get going.

— «» —

Ilulissat was now miles behind them. Mason wasn't good at counting miles, but at least an hour had passed since they'd left town. Their ride was a muddied off-road SUV, with Eli at the wheel as they drove down a thin unpaved road, just the three of them. The path wound every which way, and the professor looked a little out of his comfort zone.

"So, umm, obvious question," said Mason. "Where exactly is Winter's End?"

Liana looked at Eli too, equally unsure.

"A couple hours from here," said Eli. "Two or three, I think. I'm just not one hundred percent, you know — it's been more than a few years. I'll check the map when we go off-road. On that note, look out for an old, wooden signpost, would you? Should be coming up soon." With his free hand, Eli rubbed his chin, newly patchy with a few days' stubble. "Yes, I'm quite sure..." He ran his fingers through his bushy hair. "Yes. This looks familiar. Then the map will show us the rest of the way."

"I miss Google Maps," said Liana, eyeing the horizon. "I'd even settle for Bing Maps."

"So, I take it this Winter's End place is pretty hidden," said Mason. "I mean, we're already in fucking Greenland."

"Yes, yes," said Eli, "very hidden. It was built seventy years ago and has yet to receive an unwelcome visitor. Not even the inquisitors can find Winter's End, did you know that? It's like, umm, an invisible needle in a very large haystack — a needle that only necromancers can sense."

"I see," said Mason, "and I guess no one would ever accidentally stumble in way out here."

"Exactly right," replied Eli. "Necromancers can make things invisible, but not untouchable."

"But this land can," said Mason, scanning the endless mountainscapes. "There must be miles and miles out here that no human has ever walked on."

"It's sort of beautiful to think about," Liana chimed in, sounding half-asleep.

"I suppose you two haven't heard of Erik the Red?" asked Eli, his tone changed. Unlike off-roading, history lessons had Eli very much in his element.

"Was he a necromancer?" asked Liana.

"No, no." Eli shook his head. "At least, I don't think so. I suppose you can never be sure."

"That's too bad," she replied. "Erik the Red would be a wicked name for a necromancer. Because of, you know, the red part, and our spells are, like, red and stuff. Don't mind me. Continue."

"Well, Erik the Red was an explorer," said Eli, talking with his free hand. "A thousand years ago, he sailed to this land — to Greenland — or so the story goes. This was after he was kicked out of both his homes, first Norway and then Iceland."

The van shook. Eli stopped his story for a second and grabbed the wheel with both hands. It was a rough road. He relaxed and continued.

"Erik was an outlaw," he said, "an accused murderer, and eventually sentenced to exile. Lacking options, he decided to sail west. You see, a man named Gunnbjorn Ulfsson had spotted another island, but Gunnbjorn, he had never made it to shore. So it was, you can imagine, quite a risky endeavor, coming here. Yes, yes. But Erik took his chances, and sure enough he found this fabled land. He found Greenland. Of course, it was not yet called Greenland. That was the name Erik eventually gave it. I suppose he thought it might attract more people here, make them think it was..." Eli spun his fingers around and around, like a thinking clock. "Less snowy, I guess."

"So, he was a murderer *and* a liar," said Liana.

Eli shrugged. "Different times, Liana. Different times. In any event, Erik returned to Iceland with tales of a new home, and thirty ships sailed off for this place. Half of them didn't make it. The other half formed settlements and made a life here in so-called Greenland."

"Neat story." Liana looked out the window. "Is it true?"

"Parts of it, I expect," said Eli. "The best tales tend to mix truth with fiction. As for our scoundrel protagonist, Erik the Red, well, I sometimes think there are two types of people in this world. There are those who look at a barren land like this and see nothing... and those who see — as you put it yesterday, Mason — a canvas waiting for a painter."

The canvas outside was long and bare in every direction: fields of green grass, mossy rocks, hills that slowly transformed into snow-peaked mountains, a blue sky. The base coat had been painted — but still no trees, no buildings, and certainly no people. Save for, of course, the ones in the van.

"Look," said Liana, "a river."

It wound its way down a hill and toward their solitary road, a skinny river with crystal-clear water. Shallow too, and Mason could see smooth rocks beneath its shimmering surface. It was strangely hypnotic, that river, so much so that they almost missed what they were looking for — right in front of them, just past the water.

"Whoa, dudes, forget the river and slow down." It was Liana again. "Is that the signpost we're looking for, Eli?"

Eli slowed the SUV, squinting pensively. "Yes, yes." His smile was subtle— "Yes, it is" —and then less so as they rolled to a stop.

Mason, who was in the backseat, stepped out first. The signpost was, well, hardly a signpost. More like a piece of driftwood buried upright, the top half sticking no more than three feet out the ground. Mason kneeled down for a better look, but there was not much to — wait, a marking. Deathspeak? No.

"See something?" asked Liana, shutting the side door.

"Yeah," said Mason. "Just a single letter: *W*."

It only took her a second. "Winter's End?"

Mason shrugged. "I guess so. For some reason I thought I'd find something more, I don't know, clever."

"Not everything needs to be clever, Mason," said Liana.

Eli, meanwhile, clapped his hands and got down next to Mason, eyeing the *W* approvingly. "Yes, yes. This is it all right."

"Of course, professor." Liana did a bounce. "You led us here." She stopped and shivered excitedly, or perhaps it was from the cold — though the morning had warmed up nicely. "Winter's End," she said. "We're almost there. I've been waiting years to see this place." She turned to Mason. "Years!"

He laughed. "I'm excited too."

She swiveled on her heel again, this time toward Eli. "So, where does that map of yours say we go from here?"

"Ah, yes," replied Eli. "The map. One second." He walked back to the van.

Mason and Liana waited, not speaking but trading excited glances. Liana knew how to say *eeee!* without words. Why use words when you could embody them?

Mason, of course, required his vocabulary. "Need help looking, Eli?" he called over.

There was no answer.

Another minute passed before Eli returned, empty-handed. He wore no smile this time, subtle or otherwise. "I..." He sighed, and then: "Fuck, fuck, fuck, fucking fuck!"

They could still hear the river, babbling behind them.

Eli hung his head down, lower and lower, until he was just hair. "I forgot the map," he said, and then it was a whisper: "I forgot the fucking map in Terminal fucking City."

Liana embodied that one too.

Chapter 12

Five thousand years, unvisited, unknown,
Greenland lay slumbering in the frozen zone.
—James Montgomery, "Greenland"

— «» —

"Eli, we can come back another time."

Liana was trying to make eye contact with him, but Eli wasn't having it. He was staring at the dirt on the ground instead. He kicked up some dust and shook his head.

"No," said Eli. "I know where Winter's End is, I do." Then finally he looked up at them, his head bobbing up and down into increasingly reassuring nods. "Yes, yes. Not far from here. I remember. It's been a while, but I remember. I'll sense it when we get close enough."

"Or," said Liana, "Eli dear, we can just come back in a few months — with the map. There's no harm in that."

"Liana, I know where Winter's End is."

She didn't say she believed him. It was more of a pitying look on her face, thought Mason, who didn't know either of them well enough to pick a side. So he didn't: "How about this." Mason put on his best voice of compromise. "We give it two, maybe three hours. If we haven't found Winter's End by then, we turn around and follow our tracks back to the road."

Liana, who seemed more amiable to compromise, relented first. "How much gas do we have?"

"Enough," said Eli. "I brought an extra jug." So there were at least some things Eli didn't forget.

"Well, we have come a long way," replied Mason, looking from Eli to Liana. "We'll play it safe."

"Fine." She nodded nervously. "Two hours. I'll watch the clock."

"Eli?"

He nodded just once.

Liana was the first one back into the van.

Mason, meanwhile, began wondering just who wanted to see Winter's End more, Liana or him. Mason had only just been extended his invitation, and she'd been waiting years by the sound of it, but the thing about Mason was that he was an intensely curious man. The whole reason he was here, with two strangers in the middle of Greenland — as far in the middle of nowhere as one could be in this age — was because he was an intensely, stupidly, uncontrollably curious man.

— «» —

They were driving through a valley, far away from any road, and time was almost up. There were mountains all around them and even more mountains up ahead, blocking the horizon. They came in many sizes, like great gray and white pyramids, but they all had one thing in common: they were all bigger than they seemed at first. Eli was right on the plane: you could see far through Greenland's dry air. It made everything look closer, made it look like you were almost there — whether or not you were even close. Yet still their van vroomed onward, a tiny metal bug buzzing through an ancient city of rock pyramids, as Liana sat quietly inside, eyeing her watch.

In the seat behind her, Mason took a picture on his phone — that's about all it was good for out here. They were beside a wide river, about a hundred feet away now, watching chunks of ice float downstream as they drove up alongside it.

"Delete that photo," said Eli. "Please."

"Why?" asked Mason.

"Winter's End is a well-guarded secret," replied Eli. "That photo is a clue to its whereabouts."

"It's just a river and some mountains," said Mason. "It could be anywhere on this giant-ass island."

Eli said nothing. The tension, however, said more than enough.

"Fine." Mason deleted the damn photo.

Though it wasn't the photo that bothered Eli, Mason knew. No, it wasn't anything Mason was looking at. Liana had been eyeing her black plastic watch — unbuckled and resting upright in her palm, like she was a train conductor — with increasing regularity ever since they'd reached the river. Mason knew the time too, but he wasn't being so obvious about it.

And then they were driving uphill, the van bumping over rocks and grassy mounds, and Mason just waited for it:

"Eli," said Liana, looking right at him for the first time in an hour. "It's time."

Eli kept his foot on the gas pedal. "Hold on," he muttered, his eyes locked on the prize ahead — only it was nowhere in sight.

"Hold on for what?" she asked.

"For just a little longer," he replied. "I know it's just.... It's close. We're almost there, I'm quite sure."

Liana breathed loudly out her nostrils. "No, Eli. Please, man. We've gotta turn around."

"She's right," said Mason, realizing it was time to pick a side. As badly as he wanted to see Winter's End, reason had to reign supreme, and majestic though this strange world was, the dangers they faced were anything but unreal. If they ran out of gas out here, there was no one to help them — no getting back. Simply put, Liana was right.

But Eli kept driving forward.

"Eli," said Mason. "Turn the van around."

He didn't.

"Turn the fucking van around."

"Just give me a second, would you?" he half-yelled.

"We gave you two hours worth of seconds."

And then it seemed like he was slowing down. Not as quickly as he could of, mind you, but slowing down all the same. Mason could feel the tension deflating. He could see the relief on Liana's face.

And then the van shook violently.

"Shit!" spat Eli.

"What happened?" Liana looked out the window for an answer.

"I don't—"

The van shook again.

Now they could really feel the difference: they were no longer level; the right side of the van had dropped a foot. Mason could hear rocks skittering below. He looked down. The river was thirty feet beneath them, bordered by a cliff wall that was giving way. Dirt and pebbles rolled along the rocky side into the river below, splashing and sinking, and Mason suddenly remembered why he'd never enjoyed off-roading. The thing about it was that you could never quite trust the ground beneath you. Some people liked that, he supposed, but not anyone in this SUV — and certainly not right now.

"Fucking fuck." Eli kicked the gas pedal. It made a lot of noise but not a lot of movement. Just a rubber cyclone, sending more rocks flying in every direction, some ticking against the van, probably chipping the gray paint. It was a rental, and Mason couldn't remember if they'd taken out insurance. He shook his head. There were more pressing concerns.

Like the fact that Eli was only making matters worse, for example. The van fell another few inches. For a moment, no one moved. Mason could hear everyone's breathing. He could hear the cliff slowly losing its battle with three tons of metal.

"I think we need to get out of the van," said Mason.

"What?" Eli shook his head. "No, no. We need the van."

"Eli," said Liana. "Mason's right. Listen."

Pebbles were still pattering down the cliff. Slowly but surely, the ground was falling out from under them. Come to think of it, Mason had lived through that metaphor twice now. But there was no Rowland this time, no necromancer with enough talent to protect three people in a split second.

"Eli, you're closest to the left side," said Mason. "You get out first."

Eli sighed. "Fine." He unlocked the door — the car beeped — and unbuckled his seatbelt. Eli inched his way out and then looked back at Liana, waving her toward him.

"Go on, Liana," said Mason, barking orders. "Get out."

She shook her head. "I'm barely a hundred pounds, man. Shouldn't heavier people get out first?"

They didn't have time to argue, so Mason scooted his way across the backseat to the left side and pushed open the door. Rocks were pouring like rain now, and the van started to shift sideways.

"Hurry!" Mason screamed at her, one foot out the door.

Liana hurried, but her seatbelt twisted into a lasso, snagging her arm.

Mason pushed a dumbfounded Eli out of the way and reached through the driver side door. "Grab my hand."

She grabbed it, but she wasn't going to make it out in time. The van was tipping, and Mason had to make a choice.

He dived in with her.

The first second was chaos. Mason tried to figure out where he'd landed — half on the carpet, half on top of Liana — as Liana screamed "Shit!" and Eli disappeared under the metal horizon of the van door. And then Mason did something he'd never done before. He performed a spell that he hadn't learned — a spell he'd only seen.

But it had saved his life once before, the last time he was in free fall. He pictured what it had looked like, that red barrier that had encapsulated him and Rowland two years ago, guarding their bodies from fire and rubble. And he tried to understand it. Spirit energy was like tofu: the harder it was pressed together, the firmer it got; Mason needed to make spirit energy so firm that it reacted to (and protected them against) objects in the Living Realm, a trick few necromancers could pull off. And yet he had only seconds — and no chant to guide him — before their van would hit the shallow river below.

Thirty feet.

Twenty feet.

Ten feet.

It was an imperfect creation: an oblong red bubble that covered them like a three-dimensional splatter. But it kept them from splattering. Not that Mason could tell for the first few seconds, which were a shaky blur.

His ears started ringing. The other sound was water, pouring in through the open door. Mason's barrier began to fade, and then suddenly they were both very wet.

Liana was lying on top of Mason, and Mason on the inside roof of the van, which had landed upside down. She winced as she pushed herself off of him with only one arm. Her other hung limply — injured? The look she gave him said as much.

"Come on!" he yelled.

They crawled toward the door, helping each other as much as they could, water bearing down on them, pushing them backward, pushing its way into Mason's mouth. He coughed. Fucking water. Mason hadn't realized how much he hated fucking water. Bits of broken glass floated around them. His barrier had protected them from the worst of it — and cushioned their fall — but now there was a bobbing minefield of jagged edges. And no way to be careful, so they charged ahead and, eventually, out the open side door.

Mason was underwater for only a few seconds, but still he felt like he might suffocate. Liana popped up before him, and then they were both up to their shoulders in water, the rocky river floor only a few feet beneath their heavy, waterlogged shoes — just deep enough that their van was now fully submerged. They kicked circles, their arms outstretched, and gasped for air. Even before all the water, they'd both been holding their breath.

Liana nodded toward the shore. Mason nodded back. They climbed onto the belly of their flipped vehicle. The water went up to Mason's waist, but it went higher on Liana, who was nursing her injured arm. A bad arm would make swimming difficult, and there was a current.

Mason jumped back in first and swam a few feet to shore. Clinging to the river's rocky edge with one hand, he held out his other. "Grab my hand."

Liana jumped toward him. Water splashed Mason's face. When he reopened his eyes, there she was, pulling herself up his arm as if it were a fleshy rope. He supposed, for all intents and purposes, that that's exactly what it was. And then, at last, they rolled onto dry land, their bodies heavy with water, still breathless, still panting.

"Jesus fuck, man," said Liana.

"Yeah," agreed Mason.

She looked at him. No, stared. "You saved my life."

He didn't know what to say.

But he wasn't the only one at a loss for words. After a moment, Liana's gaze wandered upward, and Mason's followed. There was Eli, standing fifty feet over them, staring down, his bony elbows pointed outward, his hands buried in his hair. From all the way down here, Mason couldn't quite read the expression on his face, but he could imagine.

— «» —

It was night time, or so their watches told them. They were exhausted, done for, couldn't move another muscle. They needed sleep, but the sun kept punishing them with its presence, refusing to set. It was 11 p.m., and it wouldn't get much darker.

"Fucking Greenland," said Mason, audibly sighing, visibly annoyed.

Eli nodded once with his eyebrows.

Liana said nothing. She hadn't said anything for the last hour.

Eli had told them a dozen times now that Winter's End was that way, just around the corner, just another mile. On foot, he'd argued — and they'd believed him — it would be easier to make it to Winter's End than back to Ilulissat. But Mason could no longer believe a damn word he said. Eli still insisted he knew the way and that they were going to make it, but his facade was cracking. Everyone dealt with the disappointment differently. Eli grew sullen. Liana, quiet. And Mason? He grew solutions-oriented, and perhaps a little intense.

"We need to start thinking about how we're going to get back to Ilulissat." Mason looked out at the orange horizon.

Eli shook his head. "It's too far," he said.

"We can ration what we took out of the van," Mason shot back. After the accident (that's what they were calling it), Mason had dove back into the river to retrieve food and water from their sunken SUV. It wasn't much, but it was better than nothing — although after a wordless dinner two hours earlier, it was also already half-eaten. So time wasn't on their side.

"Plus," added Mason, "we're necromancers. We can heal ourselves, maybe stave off hunger a little longer. Between the three of us, we can make it. There are ways. But not if we don't stop sulking and fucking figure them out, and soon. As in, like, tomorrow morning."

Eli didn't offer words. Instead, he kept shaking his head, slowly, back and forth. Somehow, that was worse.

"You've had your window of opportunity, Eli," said Mason. "We're going home."

Eli crossed his arms, knees up, head down, sitting a few feet across from them. They were all huddled underneath a rocky cliff, its shadow the closest thing to a night sky they could find out here.

Liana looked up. She was sitting beside Mason and still nursing her injured arm (not one of them knew a healing spell that could perfectly fix a sprain). "Don't be angry," she told him in a muted voice. "Anger doesn't help, man. Anger never helps."

Mason cleared his throat. "I'm not angry," he said. "I just want to fix this. I want us to sleep somewhere warm."

They weren't about to freeze to death, but even with their jackets, it had grown too cold for a good night's rest. Not that solid sleep would have been in the cards in any event. They hadn't even brought blankets.

"Here," said Liana, who then began chanting.

It wasn't a spell Mason recognized.

A red light began to shimmer in the few feet of air between the three of them. But it seemed overly complex, what she was casting, for a simple light spell — that was every necromancer's first trick. If light spells were tired one-liners, this was a paragraph of artful prose. Artful Deathspeak. And then, finally, it became clear to Mason that this was indeed far from introductory necromancy.

Mason held his palms out, toward the light. "It's warm," he said.

Liana kept casting, and the light kept growing warmer. She chanted faster and faster, her lips mechanical, but her human face grew redder and redder. A moment later, she stopped abruptly, looking like she'd gone as far as she could go with it — and perhaps just a bit further.

She lay down on the patchy grass beside him, a little light-headed perhaps. But her spell stayed, flickering like a lantern and emanating as much heat as a campfire.

"It should last for a few hours, guys," she mumbled, eyes closed. "It'll grow cooler in about two or three and out completely an hour after that. Just wake me when that happens, and I'll cast it again."

Mason stared at her, impressed, wondering where she'd learned that — and if he could replicate the spell.

Liana, after all, looked done for, and she said as much: "Okay, I think I'm ready to sleep now. Good... mmm... night."

And just when they thought she was out cold: "No... fighting."

Chapter 13

"My reality needs imagination like a bulb needs a socket. My imagination needs reality like a blind man needs a cane."

—Tom Waits

— ⟨⟩ —

Liana's hair had grown greasy, greasier than she was comfortable with, anyhow. On the street, it didn't take long for your standards to slip. You were never clean, or even if you were, your clothes weren't, or your socks smelled, or your shoes were peeling at the sole. So you were never clean. In fact, you had to be filthy in some obvious way because that's what people expected. It's what separated you from them — from what you used to be. It's what made it okay for them to ignore you. No one liked a clean homeless person because no one liked to be tricked — and Liana had never in her life wanted to trick anyone.

East Terminal City had its share of tricksters: lying panhandlers and tripped-out squeegee kids, smudging windshields and enraging the normies (Liana's term). She had watched that a thousand times: the boy who ran between cars at every red light, squeegeeing with abandon, and the people inside, who could never quite figure out where to look — only how: annoyed. Liana knew people didn't want to look at her, and she didn't want them to. She didn't need their help. She was just figuring things out. She was in transition.

But man, she still couldn't believe she'd been homeless a year now. How the hell did that happen? Before last year, she would never have imagined it, that a good kid — her twentieth birthday was weeks away — could just slip through every possible crack and end up like… this.

She just had to remember that her mind was a temple. Her body may not be, not out here, not anymore, but her mind: she still had that. It would get her out of here, her mind, and in the meantime, well, in the meantime she had a hobby that utilized that most valuable asset.

Liana was on her way there now, the place she practiced her hobby, mentally readying herself as she zipped past open storefronts in Chinatown. The fruit here was always fresh (and more importantly, cheap), and sometimes she'd wrangle enough quarters together to buy an apple or a pear — or an Asian pear, when the mood struck — and the clerks would always talk to her in Cantonese before switching to English. Alas, Liana was half-Korean, half-Scottish, and knew more French than Cantonese. Right now, however, was no time for fruit. Her mentor was an impatient woman.

Liana turned into the alley adjacent to Fine Meats, a butcher shop she hated. Of course, Liana hated all butcher shops. She couldn't help but imagine herself in the pig's place, imagine some uncaring man cutting her heart out, blood pouring over his hands, removing her liver, her tongue, because people ate that shit. And then she'd imagine them all on display, each part of her with a price tag. Liana had been vegetarian since she was ten.

Nineteen-year-old Liana, meanwhile, stood waiting at the end of an alley, out front a rusty metal door, the only opening along a century-old brick wall. She knocked three times, just so.

She waited, longer than usual this time, until two knocks came from the other side.

Liana's turn. She counted the knocks aloud: "One, two, three, four, five."

A lock clicked. The door opened. Liana stepped through.

"Good afternoon, Ms. Chan," she said.

Ms. Chan — that was the only name she'd ever given Liana — nodded. "Good afternoon, Liana."

Ms. Chan was the most serious woman Liana had ever met, and the older woman had told her once that it was because her whole life people had never taken her seriously. After learning that, Liana chuckled at her stiff mannerisms a little less often.

"I am busy today," said Ms. Chan, "so your lesson will be shorter than usual, unfortunately."

Liana looked a little disappointed. If she'd been able to learn on her own, she wouldn't have minded, but Ms. Chan kept all her books here, locked away in the back room of an antique shop. None were to leave. Liana didn't blame her — they were precious, dangerous even — but it meant she couldn't study new spells outside of their weekly sessions.

Her first mystery lesson had been about seven months ago, two months after the women first laid eyes on each other. Liana had often hung around in the same alley (the one just outside), always alone, always reading library books in the shade, and Ms. Chan would walk by sometimes, looking at her, really looking, and judging. Not in a bad way, though. Just judging. Then one Wednesday afternoon, Ms. Chan invited Liana into her back room for tea.

Ms. Chan, a conservatively-dressed woman who was probably in her late fifties (another detail she didn't reveal), bent down and poured Liana the same glass now that she had poured her that first day, the same tea she poured her every session: jasmine, in a white porcelain cup.

Liana sipped hers slowly, savoring every drop. Ms. Chan made the best tea in the world.

Ms. Chan sat down across from her, at the only table in the room, an antique, of course.

The small space was nearly overburdened with what Liana could only assume were priceless artifacts, and it would have been a mess were anything not in its proper place. Brass statues, floral vases, old paintings, and books — lots of books. A whole wall of books.

"I know I do not say this often, but you are learning quickly," said Ms. Chan. "And well."

Liana couldn't contain her smile, not even close. "Aww man, you're gonna make me blush."

"Necromancy is not for everyone," Ms. Chan explained. "It takes a certain mind. A curious mind but also a disciplined one. Learning Deathspeak takes time, takes practice. It is not for the weak-willed. Other people may not see it in you, Liana, because you do not wear it, but here" —she held her fingers against her heart— "here you are a very disciplined girl."

Liana didn't make a joke this time. Ms. Chan's kind words were a rare gift, and she didn't want to seem ungrateful. "Thank you."

Ms. Chan nodded, and then it was back to business. "I have a new spell I wish to teach you today," she said, pouring a second cup of tea for herself. "This one is more difficult than any you have learned so far, but it is also practical. It will keep you warm on a cold night. Just be sure no one is around to see you."

"Oh, that part's easy," replied Liana. "No one ever sees me."

— «» —

It was just after 1 a.m., and no one was around to see her.

Liana settled into her usual spot on the shadowy rocks under Granville Bridge, where its metal skeleton met the shore — and where she would remain hidden. Liana had rearranged a patch of rocks into a relatively flat surface, and each night, at least the nights that weren't too cold, she'd come down with her blankets and her pillow and make a bed. Her bed.

It probably wasn't the safest place in the city for a young woman to sleep, but Liana hated crowded shelters. If a little danger was the price of privacy, she was willing to pay. This plot of stone was the only privacy she could afford.

It had been a long day, and she was tired, but the night had cooled down considerably. Indeed, it was much colder than last night. Liana shuffled in her sleeping bag, pulled it up to her neck, and tightened the string. She even sacrificed the blanket that served as her mattress, wrapping herself in it, which helped, but not enough. She could still feel goose bumps on her arms and the cold in her toes.

Frustrated, Liana sat up and looked around. There were no other people as far as the eye could see. No noise but that of the ocean, soft waves lapping against the rocks. Liana bent down and recited the spell Ms. Chan had taught her that afternoon. It was long and complex, but Liana had always had a good memory.

It took more than memory to weave Deathspeak, of course. She had to feel the words if she wanted to draw on their warmth. Liana hadn't managed to in Ms. Chan's back room, which was to be expected — these things took time, took practice, took discipline, as her mentor would say — but now she needed the spell to work. At least if she wanted to get a good night's sleep. Not that desperation had ever helped her before.

So she channeled a different d-word: discipline. Chanting the words over and over, Liana grew increasingly meticulous with her pronunciation (which was particularly difficult with Deathspeak) and, perhaps most importantly, her focus. She thought not of the cold that was her motivation, but of the warmth she aimed to create, and only that. Necromancy didn't grant wishes. It was a demanding craft that only worked when understood and done right.

And then she felt it: her own little campfire, a ball of spirit energy pulsating between her palm and the ground. It wasn't quite hot, but it was warm. For about a foot around, it was warm. Then she thought quickly to hide it. Lying down again, this time on her side, Liana covered her creation with the flap of her sleeping bag. She scooted forward, until the red light was inches from her heart and hidden from the world.

And it warmed her just enough. Just enough to make her smile. And eventually, just enough that she could sleep.

Chapter 14

Mason slept shittily.

Not as shittily as he might have, though. Once, when he woke up shivering at God knows what hour — they all looked the same: a perpetual sunset that would eventually turn into a sunrise — he saw Liana. She was up and casting her pseudo-campfire spell again. It must have helped. He eventually fell back asleep, hands tucked into his jacket sleeves.

Still, Mason was tired in the morning. By the looks of it, they all were. But Eli had another look about him, too. It went beyond physical exhaustion. It was a different form of fatigue, one that led not to sleep but rather resignation.

Mason looked to Liana, who saw it too. She was even easier to read than Eli, and for some reason always worried about him, her apparent mentor. Mason wondered who was really looking out for whom.

And then, once they were all packed — a process that went by without a single word exchanged — Eli finally broke the silence.

"I suppose we should head back now," he said, "to Ilulissat."

— ‹› —

By noon, not much had changed. Liana was still massaging her semi-healed sprained arm, wincing and then pouting to hide the fact. Eli, meanwhile, had the energy of a dead battery. Things, in short, were still grim, and made worse by the fact that they weren't totally sure they were heading in the right direction. Eli was far less certain of himself than he had been the day before (justifiably so), and somehow Mason had taken on the role of lead navigator.

And while they were all on the same page now — they were going home, or at least that was the plan — it was a depressing consensus. Mason and Liana had won the war of words and Eli had lost, yet they each felt like a loser in the end. The tension was gone, and with it the conversation.

There was another reason for that: they were all incredibly thirsty. They only had one water bottle left between them, and they were drinking it slowly, agonizingly so. Marching on tired legs, Mason kept hoping they weren't far from the river they'd crashed into. He kept hoping they were walking in the right direction.

Left foot, right foot, left foot, right foot. This place was almost as spacious as the Spirit Realm.

Increasingly, even more than he thought of home, Mason daydreamed of flowing fresh water. He got thinking he might dive into the river again to see if he didn't miss any supplies the first time.

"I think we're heading a little too west, you guys," said Liana, looking at their only compass, a small silver one. Their phones were dead and useless. "We should go a little more south, I'm... pretty sure."

Mason squinted in the direction of Liana's pointed finger, toward a valley left of the mountain they were marching toward. "Yeah, maybe," he said. He didn't have a clue.

They started going a little more south.

God, they were so far into nowhere.

At one point, Mason convinced himself that a bit more chatter might be good for morale. "I was thinking about our talk on the plane." His voice was raspy, his words slow and careful as he tried not to waste a single one. Mason knew that too much talking made him thirsty, or in this case thirstier, another notch upward on the torture scale. "About evolution," he continued, "and how it underpins everything. And I was wondering: how exactly would we have evolved alongside the Spirit Realm? You know, when we weren't quite human yet? Did we still go there? And if so, do other animals? Do..." He paused. "Do dogs go to the Spirit Realm?"

Mason hadn't seen any dogs when he went to the Spirit Realm.

Liana made a noise. They looked at her. She was giggling, and then she was laughing her ass off, wiping tears from the corners of her eyes. "Oh my god," she said, "sorry guys. I don't know why that's so fucking funny. Dogs in the — *pff!*" She couldn't finish her sentence. "Little spirit dogs." She inhaled, trying to catch her breath. "Chasing little spirit frisbees."

Then Mason was laughing. "Hey," he said, "what do you call a dog that does necromancy?"

"Oh my god, man, please tell me."

"A necro-Mastiff."

Liana clutched her stomach, red-faced, chuckling. "That's so stupid." She had laughed to the point of pain.

It was like they were high. Even Eli cracked half a smile. They had all needed that. Well, mission accomplished, Mason supposed.

Once the laughter died down, Eli tried to answer his question in earnest.

"Self-awareness is key," he said. "Dogs don't recognize themselves in mirrors. Even if they traveled to the Spirit Realm, it would be a fleeting, invisible existence. Our bodies, in the Spirit Realm, they, umm, are representations of how we perceive ourselves, yes?" It wasn't really a question. "Dogs don't even know what they look like, or they have only vague notions. Smarter animals on the other hand..." Eli scratched his chin. "Perhaps a chimpanzee or a dolphin or—"

"Spirit dolphins!" Liana screamed.

But Mason hadn't seen any spirit dolphins either.

"Short answer is we don't know, Mason," said Eli. "I'm just reiterating one theory. I don't know if dogs go to the Spirit Realm, and I don't know when our ancestors started to. I'm quite sure the Neanderthals all faded long, long ago. It's unfortunate, really. Alas," he said, "some truths will always elude us. They're buried too deep, in galaxies too far away, over horizons too vast. Yes, yes, some things just can't be found."

And just like that, the burden of reality — of their current situation — fell back upon them. Everyone looked miserable again.

Not a minute later, Mason felt something. "Hold up," he said.

They stopped and turned toward him.

"What is it?" asked Liana.

"It's faint," replied Mason. "Give me a second."

And yet already he knew what it was, what he felt, though he didn't want to get their hopes up until he was absolutely, one-hundred percent positive. There were few sensations that Mason understood so exactly — the details, the nuance. The distance. Yes, it was spirit energy, somewhere far off, a couple kilometers at least. He was sure of it now.

"Spirit energy," he said, tingling with excitement, "a few kilometers that way." He pointed northwest. "At least I think it's that way." He could follow the feeling easily enough.

Liana was wide-eyed. "Winter's End! What else?"

Eli, oddly, was now the group unbeliever. "I don't feel it," he said. "No, no, I don't feel anything. Hmm."

"Trust me," said Mason. "There's something out there."

Liana squinted, looking for something inside herself. "I don't feel it either, Mason. You sure, man?"

"We're all very thirsty." Eli coughed, as if on cue. "The body does strange things when it's stressed. It could be a mirage."

"It's not a mirage."

"Then why," asked Eli, "don't we feel it too? No offense, Mason, but based on age alone, I imagine I am the more experienced necromancer here."

While obviously true, it felt like an attack on Mason's ego. Perhaps it was time he struck back with a couple truth bombs of his own. He just needed to make sure he wouldn't be caught in the ensuing explosion. For example, telling them that Joan had sent him on a mission to spy on Eli: that one could stay in the arsenal.

But there was this: "I have a closer connection to the Spirit Realm than other people," said Mason, forcing modesty. "Because..." He traded glances with both of them, trying to anticipate what their reactions might be. "Because I've been there. I died. I was killed by an inquisitor, and then I came back."

Eli looked like he was about to say something as Mason brought a ball of spirit energy into existence and said, "It's why I can cast without chanting."

Eli closed his mouth, taking his words back before he'd said them. He didn't look convinced, but now he looked unsure.

Mason decided it was time for truth number two. "And I killed Rowland," he said, knowing that one would be even harder for them to believe. "I'm sure you've heard he's dead. It's not just a rumor. It was me. I killed him. The Spirit Realm sent me back because I promised I would. That's not why I did it, but in any case, he's dead because I killed him in a moment of... vulnerability." Mason wouldn't for a second pretend there was any honor in the deed. He couldn't stomach praise for what he'd done any more than a doctor who'd euthanized a sick old man, right or wrong be damned.

"I had indeed heard that rumor," replied Eli. "I thought it was just that, a rumor." For a moment, Eli carried the disappointment of a man who'd just lost an argument, until he realized what that meant — that Mason's senses really were better, and that maybe they'd just found Winter's End. "So," he said, "which way did you say it was? The, umm, spirit energy."

Mason pointed.

"Dude, I don't even know what to say to you right now." Liana swept the wind-blown strands of hair from her face. She shook her head. "Like, seriously."

"Then save your words for Winter's End," said Mason, perhaps a little too confidently. "We're almost there."

That detail, it turned out, was less true than Mason had hoped. It was more than the couple of kilometers he had initially wagered. His senses, he supposed, really were exceptional. Like Eli had said about Greenland: nothing was ever as close as it seemed.

But they were making progress; the feeling was intensifying.

"Wait." Eli stopped them. "Yes, yes. I feel it now. The spirit energy, I feel it." For once, his smile grew unchecked, cheek to cheek. It was a smile that said, *Now I believe.*

Then it was Liana, a couple minutes later. But Mason knew the truth was she'd felt it a while ago, maybe five minutes before Eli, who'd missed the look she'd had — and then hid. "Yeah, me too!" she yelled. They were a weird duo, those two.

The signal was strong now, obvious even to Eli, who was nodding incessantly as he surveyed the landscape, repeating variations of, "Yes, yes, this looks right. I remember that formation."

And then came time for the big reveal. The empty air ahead of them screamed Winter's End. It was quite overwhelming, actually — so much spirit energy in one small, isolated place. If you believed what your eyes told you, Winter's End was a mossy stretch of land, as flat as any surface out here, at the foot of a mountain that looked like all the other snow-speckled mountains. But eyes could only see so much.

Mason let Eli do the honors.

Standing between them, the professor cast his best revelation spell, and there, abruptly, it was: Winter's fucking End, at last.

"We made it!" Liana jumped a little, clenching her fists like a kid who didn't quite know what to do with her excitement. But it needed to get out: she punched the air, a quick one-two.

Mason could hardly hold it against her. His own excitement was palpable. He grunted a loud "Yes!" —and he was a guy who generally avoided shouting. Indeed, Mason looked down on men who made a habit of yelling things, but if ever he should make an exception to his rule, well, it might as well be upon the realization that, no, he wasn't going to die out here after all. And so: "Hell yeah!"

"Come," said Eli, stepping forward.

Mason and Liana followed.

A minute later, they passed through an old stone archway, the only entrance into an uneven circle of squared hedges. There were excerpts of Deathspeak engraved in the rock, but Mason wasn't sure if they served a purpose or if they were the necromantic equivalent of graffiti.

Then warmth. They felt it immediately. Not too hot and not too cold. This was room-temperature, with a breeze. This was a mild summer day in Terminal City, only they were halfway up Greenland. And here Mason had thought the spell Liana had cast the night before was impressive. He was suddenly struck with the realization that, unique though his connection to the Spirit Realm may be, he still had so much to learn about his craft. It was a good realization.

Winter's End itself was nice but not spectacular, about the size of a small two-story mansion, L-shaped with a fountain between its wings. It looked tough, though, all made of stone, like it could survive a blizzard or maybe even a small catapult.

The property, on the other hand, was expansive. (Mason supposed real estate was cheaper out here than in Terminal City.) Hedges surrounded an acre of mowed green lawn — this was some real country-club-level turf — lined with colorful flower beds and wooden benches. There was even a peach tree. Winter's End was its own world.

Its citizens were emerging from the front door, meanwhile, a man and a woman walking briskly toward them. Eli went forward to say hi.

Now that he could finally relax, Mason felt obliterated. He fell to his knees and then fell again, resting his ass on his heels. His thighs stung with pain and pleasure. He looked over to Liana, who was already lying on her back, unfurled on the lawn, her arms open to embrace the world.

"What a motherfucking journey that was," said Mason.

Liana turned to him and winked. Then she laughed her ass off again.

Chapter 15

*Psychopathic killers, however, are not mad, accord-
ing to accepted legal and psychiatric standards.
Their acts result not from a deranged mind but
from a cold, calculating rationality combined with
a chilling inability to treat others as thinking, feeling human beings. Such morally incomprehensible
behavior, exhibited by a seemingly normal person,
leaves us feeling bewildered and helpless.*

— Robert D. Hare, *Without Conscience: The Disturbing World of the Psychopaths Among Us*

— ‹› —

Denver, 11 years earlier

Kyle had just come home for Christmas, and this year, he
told himself, this year wouldn't be so bad. For Kyle enjoyed
the company of others — even Mom and Dad — when he
had good news to share, and things were going well for him.
Three semesters in, his university grades were finally where
he wanted them to be. He'd figured out how the school system
worked, its weaknesses and how to read his professors so
that he could write what *they* wanted to read. He'd found
ways to cheat too. Kyle, in short, was thriving.

So you can imagine his disappointment when his parents
sat down at the dinner table on his first night back looking
miserable — and then accusatory. He knew those looks, and
he knew what they meant. He could feel his heart racing
even before they'd said a single damn thing.

"Kyle." Mom went first. "We need to talk."

"Do we?" he asked sharply.

Father exchanged a slow glance with Mother. Dad was
still in work clothes, his beige dress shirt sleeves rolled up

to his elbows, his brown tie loosened and lopsided. But she was dressed for this. Mom made only surgical strikes, and she believed that every detail, down to the last, sent a message. In fact, it was one of the few things that she and Kyle actually agreed on. Today her message came in the form of a cream-colored dress and contact lenses. Her glasses were a barrier, he figured, and she wanted to seem open. The dress, meanwhile, was a mix: light and summery but formal enough to be taken seriously.

Kyle wore a black sweater and jeans.

Fashion choices aside, they looked strikingly similar, as they always did: the same light brown hair, the same medium builds, the same soft features. They were one of those families that everyone could immediately tell was a family, and sometimes annoyingly pointed out. Even Mom and Dad looked alike. Kyle had taken an anthropology class last term and learned that people tended to be attracted to people who looked like themselves, which made sense to him.

Similarities in the MacDonald family were mostly skin-deep, however. Mom and Dad were at times opposites, the embodiments of order and chaos, respectively. And Kyle, well, Kyle was a fan of ordered chaos.

"As you know, we're friends with Professor Singh," said Mom, "and Professor Singh, well, he told us he had... talked to you about your final exam." She placed both hands down onto the pine dinner table, slowly and delicately, stretching her fingers out along the surface like a cat. She was a creature of such tiresome predictability. "Kyle, he said he didn't think you wrote your own exam."

"Either that or you cheated," interjected Dad. "I think you cheated."

Mom flinched a little.

Kyle feigned a yawn. He had, of course. Cheated. But they didn't know that, and neither did Professor Singh. Kyle had stolen a copy of the final exam the evening before the big test, about two weeks ago now. He'd learned how to pick locks on the internet, where he'd learned many useful things. In any event, he'd memorized the answers the night before

— Kyle had always had a good memory — and burned the stolen exam. Professor Singh, in other words, had no proof when he'd confronted Kyle (just veiled accusations), and neither did Mom and Dad.

"I don't know what you're talking about, father." Kyle's tone was biting, condescending even. He was an adult now, nineteen, which meant he didn't need to put up with this shit.

"We still pay for your tuition, kid," said Dad, "so don't think you don't owe us the truth because you bloody well do. Unless you want to start applying for jobs at coffee shops, I suggest you stop bullshitting us. You can't go through life cheating, Kyle. You're going to get caught. But more than that, it's just wrong. Don't you get that?" He was pleading. "Don't you see that?"

"I see an A on my transcript."

"An honest B, Kyle, is better than a dishonest A."

"How do you know mine is dishonest?" asked Kyle.

"Because you went from a low C on your mid-term to an A-plus on your exam," replied Dad. "That's what Professor Singh said. And because I know you."

"No, you don't," said Kyle. "You never have, and you never will. I studied hard. End of story."

"Bullshit." His father pounded the table, rattling the cutlery.

"Where's your proof?"

"Is that all you care about: whether or not something can be proven?"

"That is how our society functions, father."

"Enough," said Mom. "This is not helping. Maybe... maybe Professor Singh was wrong."

Dad scoffed. "Are you kidding me? You're buying this?" He shook his head and looked back toward Kyle, staring at him long and hard, staring in a way that only a man who did not love his son could stare. "Our little psychopath."

"Adam!" Mom dropped her fork.

"I'm not a psychopath."

"That's exactly what you are. Always have been. Why do you think we stopped teaching you necromancy?"

"Adam, enough!"

"Enough, indeed," said Dad. "He's a grown man now, isn't that right, Kyle? A grown man who can pay his own way through school."

"That is not your decision to make alone." She'd turned red, Mom, embarrassed by how quickly the conversation had fled from her control. "Now both of you, calm down." She held her right hand up like a stop sign, but it was shaking.

"You think just because you stop teaching me something that I'll stop learning? Hah," said Kyle, staring right back at him. "Hah. Hah. Hah."

"Oh?" Father leaned forward. "And what's that supposed to mean?"

For a few seconds, Kyle considered explaining himself, but then he realized that, A, he didn't want to and, B, his father wouldn't hear it. So fuck it. Kyle started chanting something instead, a spell he knew they weren't familiar with.

Then dad's hand recoiled. He gripped his left fingers, clenched his jaw, and growled, "Son of a bitch!" from between clenched teeth. More interesting, however, was what he would do after the damage was done.

Kyle let up, looked at him, grinned, and waited.

"Kyle, those spells are forbidden!" Mom got to her feet, and now it was unambiguously two against one.

"By whom?" he asked.

"By the guardians," said Dad, "and by every decent necromancer on the planet." Now he was standing too, both of them looking down at their son, at first fiery and then — Kyle could see it in their eyes — so completely disappointed. "Get out," he said in a hoarse whisper. "Just get out." His father pointed toward the hallway and at the end of it, Kyle knew, the front door.

Mom didn't say anything, which was just as bad — worse, perhaps.

Kyle stood. "You're so pathetic, you know that? Both of you," he said. "Pathetic and weak."

His father pushed him. Not hard but stiffly, and Kyle lurched backward, almost tripping over his chair, which he clutched onto to keep his balance. Its wooden legs skidded and squeaked along the hardwood. It was the sound of a home breaking at the dinner table, the sound of heresy in a church.

Half bent over, Kyle began chanting another spell they didn't recognize, and before Dad or Mom could figure out how to respond, it hit him: Kyle's father — Adam — fell backward over his chair, his old, hard head hitting the floor with a single thud.

Kyle's eyes were red, his lips still chanting. Dad tried to get up but couldn't; and then he was coughing; blood trickled from the corner of his mouth onto the floor.

Mom threw her plate. It missed, shattering on the wall behind her son. Then she charged him, circling the table, but it was too late. Kyle could feel it: Dad was dead.

She grabbed him first, her hands wringing his black sweater. Kyle gripped a fistful of her brown hair — the same shade as his own — and smashed her head down onto the dinner table. Everything shook. She fell to the floor.

Slowly, Mom crawled away from him and into the kitchen, her neat hair unfurled, hiding her face. Kyle watched, wondering what to do.

The answer, he realized, was simple, for there was one basic need that preceded all others: self-preservation. He followed her into the kitchen and flicked on the light. Finally, she turned over onto her side, one arm guarding her face — the other pushing away the air between them — crying and shaking her head, a mess of mascara-stained tears.

"Kyle." It was her voice as he'd never heard it before, in high-pitched disbelief. "Kyle, no."

Kyle kneeled, getting as close as he wanted to get. Then a moment of silence, of searching for the right words.

"You think... you think I'm something that I am not," he eventually told her. "Dad, he at least accepted that I was... different. But you... you don't, do you? Look. Mom, look at me." And for once, he looked too, really looked, looked as honestly as he could. He was trying to let her see.

"I don't feel as you feel." He laid his hand onto his heart, his fingers shaking from adrenaline. "I'm like... an alien that you think can love, but…" He shook his head. "But I cannot. You think deep-down, still, that I must love my mother, right? But I have never loved you. Not once, not when I was five, not when I was fifteen — never.

"Your love is a mirror," he said. "You can't see past its reflection. But it's not your fault that I am what I am. I was born this way." He said it as much to himself.

Kyle looked down at the white tile floor and saw two faint silhouettes, reflections from another world. Her whole body moved with every breath.

"Despite what Professor Singh or Dad no doubt believed, I actually have learned a lot at university." He kept his head down. "For example, I've learned that we are all just products of our nature. And this is mine, Mom. It always has been. And the thing is…" His breathing grew heavier. "The thing is, I can't allow myself to be caught, to be stopped. It's simply… not in my nature."

And so Kyle began chanting.

Chapter 16

There is a place, a small, unstructured academy of sorts known as Winter's End, where necromancers from every continent gather and share knowledge. It is the heart of our kind, though a small and cold one — hidden in the vast frozen wastelands of the north. And that is as much as I will say on it in this book, for while necromancy may be privileged knowledge, access to Winter's End is a privilege within that privilege. Only a third of necromancers know where to find Winter's End, and it is left to us to decide — carefully — who exactly we let in.

—Samuel Benedict, *The New Necromancer*

— ‹›› —

The dream was just like reality, if reality hadn't changed.

Mason walked and walked through the vast, rolling fields of Greenland, between mountains and around lakes. He walked until his friends had disappeared and he was on his own, he walked until it seemed like he couldn't go another step, and then he walked some more. It wasn't starvation or thirst that threatened him most, as he had once imagined. No, the thing that threatened Mason most had played a longer game: a slow sense of dread that, at first, had been an unwelcome caress growing tighter — growing until it squeezed his heart and strangled his throat. A growing sense of nowhere.

And then Mason woke up. He didn't recognize the room around him: old hardwood floors (not that laminate shit that was ubiquitous in Terminal City), tall white walls, a slowly spinning ceiling fan staring him in the face, an antique wooden nightstand piled with books he'd never read — all necromantic — and on a single black iron chair in the room's shadowy corner, his clothes, cleaned, folded, and piled into a perfect pyramid.

He was all alone.

Floorboards from a second story creaked overhead, but otherwise Mason heard very little — just the breeze from outside his window, its shutters open only a crack. It was all rather, well, nice.

He couldn't say the same for his body, however, which ached all over. Slowly, Mason sat upward and stretched every joint, each with a satisfying crack. The first thing he looked for was his phone, until he remembered where he was and what Eli had said about Winter's End: there was no reception. Right. He was in Winter's End. Where the hell was everyone?

Mason slipped out of bed and walked over to his clothes, figuring he should start the day not naked. Currently, his boxers were all he had on — and the only item of clothing that didn't smell lemony fresh, apparently. So, they used regular old laundry machines up here; not everything needed to be necromantic, he supposed.

The room's only door swung open.

It was Liana, with a jug of water in hand. She stopped as soon as she saw him, inertia swishing a clear drop onto the hardwood.

"You're up!" And then she noticed what he was wearing — or rather, wasn't. "Oh, sorry, man. I'll leave and let you get dressed."

"It's fine," replied Mason, his voice a dry whisper. He slipped on his gray sweater, sliding the sleeves up to his elbows, the way he liked it.

"I brought you some water." She held up the purple mug in her other hand.

"Thanks. I think I need it."

"I'll say. I'm guessing you didn't sleep very well out in the wild," said Liana. "It's just after nine, and you went to bed at like six last night, right after dinner. You were looking pretty done, dude. You look better now."

"I don't sleep well outdoors." Mason wrestled into his jeans. "What's that, fifteen hours of sleep? Might be a record for me."

"Nice. Mine is fourteen," she said, thinking with her whole body the way she often did. "Yes, fourteen. Here, drink."

Mason didn't come up for air. He swigged the glass in one go and signaled for more. He hadn't realized just how thirsty he was; his mind felt sharper with each gulp.

"I've been up for a few hours now." Liana refilled his glass. "Exploring, mostly. This place is pretty freaking cool. More unassuming than I had expected — you know, from the outside — but it's actually bigger than it looks. There's a whole basement level. Oh, and you should see the library here. It's crazy, man. It's like an actual library, only full of necromancy."

"I've heard about that library," replied Mason. "I'd like to check it out. Perhaps after breakfast."

"Perhaps after you, umm, shower too." Liana smiled. "No offense."

"Some taken."

— ⟨⟩ —

Clean and fed, Mason followed Liana into the library. She hadn't lied: it was big. The room itself was a cylinder, the joint that connected Winter's End's two wings. Mason recalled its turret-shape from outside. Inside, a spiral staircase circled three levels, from the basement up to the second story. The steps were old, dark mahogany — the same as the bookshelves — and the banister was formed from twisted iron.

Mason entered onto the first-story balcony, resting his elbows on the cool iron railing, looking down and then up, and then up some more, to the vaulted ceiling. Dim lights hung from a crisscross of heavy beams. Not red, though, the lights, not like in his basement. Lester had said necromantic light was good ambience for, well, doing necromancy, but Liana pointed out that there were other rooms in Winter's End for that. "This room," she said, "is for reading." Or sightseeing, as was currently the case.

Mason, meanwhile, remembered something else Lester had said: that this library put his own to shame. He couldn't disagree.

"Looking for anything in particular?" Liana extended her skinny arm, introducing him to a world of possibilities.

"I wouldn't even know where to start."

"Yeah." She twisted her mouth. "Me neither. It's kind of overwhelming, isn't it? I spent years desperate for every crumb of necromancy dropped my way, and now I'm standing in the kitchen and I don't know where to begin."

"It's really neat, though," said Mason.

"The neatest."

"Hmm." Mason scooted along the banister, closer to Liana. "Who are those people?" he whispered into her ear, nodding downward. The only others in the library were three men, or maybe one was a woman (he couldn't quite tell from above), bent over a small table on the basement floor. Their heads were bowed as if in prayer, but they spoke not a word. They wore matching red robes.

Liana pointed to the top floor — to get a bit more distance, her expression said. They walked up the stairs, each mahogany plank creaking, and then retreated to the farthest, darkest wall of books they could find.

"They call themselves the disciples of the red," she told him. "Stupid name, I know, but they're harmless. Just a little weird."

"What's their deal?" asked Mason.

"Well, according to Eli, their goal is to have a purer connection with the Spirit Realm. They think that if they can clear their minds, they'll understand Deathspeak or something. It's like, imagine the world we see is a distortion, and channeling spirit energy when you're in the Living Realm is like trying to watch a scrambled TV show from back in the day — you know, before everyone started pirating everything online. They're trying to descramble themselves, trying to see the pure picture, because I guess they think it'll make them better necromancers or something. It looks like they're meditating right now. Eli says they meditate a lot."

"Does meditation help?" asked Mason. "With necromancy or whatever."

She shrugged. "The verdict is out, as far as I understand. A lot of necromancers think everything the disciples do is all bollocks. Eli does. He's more scientifically minded about necromancy, or so he says. The disciples are a little too, hmm, something like religious. Personally, I think they just really like role-playing, you know? They're, like, stoked about being real-life mages and want to dress up and act all mysterious and shit."

"Necromancy's biggest nerds," whispered Mason.

"Basically."

"Well, that's saying something."

"Come on." Liana nudged him. "Let's go get some fresh air. It's so nice out."

— «» —

The sun was high and the outside air perfectly room temperature — just as it had been the day before and, Mason assumed, for many days before that. They weren't the only ones enjoying the predictable comforts of the courtyard. Five necromancers were relaxing on the wooden benches around the fountain, engaged in conversation over the soft sounds of pouring water. They looked younger (and less weird) than the necromancers in the library. Mason estimated they were probably in their late twenties and thirties.

"Just how many people are here with us," he asked, "at Winter's End?"

"Fifty maybe?" Liana shrugged. "I'm not totally sure. Don't think it ever cracks the triple digits, though. This ain't Hogwarts. More like an academic retreat."

"Certainly a retreat from civilization," said Mason, taking in the grounds. He'd been too exhausted yesterday to appreciate its more meticulous details, like just how neatly arranged each flower bed was, and there were these small stone statues, never more than a foot tall, placed at random along the cobblestone pathways. No two were the same, but they did share a common character: an elf, or was it a gnome, or a hobbit, or an elf-gnome-hobbit? Some sort of small humanoid with pointy ears, at any rate.

"Those are some serious lawn gnomes," said Liana.

In the backyard, a man and a woman were playing a game of croquet on the perfect green grass. Mason watched for a while; they were pretty good, or at least they seemed good to someone who didn't know a thing about croquet. One of them waved at him. Mason waved back.

"Ever play croquet?" asked Liana.

"Does mini golf count?" He turned toward her.

"Me neither, but we should play. 'Tis a very proper sport," she said in her best — or maybe it was her worst — posh accent. "I say." She did a little fist swing.

Mason chuckled. "Sure. I'll take after my old man. I think he liked croquet."

They made their way back to the front of the building.

"Check this out." Liana led him to the archway out of the grounds, the one they'd passed through yesterday. It was the only way in, unless of course you didn't mind wading through a prickly ten-foot-tall hedge. She walked outside, into Greenland — which somehow seemed like a different country than Winter's End — and then back inside. "Now you."

Mason gave it a go. Immediately, the temperature dropped 10 degrees, like walking out the front door on a cool day. "Yeah," he said. "I remember this from yesterday."

"I know," she said, "but it's still crazy-ass cool. Man, I walked back and forth through this gate like a hundred times this morning."

"A hundred times, eh?"

"Figuratively speaking."

Mason wandered a bit farther out, until he could see around the right side of the hedge wall. There were cars parked in a neat row. Presumably, it was where they would have left their SUV if only they hadn't left it upside down in a river instead. But hell, they'd made it here all the same, a fact that Mason now realized he was somewhat proud of. He stepped back inside the walls of Winter's End before he got too chilly. He'd left his jacket in the — actually he didn't know where he'd left his jacket. On the way over to the building, someone called his name.

"Mason, right?" It was a woman in the group of necromancers sitting around the fountain. Mason and Liana approached her. She looked a youthful forty, perhaps, with dark skin, black hair, and high cheekbones. "Alexus." She smiled. "We met yesterday."

"Right, right." Mason nodded. "I remember now." Alexus, along with a guy whose name he also couldn't remember, had found them out front when they'd arrived yesterday. They had also cooked them dinner and shown Mason to one of the spare rooms — which he had wasted no time passing out in.

"You look a lot better today," she told him. "Got a good night's sleep I see."

"Yeah, apparently. Thanks for everything yesterday, by the way. I needed it — both the food and the sleep."

"Basic necessities," she said.

"At a point, they feel like luxuries."

"Alexus made me breakfast this morning." Liana was balancing on her heels. "She makes a mean French toast."

Alexus shrugged modestly. "Come, sit down." She scooted down her bench to make room. "We were just talking about — nay, debating — the nature of necromancy: whether casting spells is a more logical or a more emotional endeavor."

Mason and Liana joined the circle.

"This is Rick," said Alexus. "That's Sam, Eric, Abby and... Jason, right?"

"That's right." Jason looked only a few years older than Mason. He had a round, friendly face. "Good to meet you, Mason. Liana." He nodded to each of them in turn.

"You too," said Mason, figuring he could try to remember at least two of their names.

"It's also Jason's first time here at Winter's End," added Alexus, "and already, he's disagreeing with me." Her tone was playful. "You see, I say necromancy is ultimately — at its core — an emotional art. Why? Because it is only when you feel a spell that it works. Everything else is just a means to that feeling. But Jason here, he says otherwise."

"That feeling," Jason chimed in, "is understanding. Understanding comes from figuring out how a spell works. And that, my friends, is logical."

"But we don't truly understand those spells, do we?" she shot back. "We get but a glimpse of them, a flicker from the Spirit Realm, and we chase those feelings until — after toiling away for hours, days, weeks — something finally lights up. That's more trial and error than understanding."

"Trial and error is a step on the way to understanding," replied Jason, who then looked over to Mason and Liana. "The group is divided. What do you two think: is necromancy more emotional, or is it more logical?"

Liana shrugged and turned to Mason. "I'll let you take this one, philosophy boy."

Mason pondered. "I think there's a logic to it," he said, "like there is to everything. But different people get there different ways, you know. Like writers or musicians: they can't always explain to you where their words, their rhythm, comes from. It just sort of comes out, but there's still an underlying logic to why a work reads well or sounds good — or why it doesn't. For me, when I'm figuring out a spell, it feels like I'm solving a puzzle, it feels logical, but I can't speak for everyone. We all have our own artistic process."

His words were well-received by everyone, but Jason had on the biggest smile: "I like this guy."

Mason, meanwhile, felt almost comfortable. He felt like he fit in, which was a foreign concept, fitting in. "Yeah," he replied. "I'm not bad."

It wasn't much of a joke, but perhaps humor came easy to Jason, who leaned back in his bench, one arm extended along the seat, and laughed out loud.

"Hah. Hah. Hah."

Chapter 17

It was just after dinner and Mason and Liana had toured most of Winter's End: the red-lit basement labs — they were called labs here — where fellow necromancers were toiling away on new and old spells alike, though some doors had been locked ("For safety," a stranger had informed them); the main floor great room and its even greater wood-burning fireplace, where they had unfurled like cats on the mantel's stone bench; the kitchen for snacks; the dining room for dinner; they'd even tried their less-than-skilled hands at croquet in the backyard before evening set in.

Amazingly, Winter's End's weird ecosystem darkened with each passing hour. It was an imperfect forgery of night, absent of stars, a neutered sun looming over the horizon like a second moon.

Presently, Liana was showing Mason the room she was staying in, which looked a lot like the room he was staying in, only hers was on the second story, next to Eli's apparently.

"Speaking of which, I expected to see Eli at dinner." Mason was sucking on a lime candy he'd grabbed from a dish downstairs. "Where is he, anyway? I haven't seen him, not since before I passed out yesterday."

"Endless amounts of work to do: that's what he told me this morning," said Liana. "I think he's literally locked himself in one of those private labs downstairs."

Well, that's... suspicious, thought Mason, who was suddenly reminded of the chain of events that had led him to this moment, of the mission he'd grudgingly accepted from Joan to look into a suspicious man named Eli Abelman who maybe had plans to do... something. That was where Mason was supposed to come in: find out, report back.

Liana shrugged. "He said he'd show us in a few days, his magnum opus — for real, I caught him calling it that once. I know he's a bit cagey, but that's just the way Eli is, trust me, especially when he's stressed. He wants things to be perfect before he lets them out into the world."

"So, you have no idea what it is?" asked Mason. "This project of his."

"Your guess is as good as mine."

Probably better, actually. Mason shrugged it off, doing his best *I don't care.* He pushed himself off her mattress and onto his feet. "Where to now?"

Liana was still sitting. "Hmm. Well, we've explored the basement, the main floor, and the grounds. I guess that just leaves this floor, but I think it's just bedrooms up here. Whatever. We'll find something interesting. I bet this old building is full of interesting secrets, interesting stories. Come on." The mattress squeaked as she bounced to her feet, quicker than Mason knew how. "Let's explore."

It was, alas, mostly bedrooms. But Liana was intent on adventure, and she found her magical wardrobe in the form of an attic door, partially veiled by a bookcase at the end of a quiet hallway of bedrooms. "Look." She pointed.

"An attic. So?"

"You know what they say about attics."

"I don't, actually."

"They're full of secrets. What's that saying: skeletons in the attic or whatever?"

"It's closet."

"What?"

"You store skeletons in your closet."

"Gross, man. No, I don't." Liana couldn't tell a joke without laughing at it too.

Maybe she had a point, though. Mason remembered the last time he'd ventured through a half-hidden door, behind another bookcase as a matter of fact. And, shit, it really had led him into a magical world. Still, he didn't want to get in trouble.

"Come on." She nudged him with her elbow. "No one told us that we *couldn't* go up there. What's the worst thing that could happen?"

"The floor will be unstable," said Mason, "and we'll come crashing through and land on Eli having a shower, and it'll seem kind of funny at first, but then we'll realize we've killed Eli."

"Dude, that's dark."

"I take hypotheticals seriously."

"Well, I take adventures seriously," she said, eyeing the attic door. "Give me a lift."

Mason sighed. "Fuck it." He linked his fingers together into a hand-made step. At least Liana didn't weigh much.

She grabbed a small brass knob on the ceiling and pulled. The door started to open — and then stopped. "Shit. It's hitting the bookcase." Liana looked down at her man-ladder. "We've gotta move it."

He brought her back down and did a quick three-sixty of the hallway. No one was around. "Okay, let's bring it into your room."

She furrowed her brow.

"Trust me, it makes sense," he said. "Would you notice if this bookcase were missing?"

"I didn't know it existed until five minutes ago, so no, probably not."

"And what about if someone had left it sideways in the middle of the hall."

"Well, yeah," she said. "Okay, I see your point. Let's move this ol' thing."

"Books first."

They each grabbed a handful and delivered them to Liana's closet. A few more trips did the trick. Thankfully, it wasn't a particularly big bookcase, which might have been a logistical deal-breaker for Mason, who double-checked the hallway and stairs before nodding confirmation. They brought in the bookcase, scurrying like movers on the clock, and finally dropped it behind her bed. It wasn't much of a hiding spot. Mason was having regrets.

This time, the attic door flung fully open, wooden stairs and all. They climbed up — and into total darkness. From inside, Mason retracted the stairs and pulled the door shut as Liana cast an illumination spell.

They probably wouldn't need to worry about falling through the roof, in any event; Liana's red light revealed a space full of, well, seemingly everything. Books, blankets, tables, chairs, statues — including a few rejects from the lawn gnome collection outside. Crap piled on top of more crap. A real hoarder's paradise. Mason supposed it probably wasn't very easy to get rid of stuff when the nearest anything was a few hundred kilometers away. And here, over decades, it had all collected.

They followed a narrow walkway — almost too narrow at times — that snaked through the attic, which, Mason slowly realized, was gigantic. A gigantic time capsule. Liana looked entertained by it all, a smile never far from her face.

"What *is* this?" She stopped in front of an adult-sized rocking horse. "And why would someone, why would anyone, bring it here?"

Mason smirked. "We'll almost certainly never know."

"But I want to," she said. "So badly."

They continued on their way regardless, her red light their guide, moving like Moses between tidal waves of dusty junk.

"Hey, what's over there?" asked Mason, pointing down a small path that broke from their trail, no more than a foot wide.

"Only one way to find out," said Liana.

They had to squeeze through sideways. The path turned and eventually spilled into a small nook, about six by six feet — just wide enough for a person to lie down in. The angled attic roof formed one wall, and a shelf packed with books another. Beneath their feet, Mason eyed an old, oval green rug and, tucked into a corner by the shelf, a silver lantern, an open book, and half a bottle of Scotch.

Liana bent down for a better look. "Oh my god," she said. "Somebody, like, lived here. We've found a hideout, Mason. See, I told you we'd find something interesting. Jeez. I wonder how old this stuff is."

"Let me see." Mason joined her, grabbing the bottle of whiskey. "Johnnie Walker Black," he said. The label looked old and faded, not to mention covered in dust. "Hmm. I'd guess this is from the sixties or seventies."

She looked impressed.

"My dad used to collect Scotch," he explained. "Scotch, books, and jazz records. He had an old bottle of Johnnie Walker that looked a lot like this one."

"Wow." She moved in for a closer look. "Is it like wine? Does whiskey improve with age?"

"It does, but unlike wine, not once it's been bottled," said Mason. "A twelve-year will always be a twelve-year." He shook his head. "I'm not sure why I know this shit. I'm not a booze snob at all, I swear."

"No?" Liana looked him over. "And here I was, picturing you with a tumbler of scotch and a big ol' cigar, leaning back in some swanky leather chair." She mimicked leaning back in what was presumably a swanky leather chair. "Reading your daily Ayn Rand and devising plans to, I don't know, turn the local orphanage into a Walmart."

Mason sat down across from her, leaning on outstretched arms. "Hey," he said, "children love everyday low prices too."

Liana giggled, but then her red light died. Blinding darkness. Mason could hear her chanting, repairing the spell. No, this was something new: an orange flame flickered from inside the silver lantern resting beside them. It was yet another impressive feat.

"Red light is badass and all," she said, her pretty face airbrushed in firelight, "but nothing beats a good old-fashioned flame." Then she grabbed the Johnnie Walker, twirled off its cap — which was a little tight, but she got it — and took a sip. Liana scrunched her nose in the style of someone who'd just pounded back a lemon.

"Does it taste off?" asked Mason.

"It tastes like whiskey," she said.

"Ah." He tried some for himself and responded with a satisfied shrug. Mason liked whiskey. Liana, less so apparently, but she kept drinking anyway. They were making themselves quite comfortable.

Mason reached down and grabbed the book that had been left open. It was heavy and tome-like. He closed it between his fingers with a satisfying *whomp*. *The Necromancer's Grimoire*. The cover looked at least as old as the whiskey.

"How about that. This was the first necromancy book I ever read," he told Liana. "My father left me a copy with my mom." Mason ran his finger down the fore edge. "There was a lock right here, sealing it shut. He'd told her to give it to me if ever anything happened to him. She'd almost forgotten about it. My mom, she's never been fascinated by strange books, not really her thing, which I guess is why he left it with her. I cracked it the first night."

"I wonder..." Liana trailed off.

"What?"

She hesitated.

"It's fine," he said.

"Do you think this stuff..." She looked around. "Do you think it could have been your dad's? Like, from when he was young?"

Mason had wondered that too, but he shook his head. "I don't think so. The whiskey's too old." And yet...

Quietly, he began flipping through *The Necromancer's Grimoire*, laying it on his lap, noting subtle differences from the one he had at home. And then he spotted someone's handwriting in the margins. The penmanship, it... wasn't Dad's. Of course it wasn't. Mason felt stupidly disappointed and didn't say anything. He closed the book, setting it back down on the floor where he'd found it.

"I wonder whose it was," mused Liana.

"Don't know," said Mason. "Someone who really liked their privacy, perhaps. A recluse of some sort."

"Or maybe all the other necromancers were bullying him. Or her!" she quickly corrected herself. "So she hid up here, where they couldn't find her or say mean things. Or maybe..." She looked back down the path that had led them here. "Maybe she needed that rocking horse for something."

Mason spat out his whiskey. "Sorry," he said. "I'm just imagining someone mounting that horse while drinking this." He swished the scotch. "Getting two kinds of tipsy."

"Sounds like my kind of Saturday." Liana winked. "Sucks though, that we'll never know the true identity of Johnnie Walker, necromancer extraordinaire."

She paused for a moment.

"Have you ever wondered about all the different lives you could have lived?" she asked.

Mason had. "Yeah," he said. "Like I said about hypotheticals: I take them very seriously."

She smiled at that. "I remember when I first learned about parallel universes, this theory that everything that could happen does, splitting off into new realities. Like one where I never met you, or Eli, one where I put a pink streak in my hair instead of a blue one — because I was really torn on that, man, let me tell you." She looked down at the floor. "Or, like, one where I didn't live on the street for a year... but then I think of everything I'd lose, you know. You can't take away the bad without losing all the good that came with it. Still, I wonder what she's doing right now, who she's talking to — this other me."

"Do you believe in parallel universes?" asked Liana.

"That's a good question," said Mason. "I don't know. I mean, no one does. Lately, though, I've been wondering about this idea of *choice*." He held the word with both hands. "For example, could you really have dyed your hair pink instead of blue? That moment you decided blue: was that not the culmination of everything that came beforehand, and if so... wouldn't you decide the same thing every time? If that's the case, then maybe there's just this one inevitable universe."

"You sound like Eli," replied Liana. "He said he's a determinist."

"I'm on the fence," said Mason, not exactly flattered by the comparison.

"He's not so bad, you know."

"Huh?"

"Eli," she said. "I know he can be a bit... well, a mess. But he's also brilliant and kind. He's always been there for me. Some people, they seem nice at first, talking about how they want to help you and all that jazz, but then you realize they just want something, or you can't rely on them. Eli's rough around the edges — and yeah, bad under pressure — but at his core, Mason, that bastard is pure gold."

"You seem to feel strongly about this," said Mason.

She nodded. "I do. I really do."

"If you don't mind me asking, why?" He was digging a little.

Liana looked like she wasn't going to answer, but just before Mason could change the subject, she began:

"Okay, so, my mom, people loved her. Total coke head, alcoholic, the whole shebang, but she had a couple good years — and people like that, well, when they're good they're great, you know — but then she met this guy, this asshole, not that she was any better. Anyway, she was going to pay for my first year of university. It was her way of saying sorry for being such a shitty mom. A year of no student loans might not sound like much, but coming from her, it was unbelievable. Too unbelievable, it turned out. She and her new boyfriend, Jim — fucker — up and moved to Florida, stopped paying our rent, and took all of my tuition money with them. They left me with nothing — no home, no money. I was fucking eighteen. I told that bitch I'd missed the deadline for student loans, and she just said, Liana, you're an adult now.

"I don't hate anyone, man, but..." Liana grabbed the bottle out of Mason's hand. "I hate her." She took more than a sip.

"I ended up living on the street for over a year," Liana continued, calming down. "Never thought that could happen to someone like me. Little did I know, right? But I made a friend, Ms. Chan. She was a swell lady. She taught me necromancy and eventually introduced me to Eli. Eli gave me a place to stay while I sorted out student loans, and you know what: he never asked for anything, never hit on me, never asked when I was going to leave, never even complained. He was the total opposite of my mom, inside and out."

Then she looked up at him. "That's why I like you, Mason," said Liana. "You're like that too: stiff on the outside, pure gold on the inside."

Mason let out a single chuckle. "I'm not so sure about that." He really wasn't.

"You saved my fucking life, man," she replied, "and you could have died doing it. So you can say whatever you're going to say, but you're not going to convince me. Eli, he's an ocean of generosity. You're something different. Principled. Solid. One of the toughest sons of bitches I've ever met, man: that's what you are."

"Come now," he replied. "I'm a hundred and fifty pounds wet."

"That doesn't matter, Mason," she said, smiling. "You were the one taking charge out there. You were the one who was going to get us home. You saved me, and you kept us going. Maybe you don't see it, but I bet other people do — you're unbreakable, dude."

Mason wasn't good with compliments. He forced a laugh and blushed, and then blushed even more once he realized he was blushing. He fought against the thought that briefly entered his head too. That is, what it would be like to be with someone like Liana, a necromancer, a woman who not only knew his biggest secret — the secret he kept from Asha — but who understood it fully too. Mason shook his head to signal a loss for words and to let Liana continue.

"You're like Ms. Chan," she said.

"Who?"

"The woman who taught me necromancy."

"Oh, right."

"She was unbreakable too. You're different, friendlier, but she was tough as nails, that woman. Nothing could take her down, until she got sick. She'd been sick a long time, actually — never told me from what, because that's how she was, you know, very private. Didn't want to burden anyone else. She would just keep fixing it, her problems, her sickness... until she couldn't. She'd kept it at bay for a while, though, with necromancy." Liana broke eye contact, her sudden tears catching her by surprise. "She kept going for a while, quite a long while." She wiped a drop, quickly, with the edge of her index finger. "Tough woman, tough as nails."

Mason offered a bittersweet smile.

Liana looked sad and tired, the corners of her eyes red.

They heard footsteps from the floor below, but otherwise they heard very little, lost in their own world up here — a forgotten world they had found by accident. A world of old memories and secrets that had been packed up and abandoned to the attic, out of sight, out of mind, collecting dust in existential exile. But few things are ever truly lost.

"I'm sorry," said Mason. "She sounded... strong. Unbreakable, like you said."

Liana sighed. "Yeah. Well, no. Almost unbreakable. She did, in the end, said some things that were... yeah. Doesn't matter. I guess even the Ms. Chans of the world break sometimes. We're only human, right?"

She poked his chest.

"Yeah," he said. "Squishy apes, all of us."

Chapter 18

Necromancy, for now, remains the world's biggest secret. But in the information age, in which conspiracies are exposed across the globe in mere minutes with the click of a mouse — in this world, can we hope to keep necromancy hidden? And in this world, what would exposure mean?

—Samuel Benedict, *The Future of Our Kind*

— «» —

It was late, just after 2 a.m. last Mason checked, and Liana, he assumed, was fast asleep. So too was Eli, which was the more important thing for what Mason was about to do.

He turned the corner into the backyard, walking slowly with his hand to the wall and his eyes to the ground. As far as Mason could see, he was the only person outside, though Winter's End's fake night sky could have veiled others — as he hoped it would veil him.

So, here was the problem: the door into the basement lab Eli was occupying was locked in two ways — the old-fashioned one and with a spell. Mason figured he could have overcome one or the other, but together, for some reason, they were a bitch to get past. Mason had seen Eli head to bed an hour earlier and, just ten minutes ago, had attempted to break into the lab where the professor was working on... whatever the hell it was that he was working on. Regardless, he couldn't get in.

That being the case, here was the plan: go in through the basement window. Every room had one; he remembered seeing them earlier in the day during his tour with Liana. They were small and wide, barely a foot off the grass, and most had their blinds shut. Mason was quite sure he knew which room was Eli's because it was the only one still locked. Plus, the other rooms he'd snuck into were all too, well, organized for Eli. Which brought Mason here, counting windows until — yes, that should be the one. Or so he hoped.

Mason crouched down for a better look. The blinds were closed, but he could see the lock, an old black lever poking out from underneath. He tried to move it open with the only spell he could think of: a sort of cross between an invisible hand and a strong gust of wind. Necromancy had its limits when it came to moving matter; there were no metal locks in the Spirit Realm, after all. Alas, the angle was weird, and he couldn't quite make this one click.

"Son of a bitch."

Then Mason realized there was one thing he hadn't yet tried — and pushed the window open.

"Jesus Christ, Eli."

Mason squeezed his body through the window, which, it turned out, was the hard part. He wiggled in backward, landing on his heels first and then his ass second. The cement floor was a bullet to his tailbone.

"Mother fuck," he whisper-yelled.

Mason took a deep breath, shook his head, swallowed the pain, and then pushed himself to his feet. It was time for him to find out what Eli was hiding from the world.

The room itself was bathed in dim red, just like his basement lab back home. No light switch needed. Mostly, there was a lot of table space. Eli had covered half of it in notes.

That, Mason decided, would be a good place to start.

Of course, the notes made little sense, he quickly discovered — presumably not to anyone but Eli himself. Mason was five pages in before he found anything coherent and maybe, just maybe, damning:

> *A mass email with the codeword will notify partners on the ground that the plan is active and to begin preparation. NOTE: Remind partners of time zones. They must be synchronized. One voice can be drowned out; together, they are a chorus. Good line. Use that.*

He read it three more times. There were too many unfilled blanks for Mason to understand what exactly it meant, but he was quite sure this messily scribbled paragraph spoke of something important — something more than a little suspicious.

A lock clicked.

Mason looked up, wide-eyed, dropping the notes in his hand.

The door swung open.

There was no time to hide.

"Mason?" Eli sounded groggy. He was wearing a housecoat, his hair tousled even more so than usual. In other words, he looked very much like a man who had not been expecting company.

"I thought you were in bed," replied Mason, as if that excused anything.

"I was. I couldn't sleep." Then his expression changed to a look that said, *wait, why am I the one answering questions?* "Why are you in here, Mason?" he asked. "And *how* did you get in here?"

"The, uh, door." Mason nodded toward the door.

"It was locked."

"I don't think so."

"Mason, I just unlocked it. You saw me unlock it."

If only necromancy possessed a spell that might make Mason a better liar. But like moving matter, mental tricks were not within the purview of his craft — nor of his personality. Then he noticed Eli's eyes tick upward, and the hour for lies was over.

The open window.

Eli shook his head, returning his gaze to Mason, looking more offended than mad. "You broke in. You… you're spying on me."

Mason could have handled anger. Hell, he sometimes fed off it. Anger was a warrior with a sword, and Mason knew how to spar. No, it was guilt that got him. Guilt was a poison that had been eroding him from the inside these past few days, up until this very moment, and all he could do now was crumble.

Mason exhaled. "I'm sorry, Eli. Shit."

"Why?" Eli closed the door behind him, but he didn't lock it this time. He also didn't come any closer.

Mason felt that the truth was his only option here. Maybe Joan should have sent a better liar. Although frankly, he wasn't entirely sure whose side he was on anyway. His own, he eventually concluded.

"Because someone asked me to," Mason said after a minute of stalling. "Because I think maybe you're up to something."

"Do you?" Eli looked curious, and then worried, and then curious again, trying to veil the more incriminating of the two emotions. "And just what is it you think I am up to?"

Mason leaned up against the metal table to his left, trying to be — or at least trying to look — casual. "You tell me."

Eli scoffed. He shook his head, half befuddled, half incredulous, wholly Eli. "Right, right, because I am going to fall for that one." Then he took a deep, dramatic breath. "Mason, I must say, I am a little disappointed. More than a little disappointed, in fact. I'd invited you here out of respect for your father, a man I held in the highest esteem. You seemed, well, not unlike him, and yet he would never have stooped to spying, to crawling through..." —Eli threw an arm into the air— "through bloody windows. No, no, not your father, not the John Cross I knew."

Mason wasn't sure what his father would have done in this situation, only that he knew his dad better than Eli did. Eli seemed to almost idolize him. Not that it mattered. His father wasn't here, and Mason wasn't John Cross: the sequel.

"I'm not my dad." Mason swallowed his anger; it wouldn't serve him here.

"No, apparently not. Now, your father..." Eli wagged a single long, skinny index finger. "I think he would have understood what I'm doing here."

"And what exactly is that?"

Eli's poker face was on par with Mason's.

"Why should I tell you?" He paced thoughtfully along the edge of the room, always keeping his distance from Mason and his face masked in crimson shadows.

"Would you prefer I assume the worst?" asked Mason. "I know you're planning something. I know... I know you want to expose necromancy to the world."

The expression on his face: Eli had taken the bluff. He stopped moving, scanning the notes strewn over the table beside him. "Shit, shit, shit." He whispered the words.

"Your move," said Mason, who was impressed with himself. And to think, Lester had once called him a bad interrogator.

Eli huffed. "To hell with it," he said. "Fine, I'll tell you. I'll tell you because, Mason, it's right, what we're doing. It needs to happen, and if not now, then when?"

"Are you asking me?"

"Yes, I am."

"Can't say I have a good answer to that," replied Mason, "though some people think it shouldn't ever come to this: exposing us to the world."

"And what do *you* think, hmm?"

Mason realized he didn't know. "I'm still processing," he said, "but what I do know is that if you do this — whatever your plan is — people are going to suffer."

"Are we not suffering now?" asked Eli. "Lying to our families, hiding from inquisitors. The daylight stings at first, sure, sure, but, Mason... just imagine. Imagine what science could do with necromancy. What doctors could do. We're withholding the next electricity. Yes, the world fears what it does not understand, but it will understand it, eventually, if we let it. Socrates and Galileo were convicted of heresy, but they left the world a better place. It is because of what people like them did that we — that I — can now do this. The world is finally ready because brave men and women, they... they put themselves on the line. They pushed the heavy boulder of civilization forward. And now it's my turn. For once, it's my turn."

It was the most sure of himself that Mason had ever seen Eli.

"And you're not stopping me, Mason." It wasn't a threat, just a soft-spoken statement. Facts, and Eli evidently considered this to be one, weighed more than threats.

"So, what's your plan?" asked Mason.

"There have been many plans," said Eli. "This is just the latest one, conceived of by me and Samuel Benedict. His death, it… put a pause on things, but only for a while."

Mason remembered Samuel. Or rather, he remembered his dead body. Mason had never met Samuel in life, though Joan had spoken kindly of him. Joan: the woman who was now at odds with Eli. That was an interesting revelation.

"Wasn't Samuel a guardian?" asked Mason — the very guardian he was in the running to replace, if he were to believe Joan.

"He was a guardian who saw the big picture," replied Eli. "He was a visionary. We necromancers, we have no leader, but Samuel, he was a sort of spiritual leader."

Mason snickered in spite of himself. "Was that supposed to be a pun?"

"What?"

"Spiritual leader. Because, you know, we're necromancers."

"No." Eli almost smiled. "No, no. What we're doing, it is quite serious, Mason." More finger wagging. "Serious, indeed. Now more than ever. I have kept our dream alive, mine and Samuel's, and soon, very soon, it will become a reality. The pieces are already in place. I am not alone in this. We are spread across the globe, we are. I just need to give the word."

"To do what exactly?" asked Mason.

"Now, now, I think I've told you quite enough," said Eli.

"So, you have a plan with people around the world?"

"I do."

"Then why the hell are we at Winter's End?"

Eli hesitated. "I needed to look something up, a spell. Winter's End has the biggest necromantic library on the planet. It's as simple as that."

"Right. Can't exactly look this stuff up on Wikipedia."

"Obviously."

"It's a joke someone told me once."

"If you say so."

Mason scratched his head, shuffling his hair. The mood had gone from somewhat hostile to more just really uncomfortable, like he'd stumbled into Eli's sex dungeon or something. The difference was, in this situation, Mason felt he had a choice. He just had no idea what his options were.

"Is Liana in on this?" he asked.

"No. No, she is not," said Eli. "Believe me, I have considered telling her more times than I can count. But at the end of the day, she does not need to know, and more people knowing only puts the plan in jeopardy. I can only hope she understands, as I hope you can understand as well. This *is* happening, Mason, but you can choose to be on the right side of history. Much will change soon, and much will need tending to. Yes, yes, I do not deny that. I would certainly welcome your help."

Mason could see it in his eyes, even in the red dark, and he remembered everything Liana had told him about the professor. Eli was already prepared to forgive him. Eager, even.

But his eagerness ended there. When it came to the one thing that mattered most — changing his mind — Eli was unstoppable. Mason was a man of quick determination: he deduced what needed to be done and then did it. Eli's determination was a tidal wave: slow, deep below the surface, and easy to miss early on. But years had brought it crashing to the shore, surfacing into a tsunami that no one — if the professor had his way — could miss.

Eli was a mess by many measures, there was no doubt about that, but his convictions were clear and all-consuming. In fact, Liana had been right about another thing: they weren't so dissimilar, the two men staring at one another, wondering what came next. Two men who wielded similar powers very differently.

Finally, Eli addressed the elephant: "So, what are you going to do now?"

Mason meandered to the door, leaving the open window behind him. "Right now," he said, "I think I'll go to bed."

Chapter 19

Socrates: Consider this too, then. If this man went back down into the cave and sat down in his same seat, wouldn't his eyes be filled with darkness, coming suddenly out of the sun like that?

Glaucon: Certainly.

Socrates: Now, if he had to compete once again with the perpetual prisoners in recognizing the shadows, while his sight was still dim and before his eyes had recovered, and if the time required for readjustment was not short, wouldn't he provoke ridicule? Wouldn't it be said of him that he had returned from his upward journey with his eyes ruined, and that it is not worthwhile even to try to travel upward? And as for anyone who tried to free the prisoners and lead them upward, if they could somehow get their hands on him, wouldn't they kill him?

Glaucon: They certainly would.

—Plato, The Republic (The Allegory of the Cave)

—— «» ——

Eli eased into his seat, notes strewn out in front of him. He couldn't sleep, but he couldn't figure out this spell either. It had been just after 2 a.m. when he stumbled upon Mason, the spy he never saw coming. Now, the time was… he didn't want to know. Late. Or early. What did time matter at Winter's End anyway?

Eli reached into his pants pocket and pulled out his wallet. Then a small photo from the billfold: his son, Charles, squinting in the sunlight, orange hair a windy mess. Eli's dad had always kept a photo of Eli and his sister in his wallet, and while that sort of detail didn't matter to kids, and hadn't mattered to Eli growing up, his father had been one of the good ones — and that had mattered. Eli wanted to be a good father too, and so he kept a photo of his son in his wallet. He wasn't sure it was working.

Last Sunday, before Eli met up with Mason, he'd spent the day with Charles: brunch then a couple hours at the Terminal City Public Library, which was probably a mistake. Charles wasn't a reader. Eli explained that reading was helpful — nay, critical — when it came to opening one's mind, to seeing the world from a bigger-picture perspective. Charles rolled his eyes (a nasty habit he'd picked up a year earlier) and told him, Dad, stop trying to control everything. He didn't like books and stuff. Sometimes you need to just let stuff go and let it do its own thing.

Eli placed the bent picture of his son down onto the note-covered metal table in front of him, out of focus but not out of periphery. Then he started reading. He had a spell to figure out, and less time to do so every minute that passed.

It wasn't that he couldn't get it started. Some necromancers were better than others when it came to mastering the subtleties of Deathspeak, and Eli was — as much as anyone could be with a language they didn't entirely understand — a fluent speaker. Better than most, in fact. But there was always more to a spell than words, an idea that needed to be understood, and it was in this regard that Eli was failing.

This was what the spell was supposed to do: create a massive, expanding orb of red light. And not the simple light-bulb-sized spheres that every necromancer could summon on a whim; the book Eli had found at Winter's End said that once, in the fifties, in a field far from anyone, a necromancer had summoned and stretched a sphere until it was the size of a hot air balloon. Imagine that. Only his wouldn't be in a field — nor would it be far from people.

In major cities around the world, twelve in all, Eli had allies waiting for further instruction. First, he would figure out this spell and relay it to them. Then they would figure it out themselves, best they could, until the time came, until Eli gave the signal. Apart and yet together, they would chant, creating a dozen unbelievable — but undeniable — red suns, bathing just as many skylines in the color of necromancy, uniting the world in awe. Then everyone would see the video, and there would be no burying the truth this time, or ever again.

That, of course, was assuming Eli could figure out this bloody spell.

He watched his small red sphere grow and grow — but slowly — to about the size of a basketball, hovering in the center of the room five feet off the floor. That's when it all fell apart, as it always did. Making his orb any bigger grew exponentially difficult, each additional inch of diameter twice as strenuous as the last. Eli broke a sweat trying, and then he broke the spell; it imploded like light returning to a black hole from which it should never have escaped.

He tried again. It was all he could do.

Glistening red-tinted drops raced down Eli's gaunt face. He was holding it together, the orb, but knew there was nowhere to go from here, that he couldn't make it any bigger. He'd have better luck bench-pressing his own bodyweight, and Eli most definitely could not do that. Hopeless, his mind wandered to the last thing he'd been thinking about, his son, Charles, and what he'd said on Sunday: "Sometimes you need to just let stuff go and let it do its own thing."

For once, almost by accident, Eli took his son's advice.

He stopped trying to control the spell, stopped trying to solve it like a problem, stopped trying to lift it like a weight, stopped trying to mold it like a... son, and took a deep breath, expanding his lungs as the sphere at the center of the room grew with them, bigger and bigger, brighter and brighter, like a flame finally fed oxygen. Dark corners and maroon shadows succumbed to scarlet, until it was the brightest room Eli had ever been in.

He'd done it at last.

Eli did his best to not try too hard — which is more difficult than it sounds for some people, of whom he was one — letting the spell do its own thing, and by the time his sphere imploded once more, it was damn near the diameter of Liana, head to toe.

And with that, it was time to update the others. Indeed, now that Mason knew his plans, Eli felt even more pressure to pull the trigger sooner rather than later. The longer he waited, the more opportunity there would be for someone to interfere. Eli brushed a pile of paper off his laptop and flipped it open. An old IBM that took a while to boot up. He really needed a new one — another thing Charles had rightly pointed out not long ago.

Eli double-clicked his email inbox. Winter's End had an excruciatingly slow satellite internet connection, but at least he wouldn't have to compete with anyone else for bandwidth at this time of night. Then he typed up his email:

Friends,

I have figured out the spell. Attached is a scanned copy of the Deathspeak chant required to cast the orb, along with a few notes. I will also add my own here: there is a trick to this spell — you must let the sphere expand on its own. Do not push too hard. The spell cannot be forced. Just believe in it, and breathe, and... let it do its own thing.

Unfortunately, unforeseen events have recently transpired that compel me to ask you all to be ready soon. As in, very soon. Do not stray far and begin learning the attached spell immediately. I will send the codeword when it is time.

With you all in spirit,

Eli

With his email written, Eli gazed past the room's billowing black curtains and out the open window, into the darkened world beyond. Fear and excitement were bedfellows, and he felt his share of both, now more than ever. Success — that elusive idea he'd chased for so long, or run from, depending on whom you asked — scared the hell out of him, he realized, and he'd just locked in the last piece of an ancient puzzle. He had, not Samuel, not Rowland — Eli goddamn Abelman. He'd spent his life studying history, and now he would be a part of it, destined for textbooks.

Indeed, Eli had found the final answer to his life's foremost problem, so why now did he have more questions than ever before? What would Charles think?

Eli looked his email over once more and then clicked send.

The door squeaked open. Eli suddenly realized that he hadn't locked it following Mason's departure. He slammed his laptop shut and swiveled in his chair.

But it wasn't Mason, the person he was most expecting, staring back at him; rather it was another young man, if you could count about thirty as young, which Eli did.

"Hello," the stranger said. Eli recognized him from outside, but they'd never been introduced.

"Can I... help you?" Eli got out of his chair and stood tall.

"I think so," said the young man.

"I'm not sure we've met," replied Eli.

"Right. Of course. Jason," he said.

"Eli."

Jason appraised the room, his eyes moving from the window over Eli's shoulder to the table at the far end — letting the silence simmer.

"So, how exactly can I help you, Jason?"

Jason closed the door, locking it. "Oh, I lied about that just now," he said. "My name's not Jason."

Eli took a backward step toward the wall behind him. "What do you mean? Who are you?"

The young man whose name was not Jason stepped forward, closing the distance between them, and Eli got a better look at him, at his round, inoffensive face, his cordial smile — but Eli knew that Winter's End was full of illusions.

"Who am I?" the stranger repeated the question. "Simple. I am the inevitable, Eli."

Chapter 20

Alicia straightened her glasses first and her menu second, until it was parallel to the table's edge. As Clayton could tell you, the woman really liked straightening things. Then she peered up at the man looming over them, his notepad at eyelevel, responding to his fake smile with a fake smile of her own. "I'll have the veggie burger."

The server scribbled something before switching his gaze to Clayton.

"The, uh, regular burger."

"The hamburger?" He kept his pen hovering.

"Yeah, that one," said Clayton.

"It's not regular just because it has meat in it, you know," Alicia felt the need to say. "You should try the veggie burger. It's really quite good here."

Clayton shrugged. "As we've already established, I'm a meat-eating bastard."

"Are you implying, my love, that you cannot eat a veggie burger on the grounds that you are, unlike me, a barbaric carnivore?"

Clayton broke character first, with a heavy chuckle. "I'll admit it's pretty faulty logic."

"It is indeed." Alicia smiled, not the fake one this time. "I'll let you take a bite of mine."

"Deal."

They were sitting across from one another at a small window-side table, in a diner between downtown and Carwin University, or roughly halfway between his office and hers. Sally's. It was what it was: the tables were fake wood on loose metal legs, the ceiling fan overheard was broken, the white walls were peeling, revealing their blue heritage. Clayton and

Alicia used to come here more, back when they started dating three years ago. The food was good, the portions plentiful, and the service, well, questionable. But it was vegetarian-friendly and cheap, which explained the clientele, mostly students by the looks of them — Alicia said she recognized one. And she liked Sally's, said her father loathed the place, which quite obviously made her like it even more, which in turn made Clayton, who was no snob, like it even more too.

"Do you remember the first time we came here?" asked Alicia.

"Wasn't it our first date?" he replied. "If you could call it that."

"It was. We came here on a Wednesday."

That had been her choice, not his. The two had met on a dating site, and Alicia didn't quite trust men she met on the internet. So like today, they grabbed lunch on a workday: short, casual, and they both had an out at the end of forty minutes. Clayton, enamored by the pictures he'd seen online of a beautiful woman unafraid to forgo Photoshop, needed less convincing.

"I remember," said Clayton. "You spent half that date talking about how you didn't go on dates with men you met online, despite, you know, clearly being on one. I actually thought you were a little insecure, truth be told, which is funny because you're actually the least insecure person I know."

She laughed through her nose. "Then why did you ask me out on a second date?"

"Oh, that's easy. The same reason I agreed to meet in the first place: I thought you were hot."

"It really is that simple with your kind, isn't it?"

Clayton nodded his head from side to side, a wordless *yeah, basically.*

"Okay, so I have a question." Alicia said it like something she'd been holding onto, nervously, an uncommon characteristic for the least insecure person Clayton knew.

"I'm all ears, babe."

"Do you... want to get..." She cleared her throat then quickly added, "married?"

"What?" replied Clayton, which probably wasn't the response she was looking for, but it just came out, the first thing he felt in that split second, confusion.

"Don't make me say it again." Alicia squinted at him.

Clayton smiled. "You want to get married? I thought, you said... you told me you didn't believe in marriage, that it was archaic, a means of guilting unhappy people into prolonging their unhappiness. Your words, if I recall correctly."

"That does sound like something I would say." Alicia shrugged.

"What changed?"

"Nothing changed," she said. "I still don't believe in marriage as a general concept, but, hmm, you know how I don't like video games very much?"

Clayton nodded. "I don't know where you're going with this, but yes. You said they were for children — or in my case, adults nostalgic for adolescence. Not that I agree."

"Right, exactly, and you made me play a video game. That puzzle one with the robots and those ungodly creatures with the annoying laser beams that kept killing me, and anyway, what I'm saying, my dear Clayton, is that... I started to have fun. That night. I enjoyed playing that video game with you. I will never share your love of video games, and if it weren't for you, I probably would never play one again. But sometimes, experiences don't match the idea one has in her head about a thing, which is unsettling for philosophers like your partner. Like I said, as a concept, I still don't believe in marriage, but in this context, as an experience with you, the prospect of marrying you — you specifically... it's like that stupid video game."

"That's why you brought me here — the setting of our first date. You were trying to be romantic. Aw, shucks." Clayton couldn't help himself.

"If your grin grows any bigger, detective, the top of your head might fall off. And," she continued, nervous again, "you still haven't answered the question."

"Oh, right. Jeez, of course. Yeah. Fuck yeah. Shit, of course I'll marry you."

Alica looked relieved, as if there had been any chance in hell he would have said no.

"Should I get you a ring or something?" asked Clayton.

"God, no," she replied. "No rings. Well, maybe at the wedding. I don't know. I haven't thought that far ahead. I don't even know if I want a wedding. Anyway, no engagement ring. Besides, I asked you — and you know how much I hate diamonds."

"Biggest scam in the Western world," he said. "An artificially inflated depreciating asset. I know, babe. Trust me, no guy wants to shell out ten-thousand dollars on a drop of glass. I'm not fighting you on this one. Fuck diamonds."

"We're agreed, then."

"One-hundred percent." Clayton emphasized the *hundred*. "Does that mean we're engaged now?"

"I guess it does," she replied.

"I have a fiancée. Jesus H. Christ. I'm all grown up."

"At thirty-six, I'd hope so."

"I'm still going to play video games, however."

"I know."

"So, what now?" he asked.

She shrugged. "We both have jobs to get back to. We can go out for dinner tonight if you want."

"Back to work, just like that?"

"I didn't want to make a big thing out of it."

"Of course not."

Her mouth grinned, but her eyes were beaming. "I need to pee." Alicia shuffled out of her chair and walked by her stupidly smiling fiancée, squeezing his shoulder, black boots clicking on the checkered floor.

Clayton watched her disappear around the corner. "Just like that."

His phone beeped — a text message.

Clayton reached into his pants pocket. He recognized the name: Mitch, a colleague of his. A colleague he'd been waiting to hear back from. Clayton opened the text message: *Hey Clayton. The blood matches.*

He stared at those five words for too long, stared and realized, after all this time, after all his suspicions, that he'd never actually wanted to be right. But here was the unambiguous proof he'd been digging for.

Some background: Clayton had never solved the mystery on Carwin's campus two years back: that strange, fatal pool of blood in the forest. There were bullets, but no body, no clues. Just a mystery, and then a day later, Granville Bridge blows up, the sky bleeds red, and Clayton is forced to kill a man. Yet still, two years later, no one knew any more than they did then. The difference between them and Clayton was that he had never stopped caring, not by an inch. Maybe it was his fatal contribution to the evening's events, or maybe it was something inside of him that couldn't accept the impossible. Either way, he needed to know. Only now he was realizing, rather suddenly, that perhaps he didn't want to know.

She was the reason, Alicia. Mason was a student of hers, and she'd told Clayton to leave him alone. He was a good young man, and smart, and his father had just died and things were hard enough as is, and Clayton didn't disagree — he'd driven Mason home that night, after the shootout, and he'd liked him too. But facts were the building blocks of an investigation, and where he saw two that might snap together, well, Clayton had a duty to push. And so he did, and so they snapped.

A week earlier, Clayton had nabbed a blood-soaked piece of paper towel from Mason's house during an unannounced drop-in. He'd hesitated taking things further and, indeed, had almost thrown out the paper towel on his way to the office, ashamed, but no — Clayton hadn't, couldn't. He just had to know, had to prove a suspicion, and perhaps if he was wrong, he could finally move on from one soul-sucking mystery to another. Except, of course, he'd just found out that he was right: Mitch had run the blood on the paper tower against the blood they'd found in that forest two years ago.

It was a match.

Which raised more questions than it answered. Mason hadn't seemed injured that night Clayton drove him home, but with that much blood gone, he should have been hospitalized — if not dead. So what the hell was Clayton supposed to make of that, and more urgently, what the hell was he supposed to do with the information he'd just uncovered?

"Your hamburger."

Clayton almost missed the meal being placed down in front of him. "Oh, right. Thanks."

"And a veggie burger for the lady. Enjoy."

Clayton watched the server wander off and then, from around the corner, the love of his life re-emerge.

Alicia sat back down, smiling, her happiness uninterrupted by any text message. "At last, lunch. I am famished."

Clayton, who was already chewing on a mouthful of hamburger, nodded and grinned, feigning normalcy.

She took a bite, made an *mmm* noise, then held out her veggie burger before him. "Here," she said, "try it."

Clayton took a swig of water then a bite of the strange offering. He handed back his fiancée's food, chewing pensively. It was delicious.

"This is actually better than mine," he said truthfully.

"Oh, I know." Underneath the table, she kicked his foot. "You see, I'm always right."

Chapter 21

This is the way the world ends
This is the way the world ends
This is the way the world ends
Not with a bang but a whimper.

    —*T.S. Eliot, "The Hollow Men"*

— «» —

"**It's me, Alexus,** just doing the rounds. Can you open the door please?"

She knocked again. No answer.

"I can hear you in there."

"Busy." The man inside sounded annoyed.

"Don't care if you're busy. I've gotta check these rooms once a week, and it's that time of week. It'll just take a sec."

"Busy."

"Fuck this," Alexus whispered, more to herself. She had a key and wasn't afraid to use it. She fetched the key ring in her pocket and tried each of them, one after the other, until at last a small bronze one grinded through. Alexus turned her hand and pushed the door open with her other one.

The first thing she noticed was him: a disciple of the red, his robe loosened, his hood spilled over his shoulders exposing a bald, sweating head. Her second observation: books covering the floor, but not in a disorderly fashion; they were arranged, balanced upright into pathways — a maze. And the third thing Alexus saw was a rat, racing through this constructed labyrinth.

She looked back toward the stranger, the tint of necromancy fading from his bloodshot eyes, which remained red even after his spell had ended.

"Damn it!" He stomped.

"Were you...?" Alexus, who didn't make accusations lightly, hesitated. "Were you controlling that rat with necromancy?"

The stranger turned and stared at her. Alexus didn't recognize him, but then that wasn't surprising considering the disciples normally had their hoods up and, as an apparent rule, avoided speaking to anyone outside of their cultish clique.

"So what if I was?" He threw his words at her.

"That would be a nefarious spell," she said. "They're against the rules here."

"Nefarious? Toward whom?"

"That rat for one."

He scoffed, arrogantly. Arrogance, in fact, seemed central to his very being, his every word and gesture exuding it in excess.

"A rat?" he said. "Who cares about rats? When was the last time you ate a steak, a hamburger, bacon — take your pick?"

"I'm vegetarian." Alexus crossed her arms. "That's beside the point, however. The reason it's a nefarious spell, *sir*, is because it could be used against a person. So how about you tell me just why exactly you're down here practicing it?"

"Disciple business," he said. "None of yours."

"What's your name?" she asked.

He waved her off.

Alexus shook her head. "You're going to hear more about this, I hope you realize that. This is far from over. You best come up with a better response than that for the others. Word of advice: no one likes a dick."

She slammed the door behind her— "Fucking asshole" —and continued on her way, checking the rest of the rooms.

Winter's End had a basement full of private labs, accessible to whoever reserved them. They were safe spaces to practice and experiment with new spells, plus you had access to Winter's End's library, the best of its kind on the planet. While guests were, generally speaking, trusted during their stay — after all, only a seasoned necromancer

could find their way here — Winter's End wouldn't be the
fortress of secrecy that it was without a little precaution,
where warranted. And that rat-torturing asshole had just
proven that, clearly, her weekly checkups were.

As for why Alexus had volunteered herself for the
unenviable task of busting down doors (most exchanges were
cordial), it was the price she paid for spending six months
at Winter's End. Most necromancers came for a week, two
weeks, a month tops. A few, however, stayed longer. They all
had their reasons, and she had hers (mostly, a bad breakup
with her girlfriend). Well, Winter's End didn't run itself —
there wasn't a spell for everything — and so while each guest
was responsible for their own meals and laundry, general
upkeep fell to those who, like Alexus, had made Winter's
End a temporary home. And this particular task had been
up for grabs when she got here, simple as that. She wouldn't
complain, though. It was better than cleaning the bathrooms,
and the rent here, zero dollars a month, was a hell of a lot
cheaper than back in San Francisco.

Alexus arrived at the last lab, which was locked again.
She knocked. "Open up. It's me, Alexus, here for the weekly
check-in."

Again, no answer. She didn't wait long this time. Alexus
pulled out her key ring and got it on the first try. "I'm coming
in."

She pushed the door open and immediately saw another
man inside, only this one hadn't heard her. He was lying face
down on the floor.

Alexus hurried toward him, falling to her knees. "Sir?
You okay, sir?" She shook his shoulder, but he didn't budge.
She spoke louder, shook harder, and still nothing. Finally,
pulling with both arms, Alexus turned him over onto his
back (he wasn't heavy, but he also wasn't helping) and
quickly recognized his face from two days earlier — when
he'd only just arrived.

"Eli."

He looked pale. Alexus could feel her own heartbeat, but
what about Eli's? She didn't want to believe that maybe...
that he might be... She was a necromancer, sure, but Alexus

had never seen a dead body up close. Death was still an idea to her, innocently abstract, not something you touch. But now she had her hand on his cold face, moving her fingers down to his cold neck to feel for a pulse. To feel for what she already knew she'd found: a dead body.

— «» —

Mason was munching on cereal when he heard the muffled scream from downstairs, a quick one that was just as quickly silenced. He dropped his spoon, milk splashing his nose, and shot glances around the dining room for a reaction, but Mason was all alone, eating his second bowl of cereal that day in solitude.

(It had been explained to Mason that food here was communal, purchased weekly by Winter's End's long-term tenants, the money endowed by generations of generous necromancers, hint, hint. Unless, of course, there was a sticky note saying otherwise, which, in his brief experience pursuing the fridges, was often the case. Cereal, at least, was simple.)

Mason stood up and walked over to the foyer. A man he didn't recognize sprinted past him, and then Mason could hear more feet clamoring through the building, funneling down the basement stairs. He followed, taking the spiraling library staircase to the bottom floor before exiting into a hallway. The private labs: he'd been to Eli's just last night, four doors down from where he was standing now. He counted again to be sure, counted because that's where they were all headed, that's where they were all collecting — door number four. Mason took longer and longer strides, ducking and dodging his way past people shoulder first, closing in on Eli's private lab. Unlike last night, the way in was open this time, but the necromancers standing around Eli's door looked no less confused than Mason felt. He squirmed past them for an answer — and got one.

There was no doubt now: this was Eli's lab, and there was Eli, lying on his back, looking pale minus a dry trickle of blood down one side of his face. Minus all the bruises too: blue and purple and yellow, every color-coded degree of pain inflicted and marked. More bruises than you'd get from a good fall. More bruises than you'd get by accident.

Mason recognized only one other person in the room: Alexus, whom he'd chatted with yesterday by the fountain. He overheard someone say it was Alexus who'd found him here, like this.

"Is he dead?" asked a woman.

Without making eye contact with anyone, without moving her arms, which were crossed tightly around her chest, Alexus nodded.

Dead. Mason couldn't believe it. Eli Abelman was suddenly, inexplicably dead. Another problem solved by snuffing out a life. Just like Rowland, only it hadn't been Mason acting as executioner this time. As to whom it could have been, however, he racked his brain for suspects and couldn't come up with a single one. What he did have was a motive: Eli's plan to unveil necromancy to the world. If Joan suspected, surely others did too — surely Eli was on someone's hit list. Some person who felt that one life was a small price to pay for the greater good. Mason knew a few. Maybe it was a mole, someone Eli had trusted. It was definitely a necromancer, that much he could be sure of. There were no bullet holes or stab wounds. Mason supposed it could have been poison, but this was Winter's End, and everyone here was a necromancer. Occam's razor.

Jesus. What would Joan think? And then Mason realized that he didn't really give a damn. A man was dead, a decent man. Another necromancer, another member of his endangered species, gone. Those who practiced in death seemed so susceptible to it (Mason, who'd taken a couple bullets himself, could speak from experience), but surely that didn't need to be the case. And yet it was. Necromancers could have had their own Flanders Field, appropriately red poppies and all. No, Mason didn't care what Joan would think, didn't care that perhaps, on some level, she would be relieved to hear the news, the thought of which sickened him. This was a tragedy, and tragedies didn't deserve their silver linings, if there even was one. But Liana? Oh fuck, Liana.

Mason heard scuffling and murmuring. A man walked past him and knelt down beside Eli's body.

Mason didn't recognize him. He was maybe six feet, forty-something, Japanese, and handsome in that old-movie-star sort of way — a chiseled jaw, high cheekbones, sharp eyebrows, and an even sharper stare. He was wearing a black pea coat. Mason assumed he must have just arrived.

Then he started chanting, the handsome stranger, casting quick spells, his hand hovering over Eli's head and then down his limbs, looking detective-like, looking for a clue. From his furrowed brow, Mason wagered he wasn't finding any.

The stranger stood back up. "Who found him here," he asked, "like this?"

Alexus, who had slowly slinked away from the crime scene to where Mason was standing, raised her forearm.

"And did anyone else see anything — or know anything?"

This time, no one volunteered their arms, especially not Mason.

"Very well. We'll talk in a few hours, Alexus, once I've settled in. This is… tragic. Eli was a good man, as I'm sure many of you here know." With both hands on his hips, he made eye contact with each of them, Mason included. His gaze never wandered; everywhere he looked, everyone he looked at, he did so with apparent purpose. "We'll figure out what happened here," he said.

And then he walked out, briskly, before anyone else.

Mason leaned closer to Alexus. "Who was that?" he asked.

"Hiroshi Saito," she replied. "A guardian."

A guardian? Had Joan known he was coming? And perhaps more to the point, had Hiroshi been told about Mason, that he would be here on a (now aborted) mission? Mason wondered what information Hiroshi might possess and quickly concluded that either he knew everything, nothing, or, really, how the hell was Mason supposed to surmise this one? *Keep your head down, let Hiroshi make the first move*: that was the plan now. Oh, and maybe get the fuck back to Canada at some point.

Mason sighed. But God Almighty, poor Eli. He had a kid, he had…

Against the current of people leaving the lab, Liana walked through the open door. Mason wondered if he should stop her, but it was quickly too late — and, perhaps, not his place.

She sped up toward Eli, falling to one knee. Then she squeezed his arm, shaking it. "Eli?" She grabbed his other shoulder, shaking both, his limp head bobbing into passive nods.

"Eli?" she said. "*Eli?*"

Mason crouched down beside her. Up close, it was even more obvious that Eli was dead (it was hardly the first time Mason had seen a corpse). And then he told her, with as much sympathy and as little ambiguity as he could, "He's dead, Liana. I'm so sorry. No one knows what happened."

She didn't reply, not with words, not even a nod of acknowledgement. Slowly, at her own pace, Liana stood back up, staring out at memories that only she could see. She didn't scream or cry or say farewell, but her silence filled the room like the subtlest note of a symphony.

"Liana?" Mason turned toward her, but she turned away.

And then she walked out, between murmurs— "Is that the girl he came with?" —and sympathetic stares, wanting, Mason had learned from personal experience, none of it. And then she was gone. Not just from the room, but the version of her that had existed before the man she'd loved like a father was found dead. That Liana, Mason knew, was gone forever, gone with Eli.

Chapter 22

Ryooyaku kuchi ni nigashi.
(Good medicine tastes bitter in the mouth.)
  —*Japanese proverb*

— «» —

"Come in."

Alexus stepped inside, closing the door gently behind her.

"Thank you for meeting me." Hiroshi was sitting beside a small desk, his white wooden chair turned toward her. "Please, sit."

Alexus smiled with only the corners of her mouth and then took a seat on Hiroshi's bed, next to his silver suitcase. "Nice-looking luggage you got. Looks expensive."

He shrugged modestly. "I travel a lot. What makes something worth the price is how often you use it, I find."

"Yeah," she said. "Suppose that's true."

Hiroshi topped up the tumbler of scotch resting on the desk beside him. He nodded toward an empty one. "Drink?"

"I'm not really in the mood."

His next expression was carefully compassionate. "I know how hard it can be, seeing someone you know dead. There are no words, but you have my sympathy all the same."

"I didn't really know him," replied Alexus. "He seemed like a nice enough guy, though. Now that the shock's worn off, I'm more worried about that girl he came here with, Liana. And Mason, the other one, although he seemed, well, upset but okay — like he'd seen this sort of shit before."

"Mason Cross?"

"I didn't catch his last name."

"In your opinion, is he a suspect?"

"Mason?" she said. "Nah. I mean, as much as anyone here is, I suppose, but I don't think it was him."

"I see." Hiroshi paused. "Forgive my prodding, but it sounds as if perhaps there is someone you think that it was."

"Well." Alexus bit her lip. "I wouldn't go that far. Let's just say I ran into someone acting a little suspiciously this morning. Could be for entirely unrelated reasons, though."

"Could be. Go on."

"He was a disciple of the red," she said. "Bald guy, didn't catch his name. Or rather, he refused to give it to me. Anyway, I caught him casting a nefarious spell in one of the basement labs during my weekly rounds. He was mind-controlling a rat, steering it through this maze of books like some sort of... remote-controlled car."

"Was it a dead rat?"

"Nah, a living one."

"That's worse."

"I know. I told him as much, but he acted like a bit of an asshole, let's just put it that way. The disciples, they don't really like talking to us. Not trying to stereotype or anything, but yeah, he was a dick."

"A dick he may be," replied Hiroshi, "but a murderer? One does not necessarily equal the other. Still, you were right to bring this to my attention. I could once again use your help, Alexus. Can you find him for me? I don't want to confront the wrong man."

"Sure," she said. "I'll point him out. Is there anything else I can help with?"

"There is, in fact." Hiroshi took a longer-than-usual sip of scotch. "Those bruises on Eli Abelman's face. He was murdered, that much is obvious. Beaten and then, I assume, subjected to some sort of spirit-ripping spell, the most nefarious variety there is. Which means we have a murderer at Winter's End. If he or she leaves now, we will never find out who it was, and that is simply unacceptable. I cannot allow a necromancer-killer to come and go — to this of all places — as they please. No. To kill one of us is to kill family. This man, this woman, they must be dealt with accordingly and as soon as possible. However, that will require some cooperation." Another long sip.

"What kind of cooperation?" asked Alexus.

"First, the labs are off-limits."

"That shouldn't be a problem."

"No, but this next one will be," he said. "No one can leave Winter's End, Alexus. Not until we have solved this murder. As well, I want to impose a curfew. There will be no going outside after dark, otherwise our murderer will surely escape."

Alexus let out a long sigh. "These people don't like taking orders. They're not used to it. It's not how they operate. To be honest, I doubt many of them even consider guardians a real authority, no offense. Just not necromancer culture, you know. What's the saying: like herding cats. Yeah. That pretty much sums it up."

"I realize this will be difficult, Alexus," he said, "and that not everyone will agree with my method. Alas, we just need a majority to be on board, to enforce the rules. It is not... well, there is simply no other way. The alternative, our murderer escaping, is worse, wouldn't you agree?"

"Yeah," she replied. "Yeah, I know. I'll try, Hiroshi. I mean, it's going to be a tough sell, but I'll do my best."

"Our best is all any of us can do, my dear. You have my sincere gratitude." Hiroshi stood up and walked her to his door. "Hopefully, they are half as wise as you are. Hopefully, they will understand that we necromancers operate in a world of necessary evils."

— «» —

The dimly-lit library was deserted save for a single disciple, bent over a book on the bottom floor. And, of course, Hiroshi, who was eyeing his suspect over the second-story banister. Not that he could see much from his vantage point — just the back of a red robe with its hood up, veiling the stranger's face. Granted, he didn't know which one he was looking for anyway. The disciples of the red didn't make a point of distinguishing themselves. They made quite the opposite point, in fact.

Indeed, as far as Hiroshi was concerned, they were background noise, no matter how loud they turned the volume. Despite all of the complaints the guardians had received about the disciples over the years, Hiroshi had never uncovered anything truly troubling. They were talentless fools playing dress-up: that was all he'd learned. Their words were empty, their ideas silly, and their experiments fruitless. All bark and no bite. Hiroshi knew that truly dangerous necromancers didn't wear frivolous costumes. No. Truly dangerous necromancers understood the value of invisibility.

Still, a man was dead, and there were only so many suspects in the middle of Greenland. Hiroshi couldn't write anyone off. He would have words with this man Alexus had told him about, although right now he had another task in need of his undivided attention. It was the reason he had come here, after all — to this library, to Winter's End.

Hiroshi crouched down, wrists to his knees, and began thumbing through spines along the bookshelf in front of him. *Definitely not that one.* Some books he pulled out and flipped through, but each time it was to an ultimately unhappy ending. There was only one among the thousands circling him that he cared about right now, and so far he wasn't having any luck. Hiroshi had been at this for half an hour, thinking the entire time that he would find the book he was after in the next minute or two, but now his optimism was starting to wane, and book by book, he began doubting more and more that he would ever even find this goddamn grimoire, no matter how long he searched, and maybe this whole trip had been a — *ah, there you are.*

He let out a relieved chuckle. "Just a matter of time," whispered Hiroshi, who had come to learn that the single biggest barrier between people and what they wanted was time. Time was a price that needed to be paid in full, and he'd been saving a while for this one.

Hiroshi left the library with a small black book clenched tightly in his palm.

— «» —

He could feel him in the recesses of his mind. His presence, a faint flicker. His voice, distant, an echo carried from the farthest side of life's greatest canyon. But it was one thing to hear a man and quite another to transport him. It was one thing to summon a spirit and quite another to, well, attempt this. If Hiroshi succeeded, it would be a world first.

Vanity, however, played no part in this, or at least he told himself as much. The end, Hiroshi believed, was something much greater, much bigger than him — though it too was but a means to something grander still. Something so Earth-shaking that even a man like Hiroshi couldn't accomplish it alone.

Presently, however, solitude was imperative. Alexus had escorted everyone out of the basement labs and made it quite clear that the rooms were off-limits for the time being. That is, to anyone who wasn't named Hiroshi Saito. It was an understandable safety precaution, but even so he was surprised by how little resistance they'd seen thus far (the curfew, he predicted, would be another matter). But there was more on Hiroshi's agenda than solving one murder. There was the reason he had come here, and for that a lab and privacy were required, and suddenly he had the whole floor to himself. The circumstances were serendipitous — if framed in tragedy. Such, he supposed, was life.

Of course, Hiroshi really only needed one lab. He'd chosen the largest, locked the door, drawn the blinds shut, and laid out his notes neatly, in the order they were meant to be read, although by now he had everything memorized. He knew the chants like lyrics to a favorite song — or one you couldn't get out of your head. For a spell as complex as this, a spell that he himself had forged from a dozen others, memorization was necessary groundwork. Reading took effort, and he couldn't spare the neurons; casting this spell would take everything he had.

Still, his second attempt had once again fizzled and slowly, inevitably died, that distant voice — the connection he was trying to secure — fading back into the endless black hole from where he had drawn it. So close, yet so far. Hiroshi growled, low and deep, trying not to be heard, and then he breathed, long and steady. "*Baka.*" He took a swig of water, wiped his brow, and refocused.

He spoke the chants more quickly this time, mindlessly, focusing on an impossibly distant shadow of a man — like trying to capture a small wisp of smoke coiling out from a clenched fist. But Hiroshi had calmed himself, if only temporarily; frustration led to shaking and fumbling, and his task — if it were even possible — required an unnatural level of precision. He was getting closer. He could feel it, and feeling it was the only thing he had to go on. That is to say, he could feel *him*.

And then it became both of them, no longer solely Hiroshi, securing their connection. The sensation overwhelmed him like an unexpected drug. He grabbed the back of the nearest chair to keep his balance, its metal legs squeaking against the cement.

Slowly, the spell simmered. Hiroshi couldn't hold on anymore, but he realized he didn't need to. The connection was secured. *He* was in there now, in him, his voice like a rogue memory.

Hear me... do you... hear me?

"Yes. Yes, I hear you."

I see... colors, lights... blurry, but I see them... I see... the Living Realm.

"Then it is done."

Yes... it is done.

"Good," said Hiroshi, catching his breath. "Good."

He only hoped that it would be reversible — and that some thoughts were still private.

Chapter 23

"Hey, it's me."

No answer, but Mason knew she was inside. There was nowhere else at Winter's End she could be — he'd looked.

"I brought you some dinner. Soup. It's really good actually, and I'm not normally that into soup. But yeah. Some sort of bisque maybe? I'm not totally sure what a bisque is, to be perfectly honest with you, but it's yellow and tastes good. I didn't make it."

He thought he heard her laugh.

"Liana?" Mason knocked with just his knuckles.

"I'm not hungry."

She was speaking to him now. Progress.

"I know," he said, "but you gotta eat or you'll feel even worse. Biology is a bitch that way."

For a while there was no response, and Mason thought he'd lost her again, and then he heard a click from behind the door. She opened it just a crack and went back to her bed. Mason let himself in, shutting the door behind him. He locked it for good measure; he wasn't sure she wanted his company, but he was quite certain she wouldn't want anyone else's at Winter's End. Strangers, all of them.

And then Mason remembered that he too was a stranger to her, that they'd only just met a week ago. It sure didn't feel that way.

Liana wasn't crying, though she had all the hallmarks of someone who had been: tousled hair and mascara lines, wiped away but not completely. Her bed had been transformed into a nest, its sheets coiled into a circle around her. There was a book in the middle she'd been reading; Mason couldn't see the title, but it looked like fiction — certainly, nothing necromantic.

He handed her the soup and a spoon. "Here."

She took it from him like a vaccination needle — a means to an end — with a monotone "Thanks."

"Yeah. No problem." Mason sat down on a small white chair in the corner, a safe ten feet away.

Liana poked the soup with her spoon, as if testing it, and then took a small sip. She took another thirty seconds later, eating at a pace that all but guaranteed leftovers.

"This is quite good," she finally admitted.

"Alexus made it," Mason told her. "There's a big batch downstairs. I think she's trying to win allies. Soup's one strategy, I suppose."

"What do you mean she's trying to win allies?" asked Liana.

"Oh yeah, I guess you haven't heard." Mason scooted forward in his seat. "Hiroshi, that Japanese guy who just showed up, well, apparently he's a guardian. And now... given what's happened... he's decided to implement a curfew. The labs are off-limits, no can go outside at night, and no one can leave. Alexus is helping him enforce all of this, but she needs people on her side. Thus, the soup."

"Good." Liana nodded empathetically. "That's good. I want them caught. Whoever fucking did this. Whatever it takes, man."

Mason was less keen on the curfew. He was hiding something from them, something related to Eli — his mission to investigate the man — and worried that, somehow, someone would find out. He was quite sure he hadn't left any clues, but these were necromancers, and they had their ways. That Hiroshi guy certainly seemed to have his. Still, Mason got where Liana was coming from. He wanted the bastard caught too.

In the meantime, however, he wanted nothing more than to make Liana feel better, even if it was only a little — even if it wouldn't last.

"Want to hear a story?" he asked.

Liana shrugged.

Mason took that as a yes. "My dad, he had this record player," he began, "an old one from the eighties that he kept fixing, sitting on this small table in his den. I loved that den. He had a whole library of books, this beautiful oak desk, an old brown globe his father had given him, a bar cart, every den cliché you can think of — and this record player. My dad was really into jazz — Coltrane, Davis, Brubeck, all those guys — and he'd listen to these jazz records late at night, and I'd hear them down the hall from my bedroom as a kid, and I liked it, you know. When you're an adult you want silence when you're trying to sleep, but as a kid, that music let me know my dad was just down the hall.

"Anyway, he'd told me once that you should always put records away after you're done listening to them, snug in their sleeve, to preserve them. Don't leave them on the turntable, he said, because it's bad for the record. Now, this is ironic because he forgot all the time. He'd get distracted by whatever he was working on and, well, tended to forget the little things. So the next morning or afternoon — that's when he was gone and the room became mine — I'd wander in with a book or some paper and a pen, whatever I was working on that day, but the very first thing I'd do, every single time, was check that record player. Sure enough, at least once a week, he'd left a goddamn record on the turntable. But I remembered what he told me, so I took the record off, found the right sleeve, and put it away. I don't think he ever realized I did that for him, but I did. Every freaking time.

"The funny thing is, after he died, I didn't stop. I'd walk into that room and my eyes would just immediately lock onto that record player like some magnet. I couldn't help it. But, of course, there would be no record waiting to be put away. Not anymore, not ever again. But for nine months, until I left for Carwin, I kept looking. And each time... each time was a little disappointing.

For a moment, Mason paused to remember where he was going with this.

Quieter, he continued: "The thing was, I hadn't taken my dad's death well. Which is to say, I hadn't really taken it at all. I mean, I didn't cry, nothing. I was stunned, and then I was in denial, I guess. I don't know what it was quite frankly, but it took me almost a year before I finally had a good cry.

And it wasn't until sometime after that moment, that cry, that I stopped looking at the empty record player every single bloody time I entered that room."

Mason hadn't told this story before, not even to Asha, and it hit him harder than he saw coming. He cleared his throat, suppressing any signs of sadness as best he could.

"So, what I'm saying," he said, "is that if you feel shitty right now, if you feel just awful, if you've been crying all day — good. That's good. That's how you need to feel."

"Eli's not my father," she said, but he could tell from her eyes that she'd understood anyway.

"I know," he told her.

"I thought..." She hesitated, wrapping her blanket tightly around her shoulders. "I thought things had finally leveled out for me, you know? That reality had done its worse — left me on the fucking street, but I got through it, got stronger, proved myself — and now things would be... not amazing but normal. Just normal. That was all I wanted. I'd earned normal."

Then the tears started again. Liana wiped them away with the backs of her hands, aggressively. "I just keep thinking about everything he did for me. All the nights he gave me a place to sleep, all the books he lent me, the things he showed me, the people he introduced me to, the way he encouraged me to... be the best me. But without judgment, you know? Eli was the most patient dude on the planet." She sniffled.

"Sometimes someone does so much for you, but..." Liana searched for her words. "But you don't realize it at the time. You just see the individual acts of kindness, not the whole. It's like, hey, that was a nice thing you just did, thanks, but you forget about all the other shit. Until one day that person is suddenly gone, and you're left trying to piece them back together with nothing but memories — and then you realize, holy shit, that guy, that fucking guy and everything he did for me."

Liana shrugged, defeated, and looked out the room's only window, off into the distance through the manufactured nighttime bubble that encapsulated their strange, new reality.

"Maybe," she said, "maybe he's still alive in some parallel universe, and we're hanging out right now, and none of this shit ever happened." She laughed, bittersweet, and then asked: "What's it like?"

"What's what like?" replied Mason.

"The Spirit Realm. You said you'd been there. What's it like when you die?"

"Ah." Mason wasn't sure he knew himself; it had been a confusing ordeal more than anything, and he imagined his history-making hour in the afterlife wasn't a good general indicator of what one should expect. Still, he tried to be helpful. "It's dark," he said. "I mean, like, perfectly dark. Just this... sea of black. Until you realize you don't walk to places — you use your mind to get there. It's like learning to, well, walk all over again, minus the walking part, of course.

"And the places that do exist, once you find them, they're pretty magnificent. It's all perception in the Spirit Realm, and people have imagined up some pretty amazing shit. It's like... imagine being stuck in a dream. One of those lucid dreams, where you know you're dreaming, although I think people forget after a while — where they are, who they are, and that's when the dream can turn dark. That's when they start fading. Yeah. It's not awful, though. I think it depends a lot on your" —Mason poked his temple— "mind."

"Well," said Liana, "Eli always did have a brilliant imagination."

"No! No! No!"

The voice was a woman's.

At once, Mason and Liana both turned their heads toward the door.

"Jim! No!"

The cries were coming from down the hall.

Liana planted her silver spoon back into the bowl of soup, which was still not even half-eaten. "What the hell was that?" Her eyes were wet with tears, but Liana had stopped crying. She looked alert — and then toward Mason for an answer.

"I have no idea," he said — but it couldn't be good.

They waited another minute, but the yelling had stopped. Mason thought he heard sobbing.

"I think I should go check it out," he said.

Liana looked back toward him, worry in her eyes. "I don't know, Mason. It could be dangerous, given all that's happened. I know you're a tough dude, but maybe let someone else handle this."

"Like who?"

"Like that guardian. Hiroshi or whatever."

She had a good point, but what she didn't know was that Mason was being considered for a similar role: guardian of North America (assuming his chances hadn't died with Eli). This was an opportunity to show Hiroshi, whose support he'd surely need, that he was the right man for the job. But more than that, someone was in trouble — or at least it certainly sounded like someone was in trouble — and when someone was in trouble, Mason believed you shouldn't expect other people to step in. Often they did not. That's how the bystander effect worked. And Mason didn't consider himself to be a bystander.

"I'll be right back," he told her, "just give me a minute."

"Maybe I should join you," she replied.

But Mason knew she wasn't in the right state of mind for conflict resolution; she had her own battle to wage right now.

"I'll be fine," he said. "Just stay here, Liana. I won't be long."

"Okay, whatever. Just be careful, please."

"I will. And I'll be right back, I promise."

With that, Mason left Liana's room, closing the door slowly, until it clicked.

Chapter 24

Our eyes, they lie. Our noses, they deceive. Our fingers, they fool. The world you see and smell and touch is but a coat of paint brushed over reality. There is a way to see past this layer of delusion, however. The true path — the path of a disciple — can seem a lonely one at first, but your brothers and sisters are here to help. As a disciple of the red, you are not alone, and together we will peel back this facade. Together, we will discover the great inner workings of the universe. Spirit energy is only the start — necromancy but a crack in the hull of the cosmos.

—Jim Lightbringer, The Book of Red

— ‹› —

She was definitely crying, the woman in the room at the end of the hall. Mason could hear her muffled sobs coming from around the open door twenty feet ahead of him. Yellow light poured into the corridor from the hidden scene, distorted shadows flickering on the floor like a fan blade. The inhabitants. How many people were inside? Mason heard only one woman crying.

He moved slowly against the edge of the wall. In his mind, Mason recited a self-defense spell he'd taught himself months earlier (which immobilized people rather than killed them) and kept it at the ready. He wasn't sure who, or what, he would find. He half-hoped for danger, hoped for the person who had killed Eli. Let them try Mason instead. Let them try the man who'd taken down Rowland. In his head, Mason was getting cocky, and he knew it — but hey, necromancy was all perception.

Finally, Mason turned toward the open door and stepped through.

"Mason." It was Alexus, jumpy and undeniably on edge. "Shit... umm... maybe close the door behind you."

"What... oh."

Mason saw the man first. He was bald, wrapped in a red robe, and lying on his stomach. Without even asking, Mason knew he was dead. He could feel it, for one — his lack of presence, his lack of spirit energy — but it was also the woman. She revealed more about what had happened here, keeled over his body, sobbing into the sleeves of her equally red robe. They were disciples.

"The door," Alexus reminded him.

"Right." Mason nearly slammed it shut.

The crying disciple looked up just then, at Mason, sorrow in her eyes — but rage lining her brow. "Who are you?" she spat.

"I am... Mason. Mason Cross."

That, apparently, didn't mean anything to her. She turned her attention to Alexus and began shaking her head. "You... this is partly your fault."

"Excuse me?" Alexus took a step back.

"You heard me. You're running around, telling everyone they can't leave, keeping us here like penned animals for this butcher to slaughter. What did you think would happen?"

"Listen, Claire. People leaving wouldn't make anyone safer," Alexus explained with both hands. "There would just be fewer sets of eyes and, what's more, the killer would escape. I know you're upset, and you should be. That's why we need to find this son of a bitch."

Claire shook her head and changed the topic: "Jim told me about your... run-in this morning." She squeezed Jim's dead arm. "About how you accused him of casting a nefarious spell on a... rat? A fucking rat?"

"A nefarious spell is a nefarious spell," replied Alexus.

"And a disciple is a disciple!" Claire yelled back. "That's all you see, isn't it? A disciple. You think I don't detect your contempt for our followers? Well, I bloody well do. We all know what people like you think of us — how you distrust us. I'm sure you thought it was Jim who was the murderer until now, am I wrong? One of our brothers had to die for you to realize his innocence."

"I didn't assume—"

"Bullshit! People always assume." She shook her head and looked back down toward Jim, petting his bald spot. "You should be ashamed," she said quietly. "Ashamed."

Alexus crossed her arms and sighed, but Mason could tell she'd lost the will to respond.

"What happened here?" he asked her.

She gestured toward Claire and Jim. "I came over to talk to Jim about this morning, knocked first. He didn't respond, but I could see the light was on, so I opened the door and stepped in and… yeah. Saw this. Claire showed up just before you got here."

"Looks like what happened to Eli," said Mason, grimly.

"Yeah." Alexus sighed the word. "Yeah, it sure does."

Claire kept her gaze glued to Jim as she spoke. "Of course it does," she said. "There's a goddamn murderer on the loose. And you better… you better find them."

Mason and Alexus exchanged a wordless glance, and then she asked him, "Can you do me a favor?"

"What is it?"

"Fetch Hiroshi," she replied. "I haven't seen him in a few hours. I'm pretty sure he's in the basement labs, investigating or whatever, I'm not entirely sure, but he obviously needs to know about this. Someone needs to go down there and tell him, and I need to… stand guard here, I think."

"Sure," said Mason. "I'll be right back."

— ⟨⟩ —

As soon as he stepped onto the main floor, Mason heard footfalls overheard, presumably from people who'd picked up on the commotion and were about find out that, yes, another guest had been murdered. He didn't envy Alexus. Mason had his own role to play, however: finding Hiroshi. Alexus had said he was downstairs in one of the basement labs, which, technically, were off-limits. But every rule had a reasonable exception, and someone needed to tell the only guardian here what had just happened.

Passing by the living room, Mason gleaned gossip from a group gathered around the fireplace.

"We're not safe here. This curfew is ridiculous."

"It's necessary."

"It's dangerous. We should be escaping, not jailing ourselves for the executioner. I know I won't sleep a wink tonight."

A third voice agreed: "I'll say this, if another one of us is killed, I'm as good as gone. I don't give two shits what Hiroshi wants, frankly. The guardians have no real authority, and I have two very real kids at home."

The situation, Mason realized, was about to get a lot worse in five minutes, once everyone learned about victim number two. Then one of them — the guy with two kids at home, silver hair, red cheeks, and a potbelly that poked out from under his green turtleneck — saw him standing in the hallway, listening to them. The look he gave Mason was anything but friendly. The man viewed him as a suspect, he gathered. They all were, strangers especially, and half of the people Mason knew here had died this morning, a fact that this guy was most certainly not overlooking. Well, Mason supposed he sort of knew Alexus now. She seemed to trust him for some reason.

On that note, Mason continued his journey to find Hiroshi. There was a stairwell up ahead, where the hallway arced into Winter's End's other wing, but when Mason arrived at the way down, planting his foot on the first heavy hardwood step, a man barked from behind him.

"Hey." It was the baby boomer in the green turtleneck, eyeing him with an indignant expression carved in decades-old wrinkles. "No going in the basement."

So, it turned out he did follow some of Hiroshi's rules — or at least didn't mind enforcing them for other people.

Mason turned toward him. "I'm just getting Hiroshi," he said.

The old man squinted. "Is that so? How do I know you're telling the truth, eh?"

"You don't." Mason didn't have time for this — or the patience. "If you don't believe me, fuck, I don't know, feel free to tell Hiroshi the next time you see him."

The stranger grumbled something that sounded like "punk" and ambled on back to the living room. Mason let out a single, silent chuckled. It was nice to have the truth on his side for once, to not have something to hide — to actually be doing what he said he was doing.

Mason wasted no more time and made his way down the wooden stairs, into the chilly basement below. The cement hallway was dim and deserted, and every lab door was closed. Behind one of them, he assumed, was Hiroshi.

Listening carefully at every step, Mason walked down the cave-like hall, a red-lit corridor that felt more fantasy dungeon than necromantic workspace. It quickly dawned on him that the two weren't mutually exclusive — and what his life had become. Briefly, Mason had one of those out-of-body moments where you suddenly become hyper aware of where you're standing right now in relation to the rest of your life, and you wonder how the hell you got here, to this place, into this situation, and Jesus, life takes some strange turns. But the basement remained deathly quiet, save for his internal musings.

Mason put his ear to each closed door, listening for any signs of a second life. If Hiroshi was down here, he was being awfully quiet. Maybe that was to be expected. Mason didn't know anything about the man he was trying to find.

"Hiroshi?" he said. And then once more, a little louder: "Hiroshi? My name's Mason. Alexus sent me. Something happened upstairs that you need to see. It's... urgent."

Proverbial crickets. One by one, Mason put his ear to the remaining doors. It wasn't until he reached the last one, at the end of the hall, that he finally heard something.

He'd almost missed it. Breathing? No. Whispering. The man inside, presumably Hiroshi, was chanting under his breath. Mason listened for a while longer. Red light flashed from the space beneath the door, illuminating his toes. What spell was he casting? From out here, Mason couldn't tell.

So he knocked, and the chanting stopped.

"Hiroshi?"

The silence returned, an uncomfortable quiet that filled the dark hall like the presence of an unseen predator. Mason waited thirty more seconds.

"Hiroshi, you're needed upstairs. I know I'm not supposed to be down here, but it's important. The murderer... someone else is dead. One of the disciples. People are just finding out now, and I don't know, but it sounds like some of them might take off when they find out."

If that wouldn't get his attention, well, then Mason was out of ideas. He waited a full minute — though it felt like longer — before the chanting began once more, whispers that he could only hear the sharp edges of, and then a second soft red glow lapped at his feet.

"Screw it," sighed Mason. Whoever was in there wasn't coming out. Given the situation upstairs, Mason couldn't imagine what might be keeping Hiroshi — assuming that was Hiroshi — behind his locked door (and it was locked; Mason double-checked), but he'd done what he could. So yeah. Screw it.

And then Mason was hit with a strange sensation. Déjà vu? Maybe, though he'd certainly never been in a similar situation before. It was weird, but then everything about this place, this moment, was weird. His life was weird, even after two years of trying to get it back to normal. Indeed, here he was beckoning a necromancer he hadn't even properly met from a locked laboratory in the middle of Greenland of all goddamn places. Hell, Mason was forgetting what normal was supposed to feel like — probably not like déjà vu.

He shrugged, defeated. If Hiroshi didn't want to lend a hand, he'd offer his own. Alexus could surely use the help.

And then he remembered his other unfulfilled promise. He'd told Liana he'd be right back. "Just give me a minute," he'd said. It had been more than a minute, that much he was certain of.

"Shit." Mason eyed the locked door one last time and then walked away. *All right, Liana, I'm coming back.*

Chapter 25

Outside Liana's window, nothing moved. Night had descended over Winter's End, over its neatly landscaped yard and strange, stone lawn gnomes, but the usual late-night suspects were nowhere to be seen, grounded like everyone else. She imagined they all felt quite trapped at the moment, but not as trapped as her. She had layers on them. There were the layers they all shared: Greenland, itself a grand and beautiful prison walled in by water; isolation, being so far off the beaten path, dependent on cars and maps; the night sky, a fake ecosystem that separated their reality from everyone else's; and Winter's End, the building they weren't allowed to leave. But Liana's prison had additional walls: this room, her only reprieve from everyone else here, whom she just could not handle right now (well, aside from Mason); and herself, because the most suffocating prison of all was always your own.

Liana looked down from the window toward her dinner. She poked the half-eaten soup with her spoon. It was good, Mason was right, but she just wasn't hungry — even if her stomach suggested otherwise.

Now that the shock had worn off, Liana found herself wondering what exactly came next for her, not to mention others. Eli had a kid. Who would tell Charles, and *what* would they tell Charles? Would that responsibility fall to her? What would she do Thursday nights now (board game nights with Eli)? Who would be her best friend?

Liana wasn't certain on any of the details, but one thing, she decided, one thing she'd do no matter what was be strong. Eli would have wanted her to be strong, and that was something she knew how to do. It was something — if not the only thing, it felt like — that she could control.

The door swung open.

Liana expected Mason, more than a couple minutes overdue, but that wasn't who stepped into her room.

"Jason?" She hoped she remembered that right.

Jason slammed the door shut behind him, and Liana caught a better glimpse of the strange man who'd entered her room unannounced. He was sweating and panting, his focus darting around the room like a cornered cat's, until it found her. There was blood on his upper lip.

"Can I help you?" asked Liana.

Jason wiped the blood trickling down from his nose with the sleeve of his black sweater. The look he gave her wasn't menacing nor frightened — more contemplative.

Liana didn't know what to make of him. He was in trouble, or so it appeared, and had it been any night before this one, she would have extended nothing but unconditional hospitality. Maybe he was a victim, maybe he'd just been attacked, maybe he was somebody's scapegoat. Or maybe Eli's murderer had just stepped into her room: that possibility hadn't eluded her either. Liana racked her brain for every defensive spell she knew.

Then Jason finally said something: "Where is Mason?"

"What?"

"Mason," he repeated sharply.

"What do you want with Mason?" she asked.

Jason looked past her, pensive again, weighing options unknown to Liana. "I want Mason," he said, "because he is different, because he is unlike anyone I've ever sensed, and because I am running out of time."

Well, that clarifies nothing.

"Look, dude, I don't know what you're talking about, but Mason isn't here, as you can see for yourself," she said. "I think maybe you should leave. This is my room, and I would very much prefer a little privacy, if you don't mind." Liana certainly minded.

Jason shook his head, pinning his back against the door to, she could only assume, bar her escape. "No," he said. "No, I can't do that. A couple of them are on to me. I can't go out there now. I need to leave another way. But first, Mason."

He was crazy: that was Liana's first thought. But maybe crazy was rational in the right context. She didn't know Jason's story, only her brief part in it, and this chapter frightened her. *He* frightened her, but Jason wasn't the only one with secrets, for little did he know, Liana was strong, stronger than most of the necromancers here she bet. Liana knew her shit, she'd learned from the best, and if he pushed her...

"Mason's not here," she told him.

"Then I'll wait." Jason had his ear to the door, listening for whatever might be coming down the hall.

"And then what? If Mason comes, then what?"

"Then," he said, "reality plays out as it is destined to."

"What the hell is that supposed to mean?"

He turned and took two strong steps forward, carrying himself like a man who had patience for only one person, the one walking toward her.

"It's painful at first," he said, looking madly calm. "Just after you consume someone's spirit, but it leaves you stronger." He let that linger. "Like surgery, and I am the product of many surgeries, Liana. There is more power coursing through my veins than exists in half the necromancers here combined. But the thing about power, greatness, is that if you want more — and believe me, I do — it only gets harder and harder.

"Most people, they are not built to climb," he continued, curling both sets of fingers, sweat still pouring down his round face, "but I am, and I need to know just how far my limbs will take me. Such is my nature. And I have never sensed anyone else like Mason. Whatever he has, it's something I don't, something more, something I need."

Jason took another step forward. She could see the muscles in his wrists tensing.

"I know what my nature requires me to do," he said. "Mason's, I'm less sure. And yours, your nature, I don't know. Tell me, Liana, what does your nature compel you to do at this very moment? At your core, what kind of creature are you?"

Liana squinted. "The kind that will kick your fucking ass if you don't step the fuck back right now, you fucking weirdo."

Jason didn't budge an inch.

"I'm serious. Get the fuck out of my room."

His lips curled into soft-spoken words, a chant. But Liana was already one step ahead of him. *Her* chant had been on repeat for a minute now, running through her mind, simmering to a boil, and as soon as the words spilled out of her mouth, it hit him square in the chest: red heat, like heartburn from hell.

Jason stumbled backward, his shoulder blades rattling the wooden door, his calm veneer stripped bare. He scrunched his nose like a hurt, angry dog. Good, thought Liana. That would teach him.

Or maybe not. Jason pushed himself off the door and launched himself forward, chanting just as quickly. Liana cast the same spell, but this time Jason was ready; her red heat circled him like the fire of an eclipsed sun as his newly-cast barrier protected him from any real harm.

Shit.

Jason grabbed her. Liana nicked his chin with a quick uppercut. They both fell onto her bed, bouncing, then rolled onto the hardwood as one. Jason landed on top. He pinned her body every which way he could, his hands holding her wriggling wrists like handcuffs, one knee digging into her thigh. She kicked the air with her only free limb. She flailed and made holding her as hard as humanly possible — for a one-hundred-pound woman, anyway.

"Get the fuck off me!"

He cupped her mouth. She bit his fingers.

"Shit," he grunted, keeping painfully quiet.

She bit harder.

Then Jason grabbed her throat with his other hand and squeezed.

Liana couldn't breathe, but her arms were free. She felt around for something, anything. The bowl of soup: it was lying on the ground beside them, upside down over a slowly spreading splatter of yellow. She grabbed the bowl and swung for his head. The impact fazed him, but Jason didn't move his hand. And now it looked like he was casting something. Liana swung again, this one a weak slap to his reddened face, and then again, weaker still. She was running out of oxygen.

Liana needed a plan now or never again. She needed a real weapon. Furiously, she swung downward, smacking the floor with her bowl, which made a loud knock — but didn't break. She smacked again. Fuck. Then she noticed the metal wheel under her bed frame. Liana hit it against that, and this time the bowl cracked in two. She swung at Kyle's throat with the jagged edge.

Liana felt the impact, but it wasn't until a drop of blood flew into her eye that she realized she'd got him good. Jason yanked his hand from her throat and began cupping his own. She gasped for air. He tried to stop the bleeding. She hit him again and again until he rolled off her enough for Liana to wriggle free. She crawled toward the door, determined to make it out of here.

And then she couldn't move again. Liana twisted her head and saw him over her shoulder, loose strands of sweaty hair dangling over his mad, crimson eyes, blood running out his neck. But not pumping out. She'd missed the jugular, the fatal knockout she'd needed, and now he was casting something. Liana kicked at his face, but her leg was too short.

"Get off me!" she screamed, dragging him forward a foot as he held onto her leg. "Get the fuck off me!" She kicked again, hitting air. He was relentless.

And then Liana felt a tug. This one wasn't on her leg, however, or any other limb for that matter. This was a different sort of tug. Something was pulling *her*, the woman inside her body, gripping deeply like the claws of a night terror. His spell. Jason was still chanting, and now it was starting to take hold.

At first she felt dizzy, too dizzy to fight — the drug before an operation — and then came the proverbial scalpel: unimaginable pain. Yet somehow worse than unimaginable pain was the fact that Jason was back on top of her, pinning her effortlessly.

She was being consumed by him, by Jason, by this goddamn stranger. Liana screamed until even that grew too difficult, until she felt too far removed from her limbs to make them do anything at all. She felt the tears that welled up in her eyes, though. Her body mourning her. It was so fucking unfair, after everything she'd already been through.

As darkness swallowed Liana, she looked into her attacker's eyes and was reminded of the butcher in Chinatown.

Chapter 26

Mason picked up his pace, taking the second-story stairs two steps at a time, hoisting himself up the banister. He thought he'd heard a scream. It could have come from anywhere, but Mason didn't like uncertainties. He hurried down the hallway of bedrooms, eyeing the crowd that had collected outside the murder site. He could overhear Alexus arguing with someone.

But first, Liana. Mason made his way to her bedroom and opened the door.

He saw the man first, lying on the floor with his back against the bed, panting, pressing bed sheets against his bleeding neck. He looked familiar, if in a different context. Jason, was it?

And then Mason saw Liana.

She was flopped over, lying on her side, her legs — faded black jeans — crisscrossed, her hair — dark and tussled — poured over her face. Mason spotted a speckle of blood on her gray T-shirt.

"Liana." He immediately crouched down beside her and shook her shoulder, lightly. Then he shook it again, less lightly. "Liana, wake up."

But Mason could feel dread shaking him even harder. He'd been here before, like this, keeled over someone as if in a desperate prayer, hoping against reality, against cruelty and senselessness — against what he knew he was about to realize he'd lost. Though never had the stakes been this high, the truth so threatening. Mason eased Liana onto her back. Strands of black hair clung to her face. He brushed them away but saw even more blood; he couldn't tell if it was hers. "Liana?" He checked her pulse. Her still pulse. The next time he tried to say her name, the word stayed stuck in his throat, caught in a storm of anger and sadness and utter disbelief.

"There was another man." The voice, quiet and craggy, was Jason's.

Mason turned toward him, still wobbling on one knee, still holding Liana's soft face. But his own was jagged with rage, his jaw too clenched to let through a single word.

Jason continued the conversation for him. "I heard her calling for help," he said, "so I came into the room, and then the guy, he attacked me."

Mason finally mustered three strained words: "Who was he?"

"I'm not sure," replied Jason. "I didn't get a good look before he cast something on me. He had one of those red robes on. A hood" —Jason lifted his hand, which shook from the effort, over his eyes— "covering his face."

"A disciple?" said Mason.

"I guess so."

"Why didn't he kill you too?"

"I don't know," said Jason. "I think he tried."

Mason shook his head. "And why did he kill one of his own?"

Jason flinched at that fact. "Eh?"

"The victim down the hall," replied Mason, "he was a disciple. If the murderer is a disciple of the red, like you say, why did he kill one of his so-called brothers?"

Jason heaved his body backward with both hands, until he was sitting up straight. "I don't know, Mason. Maybe it was some sort of internal power struggle? I don't claim to understand those weirdoes."

"Maybe," said Mason. He didn't trust anyone right now, least of all Jason.

The quiet quickly returned, like the sudden silence of a showdown, only Mason didn't know whether or not this man was his enemy. If he was, if he had done this to Liana, Mason would destroy him — that much, he told himself, he was sure of.

And then someone barged in. Scratch that — two someones. The first man was intensity incarnate — and probably younger than he looked, balding and frothing as he was — and the other was the guy from downstairs, the one who'd acted like an asshole to Mason on his way into the basement. Mason and the silver-haired boomer met eyes, but it didn't last. The bald one pointed his finger past Mason, toward Jason.

"Him!" He yelled the word. "I saw him do it — I saw him kill that disciple."

Jason got to his feet, cautiously and less injured, apparently, than he had seemed only seconds earlier when he was alone with Mason. "Hold on, fellas," he said, hands forward like two stop signs.

Mason was instinctively wary of mobs, of democratic accusations of guilt, and yet he felt convinced, felt it in his blood, felt the heat flow through him, adrenaline and rage, the first spark of a fiery reckoning.

No doubt Jason felt it too, from the way he was tensing up.

"What about him?" asked the one who'd acted like an asshole downstairs, nodding toward Mason, but in that same second he saw Liana, lying on her back at Mason's feet, and then he looked up and saw Mason, saw the hard expression in his eyes. "Shit, kid, I'm sorry."

Mason didn't say anything, but he turned his attention back toward Jason, the real enemy here — or so everything suggested.

"You're coming with us," said bald one.

"Where?" Jason made no effort to come.

"Downstairs. It's time for your trial."

"I think I'd prefer to stay up here, if you don't mind." Jason feigned an awkward smile.

"I wasn't asking, you little shit."

"Either way," replied Jason, "I think I'll stay put."

Then it was the silver-haired man who responded. "Listen, you little punk," he said, "there are three of us, and there is one of you. That's the only equation that should matter to you right now, so I suggest following us downstairs. Because if you don't, if you resist, I will just have to assume you're guilty. Guilty of killing multiple people, guilty of killing good necromancers, guilty of killing an innocent young woman." He spoke in a manner that gave weight to every word. "And if you're guilty of that, don't think for a second that I won't personally rip your spirit from this world. And don't think you can pull a fast one on me either. I've got decades on you, psycho, and I've seen it all, but it's your choice. Frankly, I don't care which option you pick."

Jason smirked. "So be it." He held one hand out. "Lead the way."

Mason exchanged a glance with everyone in the room. "I'll take the rear."

Jason shrugged and stepped forward. All together they walked out, the two elder necromancers in the lead, with Jason two steps behind them and Mason two steps behind him. There was nowhere to run, or at least that was the idea. Mason looked toward Liana one last time before stepping out of the room.

"Twenty-five," said Jason, strolling down the hall at leisurely pace. "That's the age at which a person's brain stops developing. Did you know that?"

"Shut up," the boomer replied.

"I'm going somewhere with this." Jason didn't shut up. "What that means is that if you're an idiot at twenty-five, you'll still be an idiot at fifty-five, sixty-five. Sure, you might learn a few new tricks, but..." He poked his temple. "You're working off the same hardware."

"I said shut the fuck up."

"I'm almost finished," said Jason, and for the first time his anger slipped through, ever so slightly, but it was an anger Mason recognized, the anger of a man who lived in it constantly and had learned only how to hide his fury — not calm it. "It's something I've noticed with your generation," he continued, "men in particular. Men old enough to be my dad. Men who grew up in a world where they were always on top. Men who can't handle the truth: that their children have outgrown them, surpassed them. Men so blinded by a life of... undeserved power and entitlement that, well, they don't even realize when they've lost the upper hand."

They arrived at the stairs, the four of them, and it was the bald man who spoke this time. "All right, Jason. Down you go."

Jason smiled, a toothy grin this time. "Name's Kyle," he said.

"What?"

The bald man went down first, in the same intense moment that Mason heard faint chanting. It all happened in similarly short order: a quick cough, a mouthful of blood splattering his friend's face, a backward fall, his body tumbling heels over head until, abruptly, his skull smacked the main-story hardwood floor like a dropped bowling ball.

The first few seconds were spent processing what had just happened: the bald man had been murdered quickly — incredibly quickly — and the killer, well, there was no mystery this time. And the first few seconds were all Kyle needed to ready himself once more, now with a protective red barrier.

Kyle glared tauntingly at the silver-haired survivor, and Mason knew then why he had killed the bald man first. Because killing this one wasn't enough, because he needed the man who'd threatened him to know he had been terribly mistaken — and would pay for it. And most of all, Kyle needed him to know that he was less. Less than Kyle.

Just as Mason cast his own barrier (defense before offense was a good general rule), the elder necromancer attacked Kyle with a malicious spell of his own, one no doubt intended to do to Kyle what Kyle had just done to the bald man. It didn't work. Kyle's barrier held, and then he took his turn. Unprotected, the red-faced boomer went down just as quickly as the man at the bottom of the stairs. He collapsed into a dead heap.

And then there were two.

Kyle turned his attention to Mason, who was already staring right back, planning his next move but also processing his anger, for he now knew with certainty that he was standing five feet from the man who had killed Liana and Eli. Self defense be damned; this was a man Mason would murder without excuse.

Mason made the next move. Without chanting, he cast the spirit-ripping spell he'd learned from Rowland, a spell he hadn't tried since the night he used it *on* Rowland. Kyle staggered backward, the grin wiped off his face — but not dead.

They were both taken aback in that moment. Mason was shocked because he'd felt the spell work, felt himself tear spirit from body, from Kyle, and yet there he still stood. Kyle, meanwhile, couldn't believe that Mason's spell had penetrated his barrier, that he might just be the more powerful of the two, or so said the expression on his face.

Mason struck once more. Kyle resisted — it became a sort of spiritual arm wrestle — but again Mason proved stronger as Kyle stumbled backward into the wall behind him. But still, he was not dead. Finally, Kyle took his turn, no longer looking in control of the situation, but unlike Kyle's, Mason's barrier held.

Mason was winning, but why hadn't he already won? How had Kyle survived two completed spirit-ripping spells, something not even Rowland could have done? It baffled Mason, and that uncertainty was the one advantage his enemy still possessed. Kyle seized it and charged forward, shoving Mason with both hands and all of his body weight.

And here was the thing: there were two commonly used barriers in necromancy, one that protected you from necromancy (spirit-ripping spells and such) and another that guarded you from threats in the physical world (bullets, cars falling off cliffs in Greenland, and so forth), and while Rowland had learned to combine the two into a single spell, Mason had not. The barrier Mason had erected to protect himself against Kyle was of the first variety — spells only, not stairs.

And so Mason flew backward. He grasped for a railing, something, anything, but found no savior to stop his descent, nor did he find the focus to cast a barrier that *would* protect him (and wouldn't risk taking down the one he had up anyway). Instead, he fell. What followed was a painful blur, the promise of damage without the full report.

He hit the ground with a thud, and suddenly the bald man's head was two feet from his, its dead eyes staring at the ceiling, its pool of blood growing and inching closer to Mason, who tried to get up and failed miserably. He was injured in ways he hadn't yet realized, and so he tried to move one limb at a time, starting with his closest arm. He looked down and saw it, saw — shit.

Fucking shit. The bone in his right forearm was jutting through his skin, an inch from where it should be. Even through all the blood, he could see the white of bone. Fucking shit, indeed. That's when he began to feel woozy. There was nothing worse than dizziness in Mason's mind because it was a weakness no amount of willpower could overcome. If your body had decided to faint, you would faint, end of story — and possibly Mason.

He growled unintelligible protests, red spit dripping from his bottom lip. He was stuck on his stomach like a soldier under barbed wire, his own body treating him like the enemy. His real one, Kyle, was somewhere out of view.

And then all of Mason's anger — and all sense of justice in the world — seemed suddenly in vain. For Mason could feel himself losing. He could feel the darkness winning. Who was he to rage against the unpoetic nature of reality? More dizziness. Mason dropped his head to the floor.

Chapter 27

Building a better world for children.

—*World Vision*

— «» —

Each step Asha made moaned.

The old wooden staircase was rough on her bare feet, warning of potentially painful splinters, but after waiting a day to venture down, she wasn't about to turn back now. It was near pitch-black in the basement, the open door behind her providing the only light. Asha held onto the railing as she moved, each step careful, deliberate, guilt-inducing.

She'd told herself only just yesterday that she wouldn't snoop. Whatever was down here was Mason's business, and he would tell her in time, when he was ready. Hell, he'd just told her a few days ago that he would finally answer her burning questions. That is, right after he got back from wherever the hell he was. Point being, she should wait. She should trust him. Then again (and this line of reasoning had proved to be her eventual breaking point), he'd never told her *not* to wander into the hidden basement. Maybe he didn't even know about it. After all, she hadn't. Alas, Asha found that hard to believe.

Creak. Creak. Creak.

The deeper she went, the darker it grew. There were no windows down here. What a strange place, she thought. At last, Asha set a single foot down onto the basement's cold cement floor and shivered.

The basement was as dark as a coffin. Asha used her phone's bright screen to find a light switch on the wall beside her. A single light bulb, hanging from the ceiling in the center of the room, flickered into illumination — and the room into view. It was incredibly... small. Incredibly Spartan too. The space was completely empty, in fact, as seemingly forgotten as the doorway that had led her down here, into this odd little black box of a room. She wondered again whether Mason knew about its existence.

Asha tiptoed around the basement looking for anything she might have missed. It wasn't until she reached the opposite side that she spotted, well, it was hard to say. Something carved into the cement wall, chest-level, like a word, only written in another language, a primitive language, a language from another time. Either that or it was just a bunch of lines that someone bored had carved into the wall. That was probably far more likely.

Asha ran her hand across the mysterious indents and sighed. This place, this basement: it was like a book without words — wholly disappointing. A suitable punishment for snooping, she supposed.

Asha turned around, leaned back on the wall in a defeated pose, and then fell through.

She was on her elbows, stunned and more than likely bruised. The wall in front of her had... not collapsed, no. Disappeared. It had simply disappeared. She'd hit it and then gone through, like splashing into a watery surface, only instead of underwater she'd suddenly found herself in another room.

Everything was bathed in red light. Asha pushed herself off the ground and took in the space, which was much, much bigger than the room outside. There were bookshelves brimming with books, tables covered in notes, and on Asha's face, a look of complete befuddlement.

—— «◇» ——

Twenty-four hours earlier, Asha was sitting on the couch in Mason's living room, classical studies 220 notes strewn over the coffee table. Her essay on the *Odyssey* (her copy rested open and spine-up, like a flattened tent, its pages flecked with yellow sticky notes) was turning into an odyssey in and of itself. Presently, dear Odysseus was losing to Facebook.

One could only work for so long, she supposed, or with so many distractions. Asha wasn't sure which line she'd crossed, only that she needed a break. She slapped her laptop shut and made herself coffee in the kitchen, black — but not by choice. Mason didn't have milk in the fridge, nor was there sugar in the cupboards. Sometimes she wondered how he fed himself.

Food shortages aside, it was a nice place to spend a few days, Mason's that is. She was taking full advantage of the key he'd given her. This house was far bigger than her studio apartment but also, she was slowly realizing, weirdly foreign — a strange doppelganger of a house she'd come to know intimately. It was Mason's absence. Just like people, spaces revealed another side of themselves when you were left alone with them.

Back in the living room, Asha flipped on the TV. She set her steaming coffee on the nearest coaster and threw herself on the couch, remote control in hand. The thing about mid-afternoon TV, though, was that it was universally awful. She supposed there was always Netflix.

Meanwhile, a World Vision commercial began to play. "Zambia is my home, and I know how deeply it is hurting," the narrator said. "Every day more than sixteen hundred children under the age of five die from diarrhea caused by unsafe drinking water." Zambian children were hauling buckets of dirty water down a dusty path. A child walked toward the screen on a single crutch. He was missing a leg. "It happened while I was out fetching water at the river," he said. "I was carrying two containers of water when I slipped and fell. I can't go to school because it's too far for me to walk."

It was all Asha could handle. She welled up — sighed, "Goddamnit" —and reached for her laptop. When she got to World Vision's website, however, ready to donate a hard-earned twenty dollars (the minimum amount she'd decided she could spend and still feel good about herself), Asha realized her purse was in the kitchen.

She took a hurried sip of coffee and made her way to where she thought she'd left it, somewhere on the counter, or maybe it was on the chair. Asha never paid much attention to where she left things. It was on the stove.

She dug through her black leather purse — a trashcan of makeup, tissue, receipts, and other invaluable items that she couldn't, for whatever reason, part with — and pulled out a wallet. Asha zipped it open and felt for her credit card. Plastic in hand, she left the kitchen and turned into the hallway.

But before she could continue her noble endeavor, Asha tripped over her toe. "Ouch, damn it." The credit card flew from her hand, bouncing down the carpet on its razor edge before finally stopping somewhere behind a bookshelf. She approached it for a better look.

Asha dropped to her hands and knees and examined the space between the back of the bookshelf and the wall, where her card should be, but quickly found herself hopelessly distracted. There was a freaking door back here, a door behind the bookshelf.

"What the hell?" she said.

Still on her hands, Asha's gaze climbed upward until she spotted a doorknob. Was it a closet? Probably, but why block it with a bookshelf, she wondered? She tried not to overthink the matter and snatched her credit card from the carpet. Asha stood back up, stretched her limbs, and stared once more into the misleadingly slim space.

After minute, she shook her head. "None of my business."

— «» —

Down in the basement, Asha inched forward like a wary intruder. After all, she'd now gone through not one but *two* doors she probably shouldn't have. And boy, look where she'd found herself.

Where the hell had she found herself? That was the question, and she hadn't any inkling of an answer. She began with the notes on the table at the centre of the room and quickly found her first valuable piece of information: Mason's handwriting. The content, however, made absolutely no sense. At the top of one page, he'd written (and underlined), "Red light that follows your finger." Beneath that, well, it wasn't English whatever it was. It looked like the writing on the wall outside, in fact — the one she'd fallen through. Mason had scratched out most of the foreign-looking lines

and circled a couple others. Beside one, in English, he'd
scribbled, "Maybe."

Of course Mason had known about this place. Asha felt
foolish for ever having even entertained the notion that he
might not. He lived here, and more than that she'd always
known there was... something. After two years, she'd finally
stumbled into it, into the secret world he'd been hiding from
her for so long. Still, she hadn't seen *this* coming. Not that
she even knew what *this* was.

Asha turned her attention to the red lights overhead
and slowly realized that she couldn't see any light bulbs, no
LEDs, nothing. Just light. Pure red light. Now she was getting
a little scared.

"What the bloody hell, Mason?"

Then Asha heard the doorbell ring. It was faint and
distant-sounding down here. She remembered she'd ordered
pizza. Mason's kitchen had been short on food, and Asha
short on time. Her essay (she was taking a summer class) was
due the next day, and she'd found herself suddenly starving.
But all thoughts of hunger, of everything, had vanished
alongside her concept of physics the moment she'd fallen
through that wall. The doorbell rang a second time.

"Shit," she spat. The pizza was early. Asha hadn't
expected it for another twenty minutes. This was not
normally something she'd complain about, mind you, but
in that moment she could hardly pull herself away from the
strange space she'd just uncovered.

She ultimately did, however. Pizza was pizza. Asha
left the way she came in, only now the wall was gone and
a doorframe stood in its place. She sprinted up the wooden
staircase to the main floor and shut the basement door
behind her. The bookshelf she'd pulled to one side (no easy
task) looked unassuming enough. Only Mason would have
recognized that something was amiss — that he was exposed.
To anyone else, it would appear to be just another bookshelf
beside just another door.

Asha marched through the foyer to the front entrance.
Not wanting to lose the person outside, or her pizza more
precisely, she unlocked and opened the door in a hurry.

"Hello?"

But the man standing on the porch didn't look like the pizza guy. He was too nicely dressed, for one, in a collared shirt and leather jacket. And for another, he didn't have a pizza with him.

"Good afternoon," he said. "Is Mason Cross here?"

"Uh, no. No, he's not. Sorry, who are you?" she asked.

"A detective." He flashed his badge. "Name's Clayton. I just wanted to chat with Mason about something that happened a couple years back. Nothing serious. Are you his... girlfriend?"

Asha nodded, still half-hidden behind the metal front door.

Clayton smiled. "I can come back later, but would you mind if I came in and asked you a couple questions first?"

She hesitated.

"Won't take more than a moment of your time," he said. "I promise."

Chapter 28

— «» —

Mason gasped for air but swallowed only a mouthful of icy black water.

He kicked and flailed in slow-motion, the water weighing down his limbs, but it all seemed for naught. Mason couldn't see the surface above — only more dark water. Still, he swam and swam, up and up. He swam until he should have suffocated and then swam some more. The cold water grew heavier — or perhaps it was his body that grew weaker — and so he swam harder.

He was going to drown.

But impossibly, Mason splashed through the surface and filled his lungs with cold, crisp oxygen. A second later, he sank underwater once more, the ocean pulling him under. Mason wouldn't have it. He fought his way back up again, wrestling for every breath of air.

Then he spotted what looked like a ledge of land, off in the distance, and swam with heavy strokes toward it, angry waves shoving and slapping him every which way — but never off course.

It was nighttime, but Mason saw no stars as he caught glimpses of the black sky above. He immediately knew why this was, though he couldn't explain how he knew. He was too far from all of the stars, from all of the other planets, from all of the other people — he was too far for their light to get here, to wherever here was. Someplace in the space between universes, he knew, someplace utterly lost.

The Spirit Realm?

But as Mason neared the dark ledge ahead of him, he did in fact find someone. He or she — he couldn't quite tell — was standing on land, bent toward Mason with a single outstretched arm. A shadowy savior, or so it seemed. Mason swam faster.

And then the man — yes, it was definitely a man — came into clarity. It was his father, looking just as Mason remembered him. His face, however, was eerily expressionless. He wasn't calling out for him either, as Mason would have expected, and Mason didn't have the oxygen to do so himself. And so he swam, wordlessly and desperately, until another wave overcame and blinded him. When Mason opened his eyes, his father was gone.

Now the man was Lester, standing there silently with his arm out. Mason was almost to shore, the swim harder than it had looked like it should have been. Before he could make it the entire way, a final wave hit him headfirst and obscured his vision once more.

His savior had transformed a third time — into Rowland.

Rowland stared through Mason with his eternally crimson eyes, reaching out toward him with one branch-like hand, his white skin turned gray in the darkness. Mason stopped swimming. As cold as he was, Rowland's presence made him colder still. He watched as each of Rowland's fingers curled inward, beckoning him forward one digit at a time. Mason had no choice. It was literally sink or swim, and so he swam, toward him, toward Rowland.

As he reached the ledge, Mason swung for the ground but quickly found himself clasping a cold dead hand. It squeezed his.

— «» —

Sound came first, like a broken symphony. Then blurry light. Sensory chaos. To make matters worse, the world was on its side.

No, Mason realized, *he* was on his side. He'd fainted a couple times before and pieced together quite quickly that he'd just fainted again. It brought with it a fleeting amnesia. Something awful had just happened, Mason was sure, but it took him a few frustrating seconds to remember what exactly.

Jason — no, that wasn't his real name. Kyle. That son of a bitch had knocked him down the stairs. But there was more. There was what he'd done before that, the thing that had enraged Mason, and as Mason remembered that important detail, so too did his anger return.

Kyle had killed Liana.

And Mason — Mason would kill Kyle. Alas, dizziness overtook him the second he tried to sit up. His body wasn't ready to fight and wouldn't be for some time. "Fuck!" The word sounded more like a growl.

Was he to sit here, awake, knowing Kyle couldn't have gotten far and that he was unable to do anything about it? It was torture. Mason would rather have remained unconscious. But that was the hand that reality had dealt him: torture.

Mason refused to play it.

Fuck his body. Fuck its limitations. There was one power that had evolved in humans for times like these: adrenaline. His was driven by rage. Unfiltered rage like he'd never known before. Uncompromising rage that wouldn't be held down by reason. It was the most dangerous emotion in the world.

Mason pushed his broken bone back inside his skin, screamed, and then squeezed his forearm as he cast the strongest healing spell he could. It wasn't perfect, but it would do. Then he sat back up and planted his palms firmly on the hardwood floor. Shaking but unflinching, he lifted himself. And as he stood up straight, half-broken but ready for war, Mason realized his rage had done the damn near unbelievable. His rage had channeled spirit energy in a way he hadn't known was possible. An emotion was wielding spirit energy, empowering him. He could feel it infused in his bloodstream, in his muscles, in his bones — a skeleton of fire. Mason felt unstoppable.

The living room, ironically, was deserted of anyone alive. Minus Mason, only the dead remained. There was the man who'd fallen down the stairs; Mason had some of his blood on his sleeve, which he wiped off as well as he could on a green couch pillow. And there was another man, much younger and lying face down in front of the fireplace, which was still roaring, still warm and inviting — still offering a false sense of home. Of security.

Mason headed for the foyer. The front door was wide open, the warm night air pouring in. He heard a yell, but the words were muffled. Mason moved toward the door and quickly spotted its source. It was like a scene from a play he'd missed the first half of: two men facing off in front of the courtyard fountain. One of them was Kyle. The other, a stranger. But there was another man he did recognize. His name was Eric — they'd met that first day at the fountain, along with Kyle — and now here he was, dead, lying halfway between Mason and his murderer.

And then the distant stranger fell, like a tipped domino, landing in the fountain with a man-sized splash. As the water calmed, his legs were left sticking out over the stone rim, toes pointed skyward. Toward Kyle, who loomed over the dead man and appraised his work.

With that, Mason didn't see anyone else outside — anyone else trying to stop Kyle. That was for the best. Mason took a step forward.

Then footsteps came thumping on the hardwood behind him. Mason whirled around and saw Alexus jogging in his direction. He wasn't the only one after Kyle, it would seem. That, however, was not for the best.

"Come on." She nodded toward the open front door, toward Kyle.

Mason didn't budge. "No," he said. "You stay here."

"Fuck that," she replied. "I've got a one-way ticket to the Spirit Realm for that son of a bitch."

"I said stay!" Mason's tone surprised even himself.

Alexus stopped, but only for a second. "You're not giving the orders here, buddy." On that note, she took one step ahead of him and froze. "The hell?"

Mason's spell would keep her frozen for a good ten minutes. It was, of course, of the nefarious variety, but as he tried to explain to her, "It's for your own good."

"Fuck you."

A fair response. Still, she was better off stuck than dead.

Mason continued toward Kyle, alone. His enemy had taken notice at this point and watched his approach eagerly. Kyle was even more of a mess now, his forehead marked with sweaty strands of brown hair, his black sweater sticking to his skin. It had been a hard night's work for Kyle.

Mason stopped ten feet in front of him. The fountain beside Kyle was still bubbling. Otherwise, it was a pretty quiet night in the middle of Greenland.

"You have something I want," said Kyle, looking almost hungry. "It's why I let you live back there. I don't know what exactly it is, Mason, but you're... unique. And I have no choice but to—"

"Oh, shut the fuck up." Mason ripped a spirit from Kyle's body — and the monologue from his mouth.

Kyle stumbled backward, almost tripping into the fountain alongside his latest victim. That look of surprise again. Kyle could hardly believe it. He composed himself and began a rapid chant. A red barrier flashed into existence, encapsulating him.

Just as quickly, Mason had his own barrier up, with no chanting required. Kyle threw the next proverbial punch, but his spell hit Mason's shield like water on rock. Then Mason took his turn and ripped a second spirit from Kyle, who still couldn't believe it.

That was also the moment it at last dawned on Mason what was going on, why the man in front of him was still alive. He'd read about spirit stealing once: the practice of tearing out the spirit of another human being and holding it captive within your own body, channeling its power at will. It was spiritual slavery, and it was incredibly difficult. It would almost have been impressive if it weren't so nefarious — and Kyle had clearly done it many, many times. Few necromancers could have accomplished as much, though even fewer were that fundamentally awful. Mason would have said evil if he'd believed in evil. But no, Kyle was irreparably broken, though that didn't mean Mason hated him any less.

Mason ripped another spirit from the vessel that was Kyle's body. And then another. And another. Kyle tried many times to return the favor — Mason only had the one spirit, after all — but each of his attempts was weaker than the last, and before long Kyle was balancing on one knee, looking like he might vomit. He appeared to be, in a word, screwed.

As Mason tore more and more spirits from Kyle's body — freeing them, or so he hoped, for passage to the Spirit Realm where they might fade on their own terms — he could sense with increasing clarity just how many spirits Kyle still held within him. When that number neared one, Mason halted his onslaught.

Down on his shins and forearms, Kyle looked up curiously. "Why did you stop?" He panted the words, his once impervious pride replaced with the confusion of someone who had no move left — and could only wonder.

"Because I'm not done with you yet." Mason cast a new spell, the same freezing one he'd applied to Alexus, and suddenly Kyle couldn't move.

His next spell, Mason hadn't cast in two years, not since his run-in with the inquisitor who'd invaded his home and killed Lester. But as bad as that guy had been, Kyle was worse. The spell in question produced a burning sensation that could range from a slight sting to absolute torture. This time around, Mason was aiming for the latter, and after only a few seconds of casting, he saw Kyle cringe.

And then he saw another look in Kyle's eyes, a more worried one. It was the realization that he wouldn't just be killed, something he had perhaps prepared himself for, but that Mason would torture him first. To what extent, neither man knew.

More burning. Mason was turning the dial slowly, making the flame that Kyle felt throughout every part of his body grow hotter and then just a little bit hotter, one degree at a time, with no end in sight.

Kyle started to squeal. "Stop!" he begged, but Mason wasn't out for answers. This wasn't an interrogation — it was a slow execution. Then Kyle tried to reason: "You told me by this very fountain that you were a logical man. What point is there in—" He was cut off by a jolt of pain.

Mason was now hurting Kyle as much as he knew how, casting the strongest version of the spell he could, pushing himself — not just his enemy — into discomfort. Stretching a spell to its limit was a migraine-inducing ordeal, but Mason was willing to buy pain with pain. He wanted nothing more than to see Kyle suffer as much as necromantically possible. It was an unquenchable thirst, his rage.

And then Kyle began to cry. His eyes grew watery and red, a color they'd grown quite accustomed to, but not like this, never like this. A tear raced down his right cheek. Kyle was a defeated man, there was no question, but still Mason didn't let up the pain. Even when Kyle screamed. No words the first time, only agony. And then a second time: "Momma!"

He whispered the same word a moment later: "Momma."

When Mason finally released him from both spells, Kyle fell belly down onto the cobblestone. He gulped for air, wheezing like a dying smoker. Indeed, Kyle sounded like death. For a second, Mason felt a spark of sympathy, and then he remembered Liana.

Mason walked ten feet to his right. He lifted a stone lawn gnome from the plot of grass it guarded — he had a more important job for it — and then returned to Kyle, who hadn't moved an inch. Mason, meanwhile, was shaking. In part, because the stone statue was heavy. In part, because he couldn't contain his fury. And then he lifted the gnome with both hands, as high as he could, and brought it down like a hammer onto Kyle's head.

The statue didn't break, but Kyle did.

More than the blood, which sprayed in all directions — including Mason's — it was Kyle's head, or what was left of it, that bothered Mason most. To destroy someone's head was to destroy their personhood. It was something more than death. In death, one still had an identity, a face that had smiled and cried and kissed, and that would be recognized. One was, in many ways, his face, and Mason had turned Kyle's into fleshy packaging, torn over a shattered skull.

He had destroyed Kyle completely, destroyed him because he'd wanted to so badly, because at the end of the day, Mason had already lost. He felt no sense of satisfaction for it, not even a sense of justice having been served. He felt only his ongoing anger, which now had nowhere left to focus. And so Mason focused on what he'd done — and the way in which he'd done it. And then once more he felt dizzy.

Mason didn't pass out this time, but he did hurl into the fountain.

Chapter 29

Over the course of only one evening, Winter's End had become an unbearably lonely place. You could be forgiven for thinking that, being at the edge of the world and all, that would have already been the case. But when Mason arrived here two days ago, Winter's End was a family retreat. No, its inhabitants were not family, technically speaking, but necromancers all shared the same secret, and that wasn't so different. You looked out for one another, or at least that was the idea. But in the last twenty-four hours, growing tension had created cracks in that concept. Now they were a broken family, the necromancers of the north. Now, as Mason walked past a speechless Alexus (the spell he'd put on her had expired) and multiple dead bodies, Winter's End was indeed an unbearably lonely place.

And so without saying a word to Alexus, Mason made his way upstairs, to Liana's room. The door creaked as he stepped inside. He closed it all the way and collapsed to both knees.

Liana was as he'd left her, lying on her back, black hair swept over one eye. But at least one important aspect had changed, Mason knew: she was no longer trapped inside Kyle. She was free. Dead, but free. It wasn't much better, but it was all he could have done for her. Well, besides not having left her alone in the first place when a murderer was on the loose. He could have done that. Mason knew even now that he'd never let that fact go, and no amount of reason — no amount of "It wasn't your fault" —would ever quell that thought. Some things you lived with.

Mason was trembling, but it was no longer anger that unbalanced him. Sorrow had taken hold. He cried, audibly.

He clung to her shoulder with one hand and ran his fingers through her hair with the other. For some reason he couldn't quite explain, he imagined, briefly, that it was Asha lying there dead.

Maybe in another world, he thought, one of those parallel universes Liana dreamed of. And then Mason hoped more than he'd ever hoped for anything that she was right about parallel universes. He hoped the physicists were right, the ones who believed there was a universe for every possibility. And this, this was just the bad universe — the one he was in. In countless others, Liana was still here. Eli too.

And yet here she was, small and still and undeniably gone. Mason wiped a warm tear from his cheek.

Then he began to wonder: why had this happened? It wasn't an existential question but rather a literal one. Winter's End was supposed to be a guarded palace of sorts, and yet a single man had come in and killed half its occupants, or a good number at least (Mason wasn't sure of the actual body count). It was unacceptable, inexcusable, and in that injustice Mason found the answer he was looking for.

There was a system, and it was broken, and this Mason knew how to handle. This Mason knew had a solution. The guardians believed that secrecy was what kept necromancers safe from the outside world, from inquisitors, from the ignorant masses who just wouldn't understand. Joan Worthington certainly believed this, in any event, and there was truth in her convictions. But secrecy wasn't solely a safeguard, Mason now realized. Secrecy was also a shadowy alley, a dangerous place to wander when predators were on the loose. And God, they always were. First the inquisitors, now Kyle. Mason couldn't imagine a more dangerous world for his fellow necromancers than the one they already lived in.

And then he realized his decision was made. Eli had been right, and Mason had been working for the wrong side. He knew this now, in his heart as much as in his head.

Before he stood up, Mason bent down and kissed Liana's forehead. "I'm sorry," he said. His soft, broken words filled the quiet, upended room that he alone occupied. "I hope, in some other universe, I did better."

— «» —

No one tried to stop Mason from going down into the basement this time. Winter's End was overcome with a quiet chaos: people sobbing, people with their heads in their hands, people looking for an answer and finding out that it was an awful, awful one. Mason slipped downstairs into the cold cement hallway, where he found himself alone again. He eyed the door that he knew Hiroshi was behind, assuming he hadn't gone anywhere. It was still closed and still, presumably, locked.

But Mason wasn't here for Hiroshi. Whatever help he could have offered was moot now. Mason had handled the situation, not Hiroshi — not a guardian. No, Mason would not be adding guardian to his résumé, not after tonight, not after what he was about to do.

He made his way to Eli's lab.

The door had been left unlocked — one less thing he needed to deal with — and the body inside had been removed. Mason wasn't sure where they'd taken Eli's corpse, nor where they would take all the others. Perhaps the bodies of Eli and Liana would be his responsibility now. It wouldn't be the first time he'd been made responsible for finding a home for the dead. He dreaded the prospect, but he would do what needed to be done. He always did and always would.

Including right now.

It might not even be too difficult, changing the world. Mason remembered what Eli had said about all the pieces being in place already and that he just needed to give the word.

On the messiest metal desk in the room, Mason spotted a device that could do just that, that could give the word to Eli's allies all over the globe. It was the professor's laptop. Mason flipped the computer open and a login screen appeared, demanding, of course, a password.

"Crap."

It turned out he couldn't avoid locks after all, and Mason didn't have a spell to bypass this one. He pondered instead. What did Eli care about? He typed the name of his best friend, Liana. The password he entered was incorrect.

Crap was right. Then Mason spotted a small photograph a foot from his hand, half-buried under a yellow notepad. He picked it up. The picture was of a boy with messy orange hair. Eli's son. What was his name? Chris? The password he entered was incorrect. Charlie? The password he entered was incorrect. Charles. The screen flickered to blue as Eli's desktop illuminated on screen.

As far as passwords went, it was not a particularly good one — nor was that fact surprising to Mason.

Now, where to look? Mason noticed his email inbox was open — that seemed as good a place as any. He maximized the window. There was one new email. Mason clicked it open.

Ready when you are. –RG

Mason scrolled down to read the email "RG" had responded to, which had been sent by Eli himself. The last paragraph in particular he read three times over.

> *Unfortunately, unforeseen events have recently transpired that compel me to ask you all to be ready soon. As in, very soon. Do not stray far and begin learning the attached spell immediately. I will send the codeword when it is time.*

This was what he'd come here to find, and now Mason knew exactly what he needed: a codeword. Once he gave them (whoever they were) that, Eli's plan, his dream, would quickly become an irreversible reality.

Mason checked the notes lying around him just in case, but he knew the codeword wouldn't be written down anywhere. In his experience, it was never that easy. Although this time, he suspected, he already had what he was looking for. Eli did not strike Mason as the sort of man who could manage many passwords in his life. He also struck him as secretly sentimental. And so Mason responded to the email with the same, single word he had typed two minutes earlier.

Charles.

And slowly, dramatically — because sending an email felt inherently insubstantial, a mundane thing one does every day, and yet in this case it was potentially historic — he moved his cursor across his one-word email like a wooden catapult being wound backward.

Mason couldn't predict the future. No one could, although they all seemed to try. But he could see the present clearly, he could see how things were now, if not how they would become after he did this. And what he saw, he'd decided, was unacceptable. That part was simple. The difficulty was in the uncertainty. Every big decision was a calculated gamble, but some people were afraid to gamble, no matter how bad their hand, and Mason had been guilty of that himself more than a few times. Because the easy truth was that no one could blame you for the status quo, for changing nothing, but everyone — every goddamn one — would blame him for this.

So be it.

Mason hit send, figuring there was about a fifty percent chance he'd gotten the codeword right. About a fifty percent chance that he'd just turned the world upside down.

Chapter 30

"**Do you want** a glass of water or something?" Asha was pouring one for herself in the kitchen.

"Sure," said the cop, Clayton apparently. "Thanks." He was sitting by himself in the living room, reclined on Mason's couch with one arm over the back while he watched the world beyond the porch window.

She walked into the room with a cup in each hand and passed him his.

"Gracias," he said.

"Yeah." Asha slid onto the armchair a good distance across from him. She had one foot up on the chair, her knee bent to her chin. She twirled a lock of hair. "So, umm, Clayton. What can I help you with?"

"Oh, just a few questions. Nothing serious, like I said."

"Uh-huh." On a different day, Asha might have believed him. But she'd just uncovered a world of oddities downstairs, and she couldn't help but put the two — this man's unexpected appearance and Mason's secret dungeon of insanity — together. Not that she had any inkling of how they might be connected.

Clayton pulled a small green notepad and a blue pencil out of his back pocket and flipped the former open. "You mind?"

She shook her head.

"Can I get your full name?"

"Asha Sarai."

Clayton scribbled something. "And how long have you known Mason, Asha?" he asked.

"A couple years," she replied. "We've been, you know, together for a little less than that."

"So, you're close."

She nodded. He scribbled some more.

"I assume Mason told you about what happened here two years ago," he said, "that a man was killed in his, in *this*, house."

She nodded again. Mason had told her. He'd told her that he had no clue who the man was or what exactly had happened. And she'd believed him. But that was then. Now, she wasn't so sure.

"Did he say anything else to you about that, about the man who died here? Did he have any opinions or... theories?"

"No." Asha shook her head. "He said he couldn't understand it."

"I see. And did you ever maybe get the sense that he was..." Clayton hesitated, searching, she could tell, for the most delicate manner he could muster. "The sense that he was holding something back, even something small?"

She had. And for the first time, Asha was forced to decide whether or not she was willing to lie to a cop. Of course, it was a lie that no one could ever prove. Only Asha knew how Asha truly felt. "I didn't get that sense, no. I trust my boyfriend."

Clayton flipped a page in his notepad. "Almost done, I promise." Then he said, "What about a man? A Mr. Someone. Mr. Humphrey, Mr. Hudson — something along those lines. Does a name like that ring any bells?"

This time, Asha had nothing to hide. She shook her head. "None, sorry."

"I see."

Clayton was starting to look a little disappointed, she thought. He made another messy note with his stubby pencil.

Asha first noticed Clayton's reaction to what happened next. The white page of paper he was writing on turned a pale pink. He looked up, they both did, and out the window.

It wasn't red rain this time, not like two years ago — a phenomenon she, and she assumed Clayton, remembered well. But the color was the same. That crimson. It poured into the house like morning sunlight. Asha stood up and went to the window, Clayton beside her.

"The hell?" he said.

The red was coming from somewhere in the sky, though she could not see where exactly. The veranda roof blocked her view. But the light was getting brighter, the red that tinged everything getting redder — that much she could see. Wordlessly, Asha walked toward the front door and opened it wide. An unreal red ray washed over her like an invitation to another world. She made her way through the doorframe as Clayton stayed standing behind the window.

Asha crossed the creaking porch and then, finally, looked up and saw it: the massive red orb, like an old star that had descended over Terminal City. Only this star produced no heat; there was simply the unbelievable sight itself. But Asha did indeed believe what she saw. She believed it like she was staring at the truth incarnate, at the answers she'd been looking for all these years — not just about Mason but life, the world, the universe. She was staring straight at the red center of it all, and though she didn't understand it, Asha welcomed the ominous orb with every inch of her being.

Not everyone shared her feelings, she could see. Behind their windows, other onlookers appeared anything but inviting. Fear: that was the expression they wore, almost all of them. But it was the most magnificent sight Asha had ever seen, and unlike the red rain from two years ago, she refused to fear it. She could only imagine what the world must look like downtown right now, red illuminating all those glass towers. Cathartic.

Clayton moved beside her, his eyes to the sky too. "I..." he said. "Yeah."

Asha smirked. "Yeah."

"What the hell is it?"

"Maybe," she said, "it's the answer you're looking for."

He shrugged and half-chuckled. "Maybe it is." He looked over to her, but Asha's eyes stayed where they were. "I'm going to go inside and turn on the news if that's cool."

She nodded. "That's cool. I wonder what they'll say."

"Not much, I expect. Whatever they said last time."

She knew instinctively to which last time he referred.

Clayton wandered back inside. A few seconds later, she heard him turn up the TV.

Overhead, the red sun was starting to recede, fading back into the nothingness from whence it came. She watched until its light was no more, until the sky returned to its usual pale blue, and then, hesitantly, joined Clayton in the living room.

"What are they saying?" she asked him.

"They... don't know," he said, shaking his head. "Apparently we're not the only city, though. London, New York, Tokyo, Toronto, and a bunch of others — bright red lights over all of them. It's a goddamn worldwide event."

Asha dropped herself onto the couch beside him.

"One moment, folks," said the news anchor, a middle-aged woman with perfect blonde hair. "My producer tells me we have a video clip." She paused, listening to her earpiece. "I'm told that fifteen minutes ago, ten minutes prior to the appearance of these strange lights, Terminal City News was emailed a video. It is a video from an anonymous source, a video from a man who claims to be behind this afternoon's... unbelievable phenomenon."

The anchor stalled again, nodding at the voice in her ear, and then looked deeply at her audience through the camera. "We here at TCN have decided to show you, our viewers, the clip in its entirety. While we cannot verify anything the man in this video claims — and the claims, I'm told, are quite fantastical — we also cannot ignore the timing."

Then the picture changed to a man.

He was lanky and slouched in his chair, indicative of one who does not normally do TV. His messy bushy hair was more gray than brown and equally un-TV-like. He looked maybe fifty. He was sitting solemnly in a dim concrete room, a touch of crimson light on the wall behind him, the only detail in an otherwise unidentifiable setting. The man stared uncomfortably into the camera before he began.

"Hello." He paused for a moment, either for dramatic effect or, perhaps, because he was nervous. He looked nervous. "If you live in one of twelve major cities across the world, you have just witnessed a miracle," he continued.

"But it is not." And then stuttered. "It is not a miracle in the way that you perhaps think it is. No, no. Today... today is a different kind of miracle. A... historic miracle."

Asha and Clayton exchanged a slow glance and then returned their attention to the screen — and the strange man occupying it.

"You have already seen the evidence with your own eyes," he said. "You have seen the light, so to speak." He snorted at his painfully rehearsed joke. "You have seen that which cannot be explained by all but a select few. But no longer. Now... now it is time for the truth. It is a truth that the world cannot unlearn. A hard truth. A beautiful truth. And I believe..."

He hesitated once more, but Asha could tell it wasn't nerves that slowed him this time. It was the weight of his conviction, the weight of knowing that his next few words would change everything.

"I believe," he said, "that the truth shall truly set us free."

Someone knocked on the front door.

"Pizza."

Chapter 31

"He who fights with monsters should be careful lest he thereby become a monster. And if thou gaze long into an abyss, the abyss will also gaze into thee."

—Friedrich Nietzsche, *Beyond Good and Evil*

— «» —

It was time for Mason to make his exit.

What he had just done, revealing necromancy to the world, was unforgivable. Indeed, he had done the one thing — the *first* thing — every necromancer was told never to do. He had broken the first rule of Fight Club, and there would be consequences.

If Mason left Winter's End quickly enough, perhaps no one would be the wiser. After all, there were no TVs here, no cable, and the internet connection was shoddy at best. And that assumed he'd given the right codeword. Maybe nothing had happened, and the world was ticking along as it always had, with little interruption. Or maybe it was already all over the news.

Mason could find out once he was long gone and far away from here. In a weird way, he didn't even want to know. The only faint desire he had left was to leave Winter's End and be alone with his thoughts, away from everything and everyone.

Unfortunately, he wouldn't be entirely alone, at least not in body even if in spirit. He couldn't just leave Liana and Eli behind. He owed them more than that. The question was a logistical one. Ignoring for now the fact that he had no fucking clue what he'd do with their bodies upon his return to Terminal City, Mason wasn't sure how to get them there in the first place. Their van was lying upside down in a river.

Maybe Mason could convince someone to give him a ride, though that might be a tough sell considering his cargo: two bodies. Or maybe one of the necromancers who'd died tonight had brought a car with them that was now up for grabs. The latter would be Mason's preference. The less he had to talk to people, the better.

As for the bodies themselves, Mason knew where to find Liana's, but Eli's was another matter. It had been moved from the basement lab, but no one had told him where it had been moved to. His first guess was Eli's room, which he recalled Liana saying was next to hers. That, Mason decided, would be his first stop.

After taking one last look around the lab — the way one does when expecting never to return to a place — Mason slapped Eli's laptop shut and made his exit, closing the door on his way out. The basement was still empty and quiet. The same doors were still closed and locked. Mason headed for the stairs.

And then he felt it. He felt... *him*.

It couldn't be. Not here, not now — not ever, in fact. It was just a phantom feeling, Mason told himself. He took the stairs two steps at a time, hurrying away from whatever the hell it was he'd just felt — and still felt. *It's in your head, Mason. It's in your head.* It was like trying to escape a panic attack, and maybe, hopefully, that's all it was.

Mason reached the main floor and stepped out into the arching hallway. He made his way to the living room, where he could overhear murmuring. Had they found out what he'd done already? Then he saw someone's body being tended to, as much, anyway, as a corpse could be tended to. They clearly couldn't care less about Mason, not yet at any rate, but still he was growing paranoid, feeling like a spy, feeling like he needed to hurry things up and make his way back to Terminal City before someone realized he had a role in all of this.

Or maybe it was that strange sensation that unnerved him. After a minute of simmering, it was back and bubbling. As Mason walked past the living room and toward the stairs to the second floor, as quietly and respectively as he could, it reached a veritable boil. And then, out from nowhere, it was like an impossibly large hand was reaching toward his back, its oversized fingers curling around his limbs. He shook himself free and stumbled forward. Mason turned around and saw the man standing across the hall.

It was Hiroshi Saito, still and stoic, the basement door wide open behind him. He was staring past everyone else and straight at — straight *through* — Mason. And it was then that Mason stopped doubting what he had been feeling for the last five minutes. *Whom* he had been feeling. The body staring at him was Hiroshi Saito's, but the stare itself, that stare was another man's.

Indeed, Rowland's presence was just as he remembered it: a volcano.

Mason stared back long enough — and he suspected transparently enough — that Rowland could see that he knew. Oh, Mason knew.

Quickly, Mason considered what this sudden turn of events meant for him, and that part, if nothing else, was clear: he didn't just need to leave Winter's End promptly — he needed to fucking blast off. He'd hate himself for it, for leaving Liana and Eli behind, but the living had to take precedence over the dead, and Mason's heart was racing.

And then so was the rest of him — though not before he cast another protective barrier (and made a mental note not to stand next to stairs; even healed, his arm still hurt from the fall he'd taken earlier).

Instead of continuing to the second floor — instead of retrieving his friends, the people who'd brought him here, good people who deserved the best in death if not life — Mason darted across the living room toward the foyer in an effort to not join those fine folks upstairs in more ways than one. Halfway to his new destination, he tripped over someone's hand. Mason landed on his knees and elbows, swore, and looked back. It was Eric. Someone had dragged his body indoors. Someone, Mason could immediately tell from the way she looked up at him — all tears and anger — who knew him. "Sorry." Mason spat out the word in a single syllable, as Canadians do. He was back on his feet and running again.

Hiroshi, meanwhile, was walking, but quickly —
with that deadly determination Mason remembered from
Rowland. Though perhaps Rowland and Hiroshi weren't
so different. Mason did not know Hiroshi, nor did he know
where one man began and the other ended. He only knew
that he wasn't interested in getting any more acquainted
with the terminator following him.

Mercifully, the front door was still open. Mason ran
through the courtyard, over bloodstained cobblestone, and
past the gruesome sight that was once Kyle. Mason's doing.
And now, hardly an hour later, here he was running. How
quickly predators could become prey.

Hiroshi emerged from the doorframe thirty feet behind
him. "Mason Cross," he said piercingly, enunciating each
letter.

His own name stung like an attack, as if there had been
some small chance Mason was wrong about Hiroshi, about
Rowland's presence within him, and only now knew for
sure. The truth, however, was that Mason recognized spirits
like most people remembered faces, and say what you will
about Rowland, the man had an unforgettable face.

Indeed, Rowland had surfaced as suppressed memories
or neglected addictions do. Mason had told himself it was
over, that everything was fine, secured, controlled, and yet
all this time he'd never felt quite safe. The Spirit Realm
would have said it was the darkness that he carried with
him, the price of being brought back to life. But maybe it
had always been Rowland, buried deep inside him like a
reoccurring nightmare. Maybe it had always been the man
who was now marching toward him.

Mason ran down the main pathway, toward the stone
exit of Winter's End's acreage of land, and finally out from
its circle of hedges. Out from those manicured walls that
separated necromancers from the real world. The fake
darkness faded, and Greenland remerged, its midnight sun
setting fire to the edges of the shadowy mountains that
enclosed this place. They formed another, much farther
wall that Mason still had to cross, and this wall he couldn't
circumvent on foot.

Thankfully, there were cars parked to the right of Winter's End, neatly with their bumpers to the hedges. It didn't matter that they had all the room in Greenland, apparently; orderly habits die hard. Of course, not one of these vehicles belonged to Mason, and at this point he couldn't possibly find out who owned what. He could only hope that, if ever he got the chance to explain himself to the person whose car he was about to steal, they would understand. They would understand that it was the car or *him*.

Unlike the last time Mason had been forced to steal a car, however, no one had left their keys in any of the ignitions. There were eight vehicles in total, and he checked the locks on all of them — without luck. Mason supposed necromancers were probably better than most about locking things. It was certainly a skill Mason had improved upon in recent years.

Lock picking, on the other hand, not so much. He found the largest stone he could on the mossy ground around him, about the size of a grapefruit, and tossed it at the window of a red pickup truck. Not *through* the window, mind you, which was his intention. The rock bounced off it instead, leaving behind a spider web of cracks. The second throw did the trick, but now Hiroshi — Rowland — was getting close. He had left Winter's End and turned the corner toward Mason.

"Fuck," spat Mason. He reached through the broken glass and unlocked the driver side door from inside, nicking his finger on a jagged edge. Another "fuck" —they came to him like breathing now.

Mason shuffled into the truck's leather seat and slammed the door he'd just smashed his way through shut. Loose gems of glass tinkled onto the floor. Then came the hard part: starting the vehicle. Brute force wouldn't work this time, and he still had yet to learn how to hotwire a car. Whatever Mason was going to do, he had to do it fast. Hiroshi was no more than a hundred feet away now.

It would have to be a spell. Mason didn't have any particular spell in mind, but sometimes he didn't need one. Sometimes he could feel his way there. It was a talent that, as far as Mason knew, he alone possessed. Correction: he would have assumed that he alone possessed that ability — at least in the Living Realm — up until a few minutes ago.

Things had changed, quickly.

And he had no goddamn clue how Rowland had done it, how he'd beaten death — no, beaten the Spirit Realm. That was the unbelievable part. Mason had come back to life himself once, but he'd done so with the assistance of the Spirit Realm, death's de facto gate keeper. There was no way in hell — no way in the Spirit Realm — that Rowland would have received similar help from down below. This was all Rowland's doing. Well, and Hiroshi apparently. That was another mystery Mason was nowhere near solving.

A mystery for another time perhaps. Presently, Mason was using spirit energy to kick-start the ignition, as if turning an invisible key. It took a few tries, but he got it — albeit with no time to spare. Mason put the truck into reverse and it lurched backward. The vehicle was a standard. Of course it was a goddamn standard. Nothing could ever be the easy version in the life of Mason Cross.

He could visit that pity party later. Mason shifted gears and spun the steering wheel until it wouldn't budge. He moved the truck forward, keeping his distance from Hiroshi, but not so much distance that he couldn't see the other man's expression.

He was smirking.

He was letting Mason escape.

That was just fine with Mason, who accelerated to a hundred kilometers an hour, rocks flicking the paintjob, clouds of dust billowing behind him. He drove as fast as that red pickup truck would take him, albeit with one eye on the man in the rearview mirror, who stood there watching him back.

It took a few minutes before Mason could no longer see Hiroshi or feel Rowland.

More time passed, and more distance was gained, yet still Mason watched for him in every mirror. Watched for the closest thing this world had to a grim reaper.

But all Mason ever saw was that unsetting sun, shining dimly and impossibly far away.

Chapter 32

Betrayed again.

Joan had discovered the betrayal just like everyone else: at first in the sky, and then on television. The red light of necromancy, which she'd recognized immediately, slipped through the blinds in her apartment, patterning her living room carpet with strips of pale crimson. She had thought, for a moment, that perhaps someone had come for her, and she prepared a protection spell just in case. When Joan finally yanked her blinds up, however, she quickly realized that reality had something much worse in store.

For Joan it was the apocalypse, and not in the poetic sense that others might have used the term to describe what they saw that day. It was not the apocalypse because the sky over London had turned red, nor because of that (astonishingly) colossal sphere of crimson hovering over the City and the district's tallest glass towers. For Joan, it was the apocalypse because she knew in that moment that the world she had spent her life protecting was truly, unequivocally over.

If the Spirit Realm was the lifeblood of necromancy, then secrecy had been the skin that held it all together — that kept them safe. And here was a gaping wound, and not just one either but multiple open wounds, pouring red over major metropolises across the world. There was no way to stitch these shut, and there would be no saving necromancy as she knew it.

The worst part, though, was that Joan knew she had it coming.

— «» —

A week earlier, Joan had found herself suddenly unable to move.

"Tell me what I want to know, and you don't need to die." He had her in his necromantic grip, the man who had just revealed himself as Kyle MacDonald. She hadn't heard of him before ten minutes ago, but she wouldn't soon forget that name. That, of course, was assuming she was getting out of this. Joan assumed nothing.

"I can't."

"You can."

She could, he was right, but she wouldn't. No one knew the locations of more necromancers than guardians, and no guardian had a more exhaustive list than Joan. That was what Kyle wanted, that list of over a thousand names, most of them with addresses. He would use that information to hunt them down one by one, not because he had an ideological opposition to necromancers — he was one, after all — but because he wanted their power. As far as Joan was concerned, Kyle MacDonald was just about the only thing worse than an inquisitor.

And yet, she also didn't want to die. Which was funny, because there had been times over these past two years — ever since Samuel's death — that she had convinced herself that maybe it wouldn't be so bad, death. She could cement the life she had lived, a life of accomplishments and one great love, and fade away content, letting someone else bear her burden. But now that the prospect was real and immediate, and worst of all out of her hands, Joan was quite certain she wouldn't entertain those thoughts again.

But Kyle was strong, as strong as she was, and he had the upper hand here. It hadn't been a fair fight, but Kyle didn't strike her as a man who cared about such things, as a showoff. What drove Kyle was far more dangerous than vanity.

"The names," said Kyle as he walked across her living room, maneuvering around the glass coffee table without ever breaking eye contact. He had done this before, that much was clear.

Joan, meanwhile, was stuck sitting on her beige couch, just as Kyle had found her the moment he'd broken in (she had dozed off, or things might have gone differently). From afar, she might even have appeared comfortable, relaxed. But up close her limbs looked impossibly heavy, forming deep crevices in the cushions. Try as she might, Joan couldn't move. There were spells that could free her, sure, but she could tell Kyle was ready to strike the second she tried something, and she didn't like her odds.

"I have a proposition," she said.

Kyle stopped five feet in front of her and nodded, *continue.*

"There is someone I need... taken care of." The words settled uncomfortably in her mouth. Joan knew she was better than this. "Eli Abelman," she said. "Do you know him?"

"I don't," replied Kyle, looking at her curiously.

"Kill him, kill Eli, and then..." —Joan shook her head, not at Kyle but herself— "and then I will give you another name to kill. How you do so is not my concern."

Kyle considered this. "No deal," he eventually said. "If I kill this Eli guy, I want all of the names, every necromancer you have on file."

"That is my best offer," replied Joan. "Take it or leave it. But if you kill me, know that you won't find the list you're after, you won't find those names. I've dedicated my life to hiding such things, and there are few hidden as well in this world. But we can make a deal."

That last part was a lie — she had no more names to give him, no other necromancer she was willing to have killed for some greater good — but it was a way to buy her time. If Kyle could be convinced that he was helping her (and perhaps he would be, this once), he might just take his guard down next time.

"So," he said, "where is this Eli Abelman?"

"Winter's End. He'll be on his way there any day now."

"Winter's End is a dangerous place for someone like me to... operate."

Joan nodded knowingly but said, "He'll be spending a lot of time alone, locked away in the basement I'm sure. You'll get your chance." Or, best case scenario, he'll get himself caught and killed (so long as he didn't implicate her).

"Three names," said Kyle. "If I kill Eli, you give me three more names afterward."

Joan hesitated and sighed out her nostrils, acting as if the deal she was about to strike was anything but fraudulent. "Fine," she said. "I'll give you three names."

— «» —

Joan was in her upstairs den, alone. Well, not entirely alone. Her cat, Mancer, was sitting on the edge of her desk, bathing his front paw in the lamplight. On the other end of the small white table in front of Joan was a gift that Samuel had given her seven years ago: a gold Buddha statue he'd picked up in China.

Samuel was no Buddhist, but he believed in karma. She remembered him once saying he sometimes wondered if spirit energy was guided by it. He claimed that when he felt he was doing the right thing, the just thing, and he called on spirit energy, it came to him more easily — as if more willing to consent.

It was bullshit, of course, but if ever there was a time Joan could be convinced that there might be something to Samuel's outlandish (if not entirely serious) theory, well, it was right now. She had done something that was most definitely not right and not just. No, what she had done fell firmly into the horribly wrong category. She had put the lives of her fellow necromancers in danger by enabling a psychopath.

And today was the reckoning.

It was as if all of the spirit energy in the world had flown from her grasp, from the woman who had sinned, and coalesced in the sky where it was far, far out of reach and yet still very much in plain sight. Hell, plain sight was putting it mildly. There was no missing what had happened today, and Joan very much doubted she would be able to find even a single human being who hadn't at least seen it on fucking YouTube. The light had been a message to all of them, after all, the common people, not to Joan Worthington.

But it felt personal. And worse, it felt deserved.

Joan scratched Mancer behind the ear as he moved two feet forward and flopped down again, purring. So content, she thought — so oblivious. The two were inseparable, she supposed. Just like necromancers and the rest of the world, it turned out.

Joan stared out through the square window between Buddha and the yellow halo of her copper lamp. She stared out into the checkered city night and wondered about all the necromancers she knew, about whether or not their lives would ever be the same.

No, she quickly concluded, they would not.

Joan had been wrong to send Kyle to Winter's End, she could admit that now, but it didn't mean she wasn't also right. Her cause had been a just one. Not that any of that mattered much anymore. She had lost her war, and the secret was out.

If Samuel were still alive, sitting down next to her as she often fantasized on nights like these, he would have tried to infect her with his optimism — and, God, she had loved him for that. And they would have agreed that the lives of necromancers would never be the same. But Joan would know, as she knew now, the real reason for that.

It was because their lives would be hell.

If you enjoyed this read

Please leave a review on Amazon, Facebook, Good Reads or Instagram.

It takes less than five minutes and it really does make a difference.

If you're not sure how to leave a review on Amazon:

1. *Go to amazon.com.*

2. *Type in Winter's End by Trevor Melanson and when you see it, click on it.*

3. *Scroll down to Customer Reviews. Nearby you'll see a box labeled Write a Review. Click it.*

4. *Now, if you've never written a review before on Amazon, they might ask you to create a name for yourself.*

5. *Reviews can be as simple as, "Loved the book! Can't wait for the Next!" (Please don't give the story away.)*

And that's it!

Brian Hades, publisher

About the Author

Trevor Melanson is the author of two novels and an award-winning journalist who's written for numerous publications across Canada. He lives in Vancouver with his fiancée and their cat, Gilmore. Having grown up wanting to be a writer, he now dreams of work-life balance.

Here's a sneak peek at Book Three in the Terminal City Saga

Reaper's Edge
(Book Three in the Terminal City Saga)

by Trevor Melanson

"**Mason, you don't** have to do this."

"Yeah," he said, "I do."

Asha breathed in with her whole body and tried her hardest to see inside him. She was digging for something, anything, to change his mind. Mason knew that look well. He also knew that there was nothing she could say, there was nothing anyone could say, that would sway him now. Not after what was said.

"You don't even know if this will work," she reasoned with him.

"No," he admitted, "but I know what will happen if I do nothing."

"Ugh. You don't. You just think you do."

"You were there. You heard him."

Asha shook her head, almost violently, sliding her red wine down the counter as if rejecting it — rather than what Mason was telling her. The merlot swished up to the lip of her glass. "Just because someone says something," she said, "that doesn't mean you should believe them. What he said, it's impossible."

"I don't know what's possible," replied Mason. "But there's a chance."

"So you're just going to risk your life on a chance?"

"Better my life than... you know."

Asha exhaled her fury. She wasn't having any of it, and now, it seemed, she couldn't even look him in the eyes. Instead, she looked out the small window of her studio apartment. Snow had cushioned the edges of its wooden frame, forming a porthole into the night sky. The world outside was dimly lit by yellow streetlights, each revealing a cone of heavy, wet snowflakes. It was only just cold enough for the rain to have turned into snow, which was about as cold as it ever got in Terminal City.

Mason and Asha had been alone for an hour now, and yet little had progressed in their conversation. Mason, in other words, hadn't budged an inch since coming over here to tell her his plan. His big, awful plan. She was wearing a purple turtleneck and jeans, and he had on his favorite collared shirt. It was black, like most things he owned.

Asha returned her gaze to him and straightened her spine. "When I was a kid," she said, "I used to give my toys away to other kids." She spoke calmly. "Sometimes I'd give them my lunch too. Not because I was bullied or anything. I just thought, hey, I'm privileged, and maybe this kid isn't, you know, so why should I have the nice new thing and not them? It didn't seem fair. I was always trying to make everything fair, even if I ended up hungry or in trouble for it."

Mason leaned forward on his metal stool.

"Eventually my dad found out," Asha continued, "and he told me this old story. I'm not sure where I heard it or if he just made it up. He did that sometimes, made up stories. Anyway, he said there was this fisherman who kept giving away his fish for free. To beggars and poor families, whoever he thought needed help, I guess. Then one day all the fish like, I don't know, stopped being fishable or something. I don't really remember how my dad told it. Point is, the fisherman gave too much away and didn't save up for when things got bad. So he had to sell his fishing gear to pay his bills, but now he didn't have anything to fish with. He quickly ran out of money and had no way to support himself. After that, he became a beggar — just like all the beggars he'd spent his life helping.

"But here's the thing," she said, sliding her wine glass closer to her chest, "the other fishers and merchants, they didn't give to the beggars. And since the fisherman could no longer fish, there was no one left to help them." She paused before continuing. "You know I'm the queen of guilt-aholics. I get it, I get wanting to make sacrifices for other people, I do. But if you sacrifice *yourself*, Mason, then you can't help anyone anymore."

Asha almost choked on those last words. She took a slow sip of wine, and then she took his hand in hers and squeezed it gently. That, for some reason, was the thing that almost got to Mason, the thing that almost broke his unbreakable resolve.

He looked up from their hands and into her eyes. Hers had grown glossy.

"I'm not doing it for just anyone," he said.

"Don't say that," she replied. "I don't want to be the reason you do this, Mason."

He lifted her hand and kissed it. "This is on me. I'm responsible for my decisions, not you. And this is decision," he said, exhaling, "is made."

It all started with…

Terminal City
(Book One in the Terminal City Saga)

by Trevor Melanson

Mason Cross never wanted to be anything like his father, a famous professor who, it turns out, was also a necromancer. But death changes people.

Now Mason is following in his dead dad's footsteps, down a dark, solitary path between two competing lives: one as a student at Terminal City's top university, the other as a necromancer.

But will he find the answers he's looking for? Or will he find only death, caught in a hidden war between necromancers and a religious inquisition?

As the gravity of both worlds bears down on him, Mason will need to discover not just new power — but what a human life is really worth.

Praise for Terminal City

"Mason Cross is embarking on a new life in more ways than just going to college. When he moves in to the house he inherited from his dead father and an odd stranger comes calling, he discovers that death is just another beginning.

"Once introduced to the world of unseen things, Mason is delivered as a complex hard-edged young man who takes joining the ranks of his father's powerful friends, the Necromancers, in an epic battle against the Inquisitors in stride.

"This is a fast-paced, well-written entertaining book and a good way to pass time. The plot never lags, and it is pleasantly easy to stay immersed in the darkish underworld of the book. I am looking forward to the next in the series!"

— A. Volmer

"When I read a book (and I read a lot of books) I want to be more than entertained. Don't get me wrong, I enjoy a good diversion in the form of words on a page (or screen, if that's your style), but I also want to think a little, learn a little, and walk away from it with the feeling that the book filled a gap in my brain bookshelf.

"Terminal City delivers. Every character had me hooked. They challenged me to think beyond popular preconceptions of protagonist/antagonist paradigms, to what shapes a person's character and their approach to their unique situations. Mason is far from perfect. He has to adjust his reasoning and beliefs throughout his journey. Rowland is sympathetic and complex. As his character unfolded, I couldn't help but empathize with his convictions (sort of).

"While the premise of the book is dark — it's a tale of necromancy and the battle that ensues between necromancers and inquisitors, after all — the tale is balanced by a believable romance. The language of, and sparing light-hearted moments between Asha and Mason (as well as the book's other characters' personal relationships for that matter) show the vulnerability of love.

— Amazon Customer

For more on Terminal City visit:

tinyurl.com/edge2086

Need something new to read?

If you liked Winter's End, you should also consider these other EDGE-Lite titles:

White Death

by Jack Castle

Ravenous Predator hunts Arctic Expedition

Coined by early explorers as the Atlantis of the North, the Arctic is a desolate, intense land colder than even Antarctica. Anthropologist Kate Foster accepts a job at an isolated research facility on a remote island surrounded by a vast ocean of crushing Pack Ice. Her scientific expedition becomes a mission of survival when she is joined by Detective Jack Decker with the Alaska Bureau of Investigations. Kate and Decker's team of criminologists race against time to solve the gruesome and multiple homicides of her colleagues while someone, or something (thought to be extinct), is hunting them.

Praise for White Death

"Chilling, both in terms of absolute terror and frigid conditions where the action takes place."
— Spokesman Review

"When Jack Castle delivers a new adventure he draws his readers in with creative story lines that unfold in realistic

settings. The descriptive nature and action packed details of his stories are riveting and spell binding. I'm anxiously awaiting his next journey through the unknown."
— Major Dennis Allen (Ret) and recipient of the Distinguished Flying Cross

"I'm not a sci-fi fan, but I read Mr. Castle's first book, Europa Journal, in one sitting, (I actually found the book on a seat at the airport on an unexpected layover). And I didn't think he could top his supernatural thriller, Bedlam Lost. But that's exactly what he did with his latest book, White Death. This time around the story takes place at a remote facility in the Arctic. A team of criminologists are flown in to investigate a brutal massacre of scientists when something begins picking them off one-by-one. I haven't been this on the edge of my seat since watching the movie Jaws as a kid. Three different books, three different genres and the author managed to knock it out of the park every time!"
— Liz Garrick

For more on White Death visit:
tinyurl.com/edge6015

Lethal Influence

by Susan Bohnet and K L Webster

Unknown to humans, a friendly alien society lives among us. Kai, a young Trebladore male, has unusual abilities that are lethal to humans. Different factions of the Trebladore Society begin to vie for the use of his powers, and he discovers disturbing things about his species and their methods. When humans start dying and the woman he loves is in danger, Kai must make desperate choices. Choices that will change the future of mankind forever.

Praise for Lethal Influence

"From the moment I read the brief description, I knew I was in for a good read. This book takes you through SciFi, Romance, Mystery, Intrigue and Suspense. With a bit of Humor here and there. I can definitely see this becoming a series (one can hope) as there is more that can be told. But if it is only to be one book, it is still worth the read"
— Amazon Customer

"I often wish/hope/imagine that some 'guardian angels' are out there, ready to influence bad guys to be better. Susan does a GREAT job of building this in a believable way. I don't want to introduce a single spoiler, but the story builds up and ends up with a satisfactory ending."
— Xubbycat

"We follow our main character Kai, who is a Trebladore and his friends; a group of aliens with the power to influence humans, as he comes to term with the fact that he is different from his fellow Trebladores and that his own influencing power is much more than he realises. We see him struggle with this knowledge and how to best use his influencing powers for the greater good as it's what's been ingrained into him since he was a small child and is the Trebladore way.

"Some action, plot twists that you may or may not see coming with a bit of romance thrown in, it will definitely make you ponder what it means to be human and how far an alien race would be willing to go in order to help us."
— MyBookishRealm

For more on Lethal Influence visit:
tinyurl.com/edge6019

For more EDGE titles and information about upcoming speculative fiction please visit us at:

www.edgewebsite.com

Don't forget to sign-up for our Special Offers